The Elusive Everyday in the Fiction of Marilynne Robinson

LAURA E. TANNER

OXFORD
UNIVERSITY PRESS

OXFORD
UNIVERSITY PRESS

Great Clarendon Street, Oxford, OX2 6DP,
United Kingdom

Oxford University Press is a department of the University of Oxford.
It furthers the University's objective of excellence in research, scholarship,
and education by publishing worldwide. Oxford is a registered trade mark of
Oxford University Press in the UK and in certain other countries

Published in the United States of America by Oxford University Press
198 Madison Avenue, New York, NY 10016, United States of America

British Library Cataloguing in Publication Data
Data available

Library of Congress Control Number: 2021931425

ISBN 978–0–19–289636–0

DOI: 10.1093/oso/9780192896360.001.0001

Printed and bound in the UK by
TJ Books Limited

Links to third party websites are provided by Oxford in good faith and
for information only. Oxford disclaims any responsibility for the materials
contained in any third party website referenced in this work.

For James, every day

Acknowledgments

This project emerges out of many formal and informal conversations about the novels of Marilynne Robinson. I presented early drafts of several chapters at the annual American Literature Association Conference, which now includes a Marilynne Robinson author society, and am grateful for the input I received there. An earlier version of Chapter 3 was published in *Contemporary Literature* 48.2 (2007) 227–52 © 2007 by the Board of Regents of the University of Wisconsin System. Reprinted by courtesy of the University of Wisconsin Press. Chapter 4 is a revised and expanded version of "Uncomfortable Furniture: Inhabiting Domestic and Narrative Space in Marilynne Robinson's *Home*," *Contemporary Women's Writing* 7.1 (2013) 35–53, doi:10.1093/cww/vpr013, and is reproduced by permission of Oxford University Press. I am grateful to Oxford University Press for supporting this book project, with special thanks to Jacqueline Norton for her interest in this reframing of Robinson's fiction and for her warm professionalism as she shepherded the manuscript through the review process.

A Boston College sabbatical allowed me to devote time exclusively to this project. Enthusiastic Boston College students read many of these novels along with me; their passionate comments have often pushed me to think harder and more deeply about Robinson's novels. Two of those students, Samantha Kramer and Colleen Reynolds, served as my undergraduate research assistants, providing valuable help for this project. The talented students in my graduate class on Everyday Fictions, including Emily Simon, Lauren Bly, and Alexandra Machetanz, helped me to think through and complicate some of the theoretical frameworks I use here. Conversations with two former students, Kristin Imre and John Anspach, have nurtured my passion for Robinson's work. Many of my colleagues in the English Department at Boston College have contributed to this book in subtle and obvious ways, including Elizabeth Graver, Kevin Ohi, Lad Tobin, Chris Wilson, Judith Wilt, and Dayton Haskin. I am particularly grateful to Ti Bodenheimer for reading my work and productively challenging my thinking about *Housekeeping*. For years, Mary Crane and I have shared the daily routines of academic life as they ebb and flow from the transcendent to the mundane; I feel very lucky to have her in my corner of Stokes Hall.

Decades after graduate school, the friends I made there, especially Allyson Booth, Susan Greenfield and Wendy Wall, continue to remind me what a privilege it is to learn, think, and reflect inside *and* outside the classroom. Anne Fleche, Jane Ashley, and Jenny Bortnick have kept me sane in the hold of their friendships; in frequently demanding progress reports on this book, Peter Regan has driven me crazy, but in a good way. For their constant support and their perceptive insights about everything from fiction to family, I thank my sister, Beth Tanner, and my mother, Nancy Clark Tanner. The grammar expertise of my daughter, Evelyn Tanner, marks many sentences here (though any mistakes are clearly my own) and I am grateful to my son, Cole Krasner, for the shared pleasure of many probing and productive conversations about gender and race. . Thirty-five years ago, I sat down for my first graduate seminar and looked across the table at a striking young man with wavy dark hair in a white button-down shirt, radiating intensity. I could never have imagined how many years we would share, bed time stories we would read, ideas we would discuss, trips we would take, dogs we would love, pages we would write. I dedicate this book to him and to the world of coffee and words and walks we are so lucky to share, every day.

Contents

1

The Uncomfortable Ordinary

On September 14, 2015, President Barack Obama met with Marilynne Robinson in Des Moines, Iowa for a conversation about her literary work. Robinson had recently completed her book of essays, *When I Was a Child I Read Books*, but Obama began the conversation by describing his affection for her fiction. "I first picked up *Gilead*, one of your most wonderful books, here in Iowa. Because I was campaigning at the time, and there's a lot of downtime when you're driving between towns and when you get home late from campaigning." As their conversation progressed, Obama expressed two ideas about the appeal of Robinson's fiction to him, and the possibilities of fiction in general: both centered on comfort.

First, Obama described how Robinson's books served as a safe retreat for him during those hectic, media-saturated days of the campaign. He found himself particularly attracted to John Ames, the central character of *Gilead*, "who is gracious and courtly and a little bit confused about how to reconcile his faith with all the various travails that his family goes through. And I was just—I just fell in love with the character." Robinson's books are in part a refuge from the "travails" of a complex world because, Obama claims, they embody the "homespun values of hard work and honesty and humility" as opposed to "big systems where everything is all about flash." After a hard day on the campaign trail, even in Iowa, such a reminder of middle-American good-heartedness brings comfort. While appeals to small-town values are pervasive in American political discourse, Obama's identification of such values (and the emotional well-being they elicit) with the operation of literary fiction is notable.

When the conversation turned toward the role of fiction in contemporary society, Obama described the potential of the novel to offer a different kind of comfort. "The most important stuff I've learned," he observed, "I think I've learned from novels. It has to do with empathy. It has to do with being comfortable with the notion that the world is complicated and full of grays." Robinson's novels enlighten us, Obama suggests, because they invite us into the dynamic lives of characters who inhabit fictional landscapes that mirror

The Elusive Everyday in the Fiction of Marilynne Robinson. Laura E. Tanner, Oxford University Press (2021).
© Laura E. Tanner. DOI: 10.1093/oso/9780192896360.003.0001

rather than resolve the social and psychological complexities of our own world. "Gracious and courtly" (Obama), John Ames never quite settles into the stability his slightly dated or otherworldly presence evokes; throughout the novel, he strives toward a reconciliation of faith and experience that, in Obama's words, leaves him "a little bit confused." The ethical power of fiction, Obama suggests, derives from its ability to make us comfortable not only in the company of people who may be very different from ourselves but with the complexity of motivation, the tentativeness of reconciliation, that underlies existence in a "complicated" contemporary world that never resolves into black and white.

Although Obama's assertions about the role of fiction in contemporary society, and of Robinson's fiction in particular, both highlight a dynamic of comfort, they point to two very different frameworks for understanding the experience of novel reading. On the one hand, fiction can soothe the mind by reassuring us that traditional values and sensibilities endure, or can at least be remembered, in the midst of a disordered and often brutal world. Such framing defines the role of contemporary fiction as a kind of oil poured on the waters of a troubled nation. This characterization of Robinson's fiction as comforting has become endemic to both its popularity and its critical reception. Readers and critics alike express intense gratitude for the novels' ability to inspire hope and spiritual sustenance both in their overall messages and in their lyrical style.

In gesturing toward the novel's power to make us comfortable with the tensions of a twenty-first-century world that is "complicated and full of grays," however, Obama points to a second, and equally important, way of reading Robinson's fiction. Even as Robinson's lyrical prose, spiritual optimism, and luminous images clear a path toward transcendence rarely visible in the contemporary novel, her works insist on the complexity of the continuing struggle for meaning and coherence. Indeed, the central focus throughout her novels is the difficulty that inevitably accompanies the complicated realities of aging and grief, social injustice, the fracture of family, the trauma of poverty, the ravages of alcoholism, mental illness, and suicide. The path toward the extraordinary that Robinson's fiction charts leads the reader through the hours and days of ordinary experience marked by a discomfort and irresolution sometimes sidelined in analyses of her fiction.

When Marilynne Robinson's second novel, *Gilead*, emerged in 2004, almost twenty-five years after the publication of *Housekeeping*, readers greeted it with passionate enthusiasm and critics sang its praises. Although the narrator of

Gilead, a seventy-six-year-old minister, could not be more different than Ruth, the teenage protagonist of *Housekeeping*, both novels share Robinson's characteristically lyrical style and textured, poetic representation of everyday objects and experiences. Praising Robinson's "remarkable writing" as "a form of revelation," James Wood observes in his review of *Gilead*, "Gradually, Robinson's novel teaches us how to read it, suggests how we might slow down to walk at its own processional pace, and how we might learn to coddle its many fine details" (1). The next two novels in the Gilead series, *Home* and *Lila*, emerged fairly quickly, to the tune of slightly muted critical praise. Implicit in some of these understated responses is the sense that the slowness or "quietness" of the more recent novels, familiar to Robinson's readers, does not always pay off in the opportunity for transcendence or heightened aesthetic experience that readers had come to expect. Holding on to the critical frameworks most often used to interpret *Housekeeping* and *Gilead*, critics seeking access to the textual worlds of *Home* and *Lila* through the lens of the illuminated particular struggle to articulate the source of their dissatisfaction, occasionally registering their own uneasiness in describing the novels as flat, repetitive, or even boring. The lyrical beauty of the early novels collaborates with critical models that stress the recuperation of loss through religious vision or imagistic revision, both of which resignify the ordinary by rendering it luminous. In contrast, the dialogue-heavy, stripped-down prose of *Home* and the uninflected, repetitive narrative voice of *Lila* sometimes situate the reader uncomfortably in the everyday worlds they create.

Despite extensive dialogue among Robinson scholars about the role of the ordinary in her fiction—including essays exploring "Ordinary Happiness," "Rituals of the Ordinary," and "Resurrection of the Ordinary"—critical attention limits itself almost exclusively to the *transformation* of the everyday, the way in which Robinson's prose renders the ordinary extraordinary (see Mauro, Horton, and Inour). Critics who have recently offered a comparative study of Robinson's novels have emphasized the productive significance of her "quiet" fiction, which Rachel Sykes frames as offering unique access to interiority, and her luminous representation of "an experience of wonder in the everyday," which Ray Horton connects to a "background of religious conviction [that] activates concentrated aesthetic attention to quotidian moments" (120). Critics of Marilynne Robinson's early novels often begin by acknowledging a plot of grief, alienation, and diminishment, but move quickly to attend to an aesthetic of transcendence in the fiction. Their efforts at critical consolidation, however, push uneasily against some reviewer responses to the recent novels[1] and brief detours in current criticism that acknowledge moments of strain when the consolations of art and belief falter.[2]

The Elusive Everyday seeks to interrogate the critical assumptions generated by readings of the early novels and often applied to all her work. The shift in narrative style in her recent fiction, I will argue, more explicitly reveals a dynamic of alienation that has characterized *all* of Robinson's fiction, and that erupts, even in the early novels, along the fault lines of the everyday. Critical trends emphasize the motion from the tragic to the sublime in Robinson's fiction, highlighting the way that death, dying, loss, and grief illuminate and transform commonplace experience. Tapping into the momentum toward transcendence in the novels, readings of Robinson's literary narratives risk settling into a singular critical trajectory that belies the tensions the novels never fully resolve. Reversing the motion toward sublimity in her works, I will focus instead on the way that loss settles uneasily into the everyday, disrupting the taken-for-granted conventions of daily life and, in the more recent novels, the rhythms of literary representation. Critical focus on the incipient transformation of the quotidian often obscures the significance of the painful way in which Robinson's characters are expelled from the rhythms of an ordinary world. In their eagerness to frame loss as tragic or its compensations as ample, many critics have pushed aside the uncomfortable ordinary and ignored the way in which loss registers in Robinson's fiction in the form of a mundane terror that manifests in the disrupted rhythms and disabled experiences of the everyday.

* * *

In *Understanding Marilynne Robinson*, the first full-length, comprehensive critical study of Robinson's work, Alex Engebretson defines Robinson's attention to everyday life as a key characteristic of her fiction; noting that "Robinson's fiction is notable for its attention to the ordinary," he traces what he describes as the "rooted, this-worldly quality" of her fiction to her

---

[1] Because this book is going to press before the official publication of *Jack*, reviews of Robinson's most recent novel have not yet emerged.

[2] See for example, Matthew Potts's interrogation of the theological implications of biblical analogy in *Housekeeping*, Robert Chodat's suggestion that Ames's assertions might not be taken at face value in *Gilead*, David James's acknowledgment of tensions in *Gilead* that provoke the consolations of style (*Discrepant Solace*), and Rachel Sykes's exploration of the varying functions of "quiet" in Robinson's fiction.

belief in Calvinist tenets of human sanctity: "Transcendence happens here on Earth, since every part of reality, including everyday human experience, radiates sanctity. Everywhere [Robinson's fiction] suggests the daily chores and mundane tasks of life have extraordinary meaning, if the right attention is paid to them" (11). Within the context of such a reading, the everyday acts and gestures that Robinson represents assume an illuminated presence that invests the quotidian with significance. Her characteristically lyrical writing collaborates with this impulse to celebrate and transform the familiar; what James Wood describes as the "spiritual force" of Robinson's words contributes to a heightened apprehension of habitual acts and familiar sensations. Her exquisite prose lends texture and dimension to moments of perception and dynamics of experience that the novels rescue from the realm of the ordinary and render luminous.

Viewed in the context of the everyday, however, Robinson's novels construct a world that is mimetic as well as symbolic or revelatory. My use of this frame of reference, then, aims not to sequester aspects of existence that are mindless, routine, or habitual, but to highlight the way in which the everyday is implicated even in the most heightened moments of the novels. Like many of her readers, I am drawn to the sublimity of Robinson's vision and luminous prose. I am equally fascinated, however, by the tensions in her work that continually emerge to haunt moments of revelation. In the pages that follow, I push back against the luminous landscapes Robinson summons so beautifully not to dismiss their power but to explore the complex dialogues they initiate when situated within the context of lived experience. Robinson's characters straddle multiple worlds, inhabiting the boundary between the otherworldly and the lived worlds of hours and days. Recently, Bryony Randall has addressed what she describes as "the fraught issue" of transcendence in everyday life studies by questioning the assumption that "casual inattentiveness" always defines the everyday experience of everyday life; she explores a series of novels "in which heightened sensitivity to microscopic detail (on the part of narrator or characters or both) does not . . . remove what is attended to from the realm of the everyday" ("A Day's Time" 598). I would extend her opening up of the everyday in the opposite direction as well; in Robinson's fiction, the heightened sensitivity to detail that fuels transcendence often emerges from and is implicated in an uncomfortable ordinary that continually destabilizes and defies the image of the everyday as grounding. Her characters' everyday is defined not by the routine quality of the taken for granted but by a heightened self-consciousness, often borne of trauma and loss, that renders the quotidian strange and unfamiliar.

The intensified perception that contributes to moments of revelation in Robinson's fiction manifests just as powerfully, if less luminously, in a disruption of the cadences of ordinary life, what Robinson refers to in "Imagination and Community" as the "stir of displacement" that troubles the ordinary (20).

Reversing the process of transfiguration in Robinson's fiction returns the reader to a destabilized phenomenological foundation seldom acknowledged in a criticism that quickly pushes past the everyday in order to explore the way that Robinson's narratives illuminate the mysteries of the commonplace. Robinson's work, Siobhan Phillips writes, turns "its full attention to 'the actual, the phenomenal'; it defamiliarizes what is most familiar so as to recognize the wonder in what might otherwise be assumed. [She] makes the ordinary uncanny so as to appreciate it more intimately" ("Merit" 164–5). In focusing on the beauty and intensity of representations that defamiliarize the familiar, I will argue, critics sometimes gloss over the psychic cost and experiential awkwardness of inhabiting the uncanny ordinary. For Robinson's protagonists, the aesthetic defamiliarization of a taken-for-granted world often translates into the intimate experience of estrangement. Thrust out of the everyday into the space of representation, Robinson's characters lose what Rita Felski describes as the comfort of routine and "the protective cushion of habit" that enables the subject to negotiate an otherwise overwhelming array of stimuli and sensations ("Introduction" 615). Reacting against critical assumptions that undervalue what Ella Ophir terms the "psychological necessity of habit and routine" (17), recent theories of the everyday have highlighted the way that the habits of ordinary life function, as Liesl Olson explores, as a "mode of protection" or a "domestic shield" (*Modernism* 113). The power of representation that critics associate with Robinson's rendering of ordinary things emerges from an intensity of perception that marks her characters' expulsion from the taken for granted. Trapped in a representational relationship to their lived worlds, Robinson's protagonists inhabit the everyday self-consciously, performing over and over a forced relationship to the ordinary that seldom relaxes into the natural or the familiar. The characteristic acts of transfiguration that punctuate her narratives originate from and anticipate the inevitability of absence: the death of loved ones (*Housekeeping*), the impending death of the self (*Gilead*), the fracture of family (*Home*), the repetition of trauma and abandonment (*Lila*), the impossibility of everyday intimacy (*Jack*).

These novels, as I explore in the following pages, complicate the model of creative defamiliarization that Phillips and others associate with the wonder of the illuminated everyday by locating what she describes as the "uncanny" ordinary in the uncomfortable lived experience of loss. As death, dying, trauma, and grief settle in the pages of these novels, the familiar rhythms of daily life absorb into routine the catastrophic dynamics of the tragic and traumatic. The threat of loss infiltrates the web of mundane acts, assumed conventions, and habitual gestures that envelops Robinson's characters. "That most moments were substantially the same," as Ruth observes in *Housekeeping*, "did not detract at all from the possibility that the next moment might be utterly different. And so the ordinary demanded unblinking attention. Any tedious hour might be the last of its kind" (166). Although the heightened apprehension of the quotidian in Robinson's novels often registers powerfully and beautifully in representational terms, its aesthetic intensity is enacted at the expense of characters who patrol the margins of the ordinary with unceasing vigilance; their capacity to be dazzled by the commonplace marks less their immersion in the textured details of the everyday than their expulsion from its comfortable realm.

Attending to the rhythms of lived experience in Robinson's fiction thus challenges the idea that the everyday can be understood only as what is taken for granted. Pushing back against frameworks that naturalize a methodology that draws attention to dramatic events, spectacular discoveries, or life-altering changes, everyday life studies typically focuses on the daily, lived worlds of work, home, and family that are often marked by repetition and routine. My use of the frame of the everyday to explore Robinson's work, however, questions the assumptions of a methodology that often defines its focus only in negative terms, highlighting only what is ignored, assumed, or relegated to the background. Even as it seeks to incorporate the rhythms of daily life, such a frame of reference excludes the disrupted cadences of an everyday that refuses to settle into the ordinary, or an ordinary that is defined by the crippling rhythms of anxiety, fear, or grief. The everyday does not disappear for the homeless and the grief-stricken, those suffering in the wake of violence and trauma, those living in old age or in poverty; instead, it absorbs and reflects an experience of loss that cannot be reduced to a singular incident. The everyday, as Liesl Olson argues, "is a mixture and ongoing flow of events" (*Modernism* 70). Although the artificial isolation of everyday experience pulls its dynamics from the margins into the spotlight, once illuminated it refuses to be contained within neat borders. "If it makes sense to see the everyday as one of the parameters of our lives," Michael Sheringham asks, "can this parameter ever be disentangled from others?" (25). Applying the framework of the everyday to Robinson's fiction isolates the category of the ordinary in order to expose its implication in other categories of being, its entanglement in the phenomenological orientation of characters and narrative alike. Scarred by grief, illness, aging, and trauma, Robinson's characters inhabit a world of transcendent beauty suffused with the terrifying threat of loss. Theories of the ordinary that concentrate on what we do not concentrate on underestimate the dynamics of lived experience that Robinson's fiction so beautifully represents: the way that consciousness and feeling are implicated not just in the moments of being that crystallize meaning and beauty but in the minutes and hours that surround, support, or interrogate them.

Theories of everyday life that characterize the everyday as what is routine, assumed, or taken for granted would thus deny most of Robinson's protagonists an everyday. In opposition, I would argue, it is exactly the lived experience of self-consciousness, the very rhythm of pivoting between transcendence and unstable ground, that constitutes the uncomfortable ordinary of many of her characters. If the transcendence that many Robinson critics highlight marks a refusal to take for granted the most routine acts or familiar perceptions, Robinson's novels repeatedly link the gift of such heightened self-consciousness to a much darker dynamic: her characters' expulsion from a familiar landscape or inability to rely on the habits or conventions of daily life others may take for granted. Situated at the margins of the lived world, Robinson's characters perceive the quotidian from a distance that renders it representational; the novels stage, again and again, scenes in which their protagonists look down at the unfolding activity of daily life from a window or a podium, summon its textures only through memory and imagination, and retreat from its touch into dim and isolated spaces that strain to echo the lived rhythms of home. Attending to the psychic complexity of Robinson's characters thus demands acknowledging rather than sweeping away their uneasy situation in the everyday world. "The psyche," as Bryony Randall observes in *Modernism, Daily Time, and Everyday Life,* "is not simply a surface text revealing a depth of dailiness, nor is dailiness a grid overlaid on an otherwise uninflected psyche" (9). As consciousness, the very force that enables the depth and beauty of much of Robinson's prose, haunts her protagonists, returning them again and again to the inevitability of loss, the everyday world that might cushion them only throws into relief their panic. In contrast to the luminous images of textured presence that critics associate with her portrayal of the ordinary, Robinson's characters also huddle, hunched and anxious, in an uncomfortable everyday. Stiffly perched on the edge of uncushioned furniture or propped awkwardly in the midst of someone else's conversation, they inhabit the margins of a lived experience they are often forced to observe self-consciously and vigilantly. Existing in a heightened state linked to the perception of loss, they occupy a defamiliarized landscape that demands the rigid maintenance of aesthetic, existential, or social self-consciousness. Robinson's novels locate their protagonists in a representational relationship to reality that renders the habitual, embodied, and unselfconscious dynamics of the everyday elusive.

*   *   *

Given the grace with which Robinson's novels transform the commonplace, rendering it anything but ordinary, it might seem counterintuitive to consider her novels within the framework of the everyday. In testifying to the powerful force of her writing and the metaphysical scope of her vision, critics often situate Robinson's fiction in the contexts of American transcendentalism, religious belief, or literary style. What Engebretson terms the "rooted, this-worldly quality" of Robinson's narratives functions primarily as a mechanism, in his view and that of others, for transcending rather than dwelling in the mundane (11). Robinson's fiction thus highlights and exaggerates a central dilemma of using theories of the everyday to approach literary representations of the ordinary.

Everyday life studies consciously sets out to explore the significance of what is otherwise taken for granted or pushed outside the frame of critical attention: as a field of study, it often focuses on what is routine, mundane, habitual, and repetitive. Everyday life, Rita Felski argues, "is typically distinguished from the exceptional moment . . . The distinctiveness of the everyday lies in its lack of distinction and differentiation; it is the air one breathes, the taken-for-granted backdrop" of existence ("Invention" 80). In attempting to "rescue" every facet of the quotidian from anonymity, in Lefebvre's words, the field of everyday life studies offers a broad spectrum of approaches that invite interdisciplinarity and diversity of approach (*Everyday Life* 2). Widespread interest in the everyday across fields as varied as literary criticism, philosophy, sociology, cultural studies, anthropology, and media studies reflects the impact of intellectual heritages from multiple traditions of thought, including philosophers William James, Martin Heidegger, and Ludwig Wittgenstein, the Marxist sociological critiques of Henri Lefebvre, the poststructuralist insights of Roland Barthes, and the intersections of history, psychoanalysis, and anthropology in the work of Michel de Certeau. Recently, literary scholars including Bryony Randall, Liesl Olson, Siobhan Phillips, Rita Felski, Laurie Langbauer, and Andrew Epstein have explored the representation of the everyday in different genres and through multiple lenses.[3] Given what Liesl Olson terms the "definitional capaciousness" of everyday life studies, work in this field might be defined by *what it does not do*, as it consistently pushes back against the tendency to prioritize heightened experience and spectacular events ("Everyday Life Studies" 178).

Robinson's fiction, in contrast, often subsumes the ordinary within aesthetic form and incorporates it within the motions of transcendence. Within such a framework, it might be argued, apprehending the everyday dimensions of human experience through the intensified lens of representation denatures the ordinary by rendering it extraordinary. Theories of the everyday often begin by acknowledging the paradox of foregrounding an experiential dynamic defined, by its very nature, as background. The representation of the everyday, insofar as it frames or highlights what is normally assumed, transforms the very essence of that which it conveys. As Felski articulates, literature

> tries to redeem the everyday by rescuing it from its opacity, defamiliarizing it and making us newly attentive to its mysteries. Yet this act of magnifying and refracting taken-for granted minutiae transcends the very dailiness it seeks to depict. Literature's heightened sensitivity to the microscopic detail marks its difference from the casual inattentiveness that defines the everyday experience of everyday life.   ("Invention" 90)

Critical projects such as Liesl Olson's *Modernism and the Ordinary* trace the complex challenges that result from literary attempts to pull the everyday from the background and foreground it without, in the process, denaturing the very routine, taken-for-granted qualities often used to define it. "If the ordinary is the nonrepresented, the overlooked," Olson observes, "then the writer's objective is paradoxical: How does a writer replicate what is overlooked, if the nature of literary representation is to look closely at its subject?" (7). The intensity of Robinson's renderings of an everyday radiant with significance, it might be argued, only exaggerates the representational dynamics that always problematize fictional depictions of ordinary life.

Critical tendencies to deemphasize the quotidian foundation of the aesthetic and revelatory effects of Robinson's novels may also stem from the way that realistic fiction often employs the everyday as a convention in

---

[3] For an excellent introduction to everyday life studies, see Liesl Olson's "Everyday Life Studies: A Review."

the process of building worlds. The reader of fiction seldom inhabits the everyday as everyday; the heightened representation of the ordinary transforms the commonplace in the process of framing it, rendering it anything but familiar, while the representation of the ordinary, insofar as it functions as a mimetic convention of fictional worlds, fulfills itself in disappearing from view. Intimations of everyday life, invoked briefly and strategically, often function to naturalize the storyworld of narrative.[4] The calculated introduction of details superfluous to the plot—the description of commonplace objects and mundane acts—may help to establish what Roland Barthes describes in "The Reality Effect" as a "referential illusion" (148) that substantiates the fictional universe the text creates. Because the everyday typically manifests in the mundane and repetitive structure of daily life, the invocation of the everyday as a representational convention for building character and anchoring plot in fiction encourages readers to relegate its dynamics to the background; in such a case, its content is subjugated to its formal role in the mimetic process of anchoring a textual world. In "Imagination and Community," an essay from *When I Was a Child I Read Books*, Marilynne Robinson herself directs us away from the mechanical motions of a narrowly conceived everyday:

> As a fiction writer I do have to deal with the nuts and bolts of temporal reality—from time to time a character has to walk through a door and close it behind him, the creatures of imagination have to eat and sleep, as all other creatures do. I would have been a poet if I could, to have avoided this obligation to simulate the hourliness and dailiness of human life. (20)

Framing the representation of everyday motions as a novelist's "obligation," Robinson seems to dismiss the simulation of hourliness and dailiness as a painful, if necessary, convention of novelistic representation, a mere platform for the more interesting work of the fiction writer.

Robinson goes on, however, to interrogate the notion that the everyday functions as a mere convention of fictional representation, a strictly empirical or formal mechanism that can be separated out from the complexity of

---

[4] In *Narrative Discourse*, Gerard Genette juxtaposes the storyworld with the narrative discourse of a text. More recently, David Herman's work on storyworld extends Genette's terms to highlight the way that the reader interacts with the textual cues to create a storyworld: "interpreters rely on inferences triggered by textual cues to build up representations of the overall situation or world evoked but not explicitly described in the discourse" ("Narrative Ways" 73).

human experience or its novelistic portrayal. Following up on her own example of a character walking through a door and closing it behind him, she observes, "This is not to say that books could not be written about walking through a door—away from what? Toward what? Leaving what wake of consequence? Creating what stir of displacement?" (20). The everyday, as Robinson suggests here, is implicated in a complex dynamic of phenomenological orientation that encompasses absence as well as presence. Locating a simple, familiar motion within less quantifiable paradigms of human motivation and effect, Robinson destabilizes the notion of ordinary acts as routine, mechanical, or strictly categorizable; her framing positions the everyday within the more dynamic model suggested by her imagistic focus on the "stir of displacement" such acts create. In "Phases of Fiction," Virginia Woolf observes that "to give that full record of life, not the climax and the crisis but the growth and development of feelings, which is the novelist's aim, he copies the order of the day, observes the sequence of ordinary things" (99). As Woolf suggests, fidelity to "the sequence of ordinary things," as opposed to the heightened realms of climax and crisis, functions not only to lend the illusion of realism to fiction but to capture the motion of consciousness embedded in everyday acts; in such a rendering, representation of the everyday is not only a formal means to an end but a way of capturing the feelings and thoughts embedded in the rhythms of lived experience.

Insofar as everyday life theory seeks to restore attention to dimensions of experience often dismissed or taken for granted, it risks the categorical reductiveness that may result from theoretically isolating actions and activities always woven into the complex phenomenological dynamics of human existence. The diffuse nature of the everyday, as Michael Sheringham highlights, defies its artificial separation from other aspects of existence; "If it makes sense to see the everyday as one of the parameters of our lives," he asks, "can this parameter ever be disentangled from others?" (25). Even as the framework of the everyday exposes an uncomfortable ordinary that escapes the sweep of transcendence in her work, Robinson's fiction, in turn, tests the boundaries of an everyday conceived of as only rote and routine. Her impatience with depicting the mechanical motions of daily life, it seems to me, emerges out of her unwillingness to reduce the dynamics of lived experience to simple binaries. Following her reframing of the mundane act of door opening, Robinson goes on to extend the parameters of human perception to define imagination as one of its necessary components; highlighting the way that "presence in absence" functions "as a great reality for all of us in the course of ordinary life," she suggests a concept of the everyday defined not only by the solidity of quotidian acts and objects but by the dynamic and destabilizing forces of human consciousness, even in the face of empirical absence (*When I Was a Child*, 20–1). Her novels, I will argue, evince an interest in an everyday that resists its status as material or psychic grounding.

Although I use both the terms "everyday" and "ordinary" as points of reference for Robinson's representations, then, *The Elusive Everyday* moves toward a qualification of the connotations of both terms. The everyday, I will argue in contrast to several everyday life studies critics, need not be routine or taken for granted. The "stir of displacement" that Robinson associates with the most ordinary of acts materializes a vision of the everyday that refuses its role as mere experiential anchor or representational convention. For Robinson's characters, who struggle to occupy the space of the "ordinary," the everyday is often marked by self-consciousness and discomfort rather than the ease of habit or routine. Patterns of thought and feeling, no less than physical habits, constitute the platform of daily life for the protagonists of her novels; often, their experiences track along psychic grooves that reinforce rather than mitigate dynamics of alienation and displacement. Even as they render the quotidian luminous, Robinson's narratives also extend the reach of the everyday in the opposite direction; her novels redirect attention to the voided spaces of a shadow ordinary that refuses to uphold its function as the taken-for-granted backdrop of everyday life. Representations of eating, sleeping, and walking through doors in Robinson's novels are haunted by consciousness and tangled up inextricably with grief, longing, trauma, and isolation.

*   *   *

Approaching these urgent issues in Robinson's fiction through the lens of the everyday not only initiates new critical dialogues in Robinson scholarship but raises larger questions about the contemporary novel's role in engaging with the psychic, ethical, and affective dimensions of lived experience. Despite being awarded numerous critical accolades and achieving immense popularity, Robinson's fiction is sometimes pigeonholed by the very terms that mark its success. Highlighting the transcendent vision of her work—her willingness to capture the possibilities of belief through the luminous images of her poetic prose—critics of the lyrical novel and scholars of literature and religion have seized upon a voice proudly out of step in a post-postmodern age of established skepticism and spiritual exhaustion. In highlighting the extraordinary qualities of Robinson's fiction, however, such approaches sometimes bypass the relevance of its contributions to literary and cultural dialogues about ordinary life. Both urgent and mundane, the everyday in Robinson's fiction embodies the rhythms of aging, family, grief, anxiety, illness, poverty, and trauma for characters whose struggles often emerge—not only through the development of plot but through the phenomenology of narrative voice—as beautifully, darkly complex. For that reason, focus on the everyday in Robinson's fiction opens up larger theoretical questions about the relationship between style and substance, aesthetic consolation and cultural critique in the contemporary novel.

In the case of Robinson's early fiction, the aesthetic rewards of defamiliarization—the lyrical rhythms of luminous prose that render the ordinary extraordinary—pull the reader away from her protagonists' awkward and uneasy relationship to the ordinary. In lingering over the consolation of beauty, such a critical agenda ignores the way that loss settles into the everyday, rendering it uncomfortable and uncanny. As characters, Robinson's narrators conspire in the acts of representation that fuel her poetic narratives; declaring their heightened experience of the quotidian as adequate recompense for their expulsion from the ordinary, they dwell in an imagistic reality that the reader is easily persuaded to inhabit. The narrators of *Housekeeping* and *Gilead* negotiate the uncanny ordinary by situating themselves in the space of representation; Ruth's ceaseless, textured images of her dead mother testify to an embodied absence the significance of which she consistently disavows, while the dying Ames seeks redress for his physical and psychical distance from lived experience in the heightened intensity of perception. The narratives of these works collaborate with such agendas of deflection. The compensations of lyrical language and textured image formally and stylistically redirect the reader, whose access to presence is always mediated through representation, away from the realm of the ordinary; in that realm, grief and loss register painfully not just in the motions of consciousness but in the breakdown of habit, the cessation or intensification of sensation, the disruption of the taken-for-granted conventions of daily life. Insofar as readers delight in the transformation of the ordinary or dismiss the everyday as a mere backdrop of mimetic convention, they collaborate with a psychic disavowal of loss that verges on self-deception for the characters and strains the boundaries of representation that distinguish the storyworld from narrative discourse.

Although I agree with the notion that experiences of loss in Robinson's fiction often heighten perception and fuel the creative sensibilities of her protagonists, I am most interested in pushing back against these aesthetic compensations to consider the location—or perhaps more accurately, the dislocation—of her characters in the everyday world. Despite her reputation as one of the most important contemporary novelists writing in English today, Robinson tends to be viewed as a bit of an iconoclast; that reputation is fueled by the strong, opinionated proclamations of nonfiction writing that takes to task the assumptions of modern thought, including the legacies of Freud and Darwin, as well as a wide range of contemporary popular scientists and materialists (and even organizations such as Greenpeace, which sued Robinson for libel) with what Parul Sehgal in the *New York Times* terms "frank combativeness." Observing that "Robinson presents herself as an unfashionable contrarian," Engebretson describes the difficulty of placing her in the canon of contemporary literature. Noting her opposition to a culture—and a literature—mired in anxiety and disappointment, he joins other critics in distinguishing her from modernist and postmodern writers. Instead, he links her to Romanticism, highlighting her belief in consciousness as a source of revelation and her "exalted, optimistic view of self" as an inheritance from writers like Emerson, Melville, and Dickinson: "In returning to these 'old aunts and uncles,' Robinson sidesteps modernism to recover and reimagine the strong, deep, optimistic self from the nineteenth century" (8). Robinson's style collaborates with this vision of her writing. Engebretson opens his volume by citing James Wood's assertion that "Robinson's words have a spiritual force that is rare in contemporary fiction" (1).

Embracing a writer who endorses optimism, beauty, and belief in a skeptical age, critics have explored, with specificity and power, the aesthetics of transcendence and the relevance of faith—what Wood describes as the "spiritual force"—of Robinson's fiction. Criticism of her works is frequently framed within the context of religion and literature, as readers and scholars alike turn to her novels as an alternative to nihilistic vision and literary exhaustion. Describing the unique impact of Robinson's fiction in a *New Yorker* essay entitled "The First Church of Marilynne Robinson," Mark O'Connell observes, "She makes an atheist reader like myself capable of identifying with the sense of a fallen world that is filled with pain and sadness but also suffused with divine grace." Declaring herself an agnostic lacking a framework for belief or conviction, Rachel Vorona Cote describes turning to Robinson's work in the attempt to "grasp for some form of structural transcendence" in a dark personal and political time:

My husband, also disinclined towards organized religion, had recently read Robinson's 2004 novel, *Gilead*. I witnessed him in the aftermath, tearful and enthralled, and thought that perhaps I had found my Virgil: a woman of faith to guide me through her theological web—and who could believe in my stead what I feared couldn't possibly be true.

Cote concludes her provocative essay, aptly titled "The Complicated Comforts of Marilynne Robinson," by questioning the certitude of voice in Robinson's nonfiction, qualifying the assurance of its assertive optimism with a theoretical critique of its assumptions.[5] Although I share some of Cote's reactions to Robinson's polemical nonfiction, which has sometimes served as an unexamined frame for readings of her fiction, the varied and distinctive narrative voices of her novels complicate their assertions of certitude. Robinson's powerful testimony to the possibilities of belief in her writing represents a welcome alternative to the nihilism of the twenty-first century; the eagerness with which critics have embraced the forms of revelation and the rhythms of conviction in her work, however, threatens to obscure the complex phenomenological and narrative instabilities evident in her fiction. In *Literature after Postmodernism: Reconstructive Fantasies*, Irmtaud Huber traces recent scholarly and artistic reactions to the limits of postmodernism: "Having reached the limits of irony and skepticism, there seems to be a general agreement that literature is struggling to recover a sense of commitment and sincerity. Such a struggle…can indeed at times seem blatantly anachronistic, desperately futile, hopelessly naïve or embarrassingly optimistic" (24). The same impulse that leads critics to embrace the revelatory qualities of Robinson's work in an age of skepticism, in other words, risks consigning it to the category of the old-fashioned, the unselfconscious, or the irrelevant.

None of these criticisms, I would argue, apply to Robinson's fiction. Although my focus in this study is not on religion, the tensions I observe throughout might be seen to reflect rather than refute Robinson's religious sensibility; her view of religion situates the dynamics of faith not only in moments of transcendent belief but in what she describes as the "lived experience" of the everyday. "To associate religion with unwavering faith in any creed or practice," Robinson observes, "does no justice at all to its

---

[5] Cote concludes her essay by saying, "Still, too much fear and doubt becomes unwieldy: lately I'm not so much grappling as flailing my arms, with feet lodged in half-ossified mud. But my eyes are chasing flecks of light. They're there, those roving glints, wild and skittish, but if I squint just right, they'll illuminate the reasons to crawl towards something better. I'm willing to be optimistic about this much: Marilynne Robinson—certain of grace, certain, perhaps, of too many things—taught me how to look."

complexity as lived experience. Creeds themselves exist to stabilize the intense speculations that religion, which is always about the ultimate nature of things, will inspire" ("Highest Candle" 131). The complexity of lived experience plays out in the novel form; attention to the everyday reveals the way her fiction uncovers the dynamics of stabilization enacted by characters and narrative alike. Her aesthetic of transcendence reveals itself as implicated in structures of perception and imagination, both in the characters' psychic strategies for negotiating loss and in the reader's apprehension of narratives marked by Robinson's characteristic lyricism and textured images. Reading backwards from heightened moments of transcendence into the patterns of the hours and days they punctuate often reveals the psychic and stylistic force required to maintain everyday postures and images of transfiguration that the novels appear to naturalize.

For that reason, I am drawn to recent readings of her work that acknowledge the way that, in Robinson's novels, both metaphor and conviction must continually renegotiate their purchase on a shifting ground. In a recent essay in *Christianity and Literature*, for example, Matthew Potts observes of *Housekeeping*:

> And although I believe the naming of the baptismal analogy is appropriate and accurate, it also raises provocative theological questions. Because however transformed Ruthie is by her passage, she remains consumed still by loss, unreconciled to her loved ones, living and dead. The passage does not release Ruth from her aching grief. Instead, [it] presents a new and cruel estrangement to consider. This moment that bulges so memorably for Ruthie may indeed be a sign of baptism, but death and loss and anguish and alienation persist so tragically in the wake of this dark passage that it should stir in the theologically minded reader some uncomfortable reflection. (489)

Such "uncomfortable reflection," it seems to me, is not a challenge to Robinson's religious vision but a testimony to her willingness to explore what she terms religion's "complexity as lived experience." Potts's desire to complicate the religious and symbolic frames applied to Robinson's fiction reflects an uneasiness with the certainty of correspondence that Robinson herself critiques in her foreword to Faulkner's *The Sound and the Fury*: "There are perils in interpreting a fiction on the basis of biblical symbols or references, a risk of finding a fixed meaning in these references that denies an appropriate attention to the complexities of the fiction as a whole" (xvi).

Attention to the uncomfortable everyday that the protagonists of her novels inhabit destabilizes but does not destroy the images of reconciliation and transformation they endeavor to sustain; operating at multiple levels, Robinson's fiction locates the challenge of lived experience in the complex negotiation of the physical and the metaphysical, the everyday and the transcendent.

In *Postmodern Belief: American Literature and Religion since 1960*, Amy Hungerford situates Robinson's complication of unwavering faith and stable creeds within the productive tension between theological doctrine and lived experience, citing her first novel as an example:

> The relentless generation of likeness in *Housekeeping* is not so much a remedy for radical unlikeness, then, as the natural response of human longing upon the perception of unlikeness. Just as Sylvie and Ruth finally cross the bridge that a doomed train spectacularly fails to cross in the novel's opening scenes, the human effort, *at great cost*, is to bridge the gap, draw difference closer, knit up the world... As we come full circle from a theology of these differences to the lived experience of difference and reconciliation in the home and in the writer's housekeeping (knitting up a fictional world), it becomes clear that difference is not for Robinson a problem to be solved but rather the occasion for living a religious life.
>
> (120–1, emphasis mine)

Like Potts, Hungerford highlights the way that Robinson represents—and even embraces—the tension she associates with the dynamics of belief. In my exploration of what Hungerford describes as "the lived experience of difference and reconciliation" in Robinson's fiction, the context of the everyday directs focus away from images of transfiguration and revelation to what Hungerford refers to briefly as the "great cost" of that attempt to "knit up the world." In relocating acknowledgment of that cost from a subordinate clause to a place in the critical spotlight, my argument highlights the hourly and daily impact of trauma and loss, pushing back against the motions of consolation and coherence in the novels to explore their origins and effects in the lived experience of the everyday.

Attending to the costs as well as the compensations of transcending loss in Robinson's fiction reveals the complexity of her representations and the contemporary relevance of her writing. If some religious studies framings of the novels risk sidelining dimensions of her writing that stir "uncomfortable reflection" in the "theologically minded reader," the opposite dynamic chances equal foreclosure. The very expressiveness of Robinson's writing registers as a form of aesthetic compensation that some secular, theoretical, or political critics approach with suspicion. Viewed within the context of current debates about the role of the novel in a post-postmodern universe, not only the focus on religious belief or the "exalted" motions of transcendence in her fiction but the lyrical beauty of Robinson's prose might appear to render it an example of a dated approach to representation. In "Two Directions for the Novel," her 2009 essay, Zadie Smith famously interrogates a genre of recent fiction she terms lyrical realism, using Joseph O'Neill's *Netherland* to identify and critique a literature that she traces to its origin in the nineteenth-century lyrical realism of Balzac and Flaubert. Specifically, Smith highlights the dangers of the consolation of style in contemporary fiction, repeatedly invoking terms such as "transcendence" and "transubstantiation" that she frames as outdated and out of touch. Hanging on to "the rituals and garments of transcendence" ("Directions" 81) that are necessarily "empty" in a culture of skepticism, fiction like O'Neill's, she argues, offers only "the nostalgic pleasure of returning to a narrative time when symbols and mottoes were full of meaning and novels... could aim themselves simply and purely at transcendent feeling" (75). Pushing back against the consolation of lyrical language that manifests in "pretty quotes," Smith describes the way that, in *Netherland*, "transubstantiation shows itself for what it is: the beautiful pretence of the disappeared remainder" (90). In our contemporary political and artistic climate, she posits, literature that "wants always to comfort us, to assure us of our beautiful plenitude," obscures the realities of limitation and loss, both psychic and social (80–1).

Within such a rendering, not only Robinson's affirmation of religious belief in a secular age but her lyrical prose style and the motion toward transcendence in her novels might implicate her in an aesthetics of consolation that ignores the lessons of contemporary theory and glosses over the complex lived realities of personal and political existence. In his response to Smith's essay, David James situates Smith's suspicion of lyrical realism, with it "reliance on lushly evoked impressions and soothing resolutions," within the context of Fredric Jameson's account of modernist moments that "could perfect themselves only by being insulated from the messy materiality of the world they lyrically transfigure" ("Defense" 77). Robinson's novels, in a line of argument running from Jameson to Smith, might appear out of touch with or insulated from historical forces or social tensions, and thus risk occupying a marginalized position in the discourse of what contemporary fiction can and should be. The otherworldliness of her fiction, it might be said, propels us into a realm where, in James's summary of Smith's argument, "style becomes a controversial counterpoint for loss, an antagonist of despair" ("Defense" 87). Amy Hungerford's broader critical argument in *Postmodern Belief: American Literature and Religion since 1960* assumes relevance here, as she traces the way that faith in literary style parallels and often replaces the force of religious belief in recent fiction. Contemporary American writers, she claims, "turn to religion to imagine the purely formal elements of language in transcendent terms" (xiii). Seen in this context, it is not surprising that postmodernism's dismissal of religious belief should extend to other forms of transcendence in the novel; as "the formal elements of language [function] as a substitute for the content of belief" (108), faith in literary style, one might argue, becomes the last battleground for skepticism.

My goal is not to argue for reading Robinson primarily as a political writer (although a recent anthology on politics has done so) (see Mariotti and Lane), but to push back against readings that, in the face of her lyrical style and luminous imagery, disregard the "messy materiality" of lived experience in her fiction. By revealing how the novels themselves unsettle the process of transfiguration they often enact, I hope to follow in David James's footsteps as he argues in defense of lyrical realism; close attention to literary style, he asserts, need not foreclose emphasis on fiction's social and psychic relevance, but can serve as a means of opening up the complex ways in which the novel offers, in Caroline Levine's terms, "a thought experiment in creating models for life" (quoted in "Defense" 86). Attending to the phenomenology of narrative voice in Robinson's fiction highlights an uncomfortable experience of the everyday that, in her novels, often fuels the impulse toward transcendence. Like the texts that James explores, Robinson's fiction stages the dynamics of consolation and critique simultaneously.

After noting Robinson's opposition to anxiety and disappointment and describing her self-presentation as "an unfashionable contrarian," Engebretson goes on to describe her as "comfortable with tension and paradox" and "most critical of epistemological simplicity and certainty" (109, 117). Indeed, I will argue, Robinson's novels stage, in part through their deployment of narrative voice, the tensions that emerge when characters struggle to accommodate or escape the daily, lived experience of trauma and loss. Even as the beauty of Robinson's prose facilitates the motion from the ordinary to the extraordinary, the physical to the metaphysical, her works strain against the coherence of their own aesthetic production. Rather than leaving the "messy materiality" of the world behind, moments of transfiguration in her fiction often illuminate the bits and pieces of doubt, desire, and devastation her unifying figures sweep into the shadows. In response to Thomas Schaub's questioning the consolations of her first novel during an interview for *Contemporary Literature*—"I think in *Housekeeping*, too, where Ruth asserts that everything that rises must unite, it's not clear, at least to this reader, whether Ruthie's engaging in wishful thinking"—Robinson responds by highlighting the constructedness of reality:

> What, in effect, anyone does...is to cast out nets or lures or whatever that they hope, that they consider are appropriate to snagging a bit of reality for them. Of course what they catch depends on what they deploy. They can never know that with a finer net or a larger net or a better lure they'd have brought in a different reality. (240)

She then goes on to invoke Emerson and Melville within a framework that attributes to the romantic tradition within which critics often situate her a self-conscious methodology critical of its own linguistic consolations and aesthetic devices:

> The masthead chapter [in *Moby Dick*] is a classic demonstration of a sort of Emersonian method which is based on the assumption of the inadequacy of the method. That's what is so brilliant about it. You can create an absolutely dazzling metaphor that seems to be resolving things and pulling things together and reconciling things and making sense of things, and then you can collapse the metaphor, and what you're left with is an understanding that's larger than you had before, but finally it is a legitimate understanding because you know it's wrong or you know it's imperfectly partial... [Language] has its own logic, because it wants to go its own way. There's always the drift toward self-invited order in language that makes resolutions that are too neat or too small or beside the point. (240–1)

The dynamics of language and literary representation, Robinson makes clear here, "drift" toward "self-invited order," the coherence of which may be facilitated by "dazzling" metaphors that only seem to be resolving contradictions and tensions. Because such resolution, in her rendering, is always too neat, understanding necessarily involves awareness of the constructedness of coherence or consolation: "finally it is a legitimate understanding because you know it's wrong or you know it's imperfectly partial." If Robinson's novels, in the terms of Zadie Smith's critique, "aim themselves simply and purely at transcendent feeling," their metaphysical trajectories are embedded in narratives that disrupt the seemingly effortless motion toward transcendence, returning us instead to the uncomfortable experience of the everyday and the awkward mechanisms of meaning making.

As the lyrical interludes in Robinson's novels become less frequent, I will argue, her more recent fiction unveils a critique present from the beginning, but often obscured by the lyrical prose of *Housekeeping* and *Gilead*. My close attention to narrative voice and style, combined with a focus on the everyday, highlights the urgency and the relevance of the real-world issues Robinson raises. Although historical references to racial inequities, gender assumptions, and climate crises situate her fiction in the sociopolitical dynamics of historical periods and specific events, I am most interested in exploring the phenomenology of narrative voice in her works. In a series of narratives driven not by plot events but by the felt rhythms of days and hours lived in the wake of trauma and the anticipation of loss, Robinson's fiction offers intimate entry to the lived experience of homelessness, aging, abuse, neglect, grief, and poverty. Pivoting away from dramatic episodes of trauma and heightened moments of transcendence to the lived experience of the everyday, I will argue, reveals how these dynamics saturate the worlds and voices of Robinson's protagonists, emerging both in the disrupted rhythms of the daily and in the lyrical cadences of epiphanic perception that strain to take their place.

Opening up the realm of the everyday to accommodate what cannot be taken for granted extends Robinson criticism to encompass not only the way human perception transfigures the quotidian universe, illuminating the ordinary, but the way that heightened experiences and traumatic events settle into daily life and ordinary acts. "What is most important is to note," as Henri Lefebvre observes in *Critique of Everyday Life*, "that feelings, ideas, lifestyles and pleasures are confirmed in the everyday" (45). The everyday is infused with thought as well as thoughtlessness, emotion as well as habit. In a desire to resist focus on narrative events, everyday theory often posits the need to spotlight the habitual, familiar aspects of the everyday that are relegated to the background of critical attention. The artificial isolation of what is routine and taken for granted, however, risks disrupting the balance of experience that everyday theory seeks to restore, of providing a definition of the everyday that, "like all definitions, tends to immobilize what it is trying to define" (Lefebvre, *Critique* 43). If dailiness, in Bryony Randall's terms, is not "a grid overlaid on an otherwise uninflected psyche," attention to the everyday should ultimately gesture toward acknowledging the embodied subject's dynamic negotiation of a lived world in which patterns of thought become habitual, while feelings and past experiences haunt routine acts and repeated gestures (*Modernism* 9). In both the storyworld and the narrative discourse of Robinson's fiction, eating, sleeping, and opening doors are seldom *only* physical motions or mere mechanisms of mimetic grounding. Both immersed in and separated from the ordinary worlds they inhabit, her protagonists' self-conscious negotiation of the everyday reveals the artifice inherent in the separation of what Lefebvre terms the "upper" and "lower" spheres; if the everyday is a level of being, restoring attention to its marginalized status should operate, ultimately, in the service of recognizing the permeability of a border that separates the abstract and the concrete only in theoretical terms. "In one sense," Lefebvre observes, "there is nothing more simple and more obvious than everyday life. How do people live? ... nothing could be more superficial: it is banality, triviality, repetitiveness. And yet in another sense nothing could be more profound. It is existence and the 'lived'" (*Critique* 47).

*   *   *

In framing Robinson's fiction within the experiential dynamics of the lived, *The Elusive Everyday* situates the insights of everyday life studies within dialogues from multiple disciplines and approaches, including the sociology and psychology of aging, trauma, anxiety, and grief, feminist theories of domesticity and space, narrative theory, race theory, phenomenology, cognitive theory, and cultural studies. By locating Robinson's representations in the intersections between such diverse frames of reference, I hope to gesture toward what Lefebvre describes as the profundity of everyday life, highlighting the depth and range of everyday experience and gesturing toward the scope and power of its representation in Robinson's fiction. For me, the stakes in such a project include not only expanding the reach of the everyday and highlighting the complexity, relevance, and contemporaneity of Robinson's fiction, but acknowledging the power of the contemporary novel to embody the lived experience of a broken world continually haunted by the presence of beauty and the possibility of belief.

The narrators of Robinson's early fiction, as I will explore in Chapters 2 and 3, conspire in the acts of representation that fuel her poetic narratives; declaring their heightened experience of the quotidian as adequate recompense for their expulsion from the ordinary, they dwell in an imagistic reality that the aesthetic appeal of the novel persuades the reader to inhabit. The lyrical beauty of *Housekeeping*, Chapter 2 argues, obscures the way in which the dynamics of grief that shape its content unfold in the interstices of the ordinary. This chapter shifts focus away from the luminous images of the novel to the lived experiences of traumatic grief those images often veil. Although the plot of *Housekeeping* centers on a series of deaths, desertions, and losses, its lyrical beauty offers stylistic reinforcement of a first-person narrative that seeks consolation in immaterial forms. Critical focus on the transfigured ordinary and its aesthetic compensations tends to substantiate rather than interrogate the project of Ruth, focusing on the vibrancy and vitality of the images that she conjures rather than her terrifying expulsion from the everyday. As a narrator whose poetic descriptions of the ordinary often obtain the power to mesmerize, Ruth conspires with such readings by continually redirecting focus away from the lived world that she inhabits uncomfortably. Even as it lends form to her abstract imaginings, however, the novel disrupts the illusions she creates to return us to the quotidian. Haunted by memories of maternal presence and incapable of resurrecting her mother, Robinson's protagonist attempts to write herself out of the everyday world and into the spectral landscape in which her mother continues to exist; rendering her own embodied existence in ghostly terms, Ruth situates herself in a phantom ordinary. Establishing a dialogue between psychological and phenomenological approaches to trauma and the everyday, this chapter highlights the narrative strategies that mediate Ruth's unfolding experience of traumatic grief in the novel. *Housekeeping*, I argue, subtly interrogates Ruth's substitution of aesthetic images for ordinary presence in a way that anticipates the dramatic collapse of aesthetic consolation in Robinson's later fiction.

Like Ruth, who observes that in the wake of tragedy even "the ordinary demanded unblinking attention" (166), the protagonists of Robinson's other novels all find themselves expelled from the habitual realm of the ordinary. The cultural force of *Gilead*, Chapter 3 argues, stems from its powerful unveiling of how dying complicates the sensory and psychological dynamics of human perception, expelling Robinson's aging and ailing narrator from the ordinary world his prose so beautifully illuminates. In his journal to his son, Ames uses language to compensate for his anticipated absence; mediated as it is through the lyricism of Ames's voice, however, the reader's experience of this first-person narrative may achieve an aesthetic transcendence that belies the aching apprehension of loss that functions as its scaffolding. Readings of the novel that focus on aesthetic or religious compensations for loss tend to accept at face value the transcendent vision of everyday experience that Robinson's narrator labors to maintain. In highlighting the "miraculous" power associated with the narrator's heightened perception of the moment, critics risk ignoring the novel's inquiry into how the anticipation of "looking back from the grave" disrupts Ames's somatosensory experience in the narrative present. *Gilead* localizes Ames's psychic struggle with his own imminent death in acts of perceptual processing that it both depicts and thematizes. Combining physiological, sociological, and psychological approaches to aging with phenomenology and cognitive theories of perception, this chapter explores how the novel pushes existential concerns into the realm of the everyday to explore the way that the lived experience of dying traps Robinson's protagonist uncomfortably in the collapsing space between perception and representation.

Although heightened sensation registers powerfully and beautifully in the narrative discourse of Robinson's early texts, it fails to protect the protagonists of *Housekeeping* and *Gilead* from the encroachment of loss into the parameters of the storyworld, a dynamic rendered more visible in the uncomfortable narratives that follow. Largely abandoning the lyrical prose of her first two novels, Robinson adopts in *Home* and *Lila* more conventional third-person narratives grounded in dialogue and detail; as these novels creep closer and closer to their protagonists' everyday experiences, dwelling naturalistically on the particulars of ordinary life, the intimacy such a narrative strategy would seem to promise dissolves into a flatness that critics sometimes register in responses ranging from boredom to aesthetic dissatisfaction. These novels stall the reader in an everyday world that is often uncomfortable and unilluminated. Although Robinson's characters consistently experience the ordinary as inhospitable, the protagonists of her earlier novels convert that estrangement into a form of heightened perception facilitated by the lyricism of Robinson's prose; *Home* and *Lila*, on the other hand, often reproduce stylistically the awkward gestures their protagonists repeat as they struggle to inhabit the everyday. As Robinson's fiction moves away from the characteristically lyrical voice of her first-person narrators, her novels challenge aesthetic expectation and unsettle assumptions about depth that link the span of consciousness to the complexity of fictional characterization. In fact, I will argue, the third-person focalized narratives of *Home* and *Lila* capture the motion of their protagonists' consciousness powerfully, if not always beautifully, by enacting in narrative terms their uncomfortable expulsion from the conventions of the everyday; these texts register the experience of alienation by denying the reader the comfortable rhythms of narrative convention and the consolation of aesthetic form.

By locating the reader uncomfortably within its circumscribed fictional world, Chapter 4 argues, *Home* highlights the confining cultural and narrative structures through which the everyday dynamics of family are often experienced and represented. Despite its focus on quotidian detail, the novel's spare plot, limited cast of characters, narrowly confined setting, and achingly slow pace resist the comforts of the ordinary. In its refusal to provide mechanisms of imaginative transcendence that would transport the reader out of the Boughtons' oppressive dwelling or make it more hospitable, the novel renders domestic and narrative space equally uncomfortable. Revealing the way that Glory, the novel's reserved and "straightforward" protagonist, remains trapped within her role as keeper of a symbolic home that she alone must literally inhabit, the novel disrupts the story she painstakingly constructs to expose the unworkable fixtures of domestic life and the forced conventions of narrative upon which that story depends. Using narrative theory, cultural studies explorations of family and memory, and feminist theories of gender and space, this chapter explores how *Home* unsettles the culturally sanctioned idea of home as an escape from the contesting ideologies of the larger world even as it reveals the force of our investment in a domestic ideal that legislates, sanctions, and naturalizes scripted performances of the ordinary.

Although *Lila* seems to promise access to the interiority of a character whose life has unfolded under the stresses of poverty, abuse, and homelessness, the novel captures the rhythms of its protagonist's existence through acts of narrative repetition and deflection that defend against intimacy. Lila's inability to feel at home reflects a self-consciousness rooted in the trauma of childhood abandonment, violence, and forced sex work. Her exclusion from the everyday is marked by a sense of being alert, unable to relax into quotidian experience or predictable routine. As the repetitive enactment of trauma-induced anxiety crowds out the comforting backdrop of the everyday, Chapter 5 argues, *Lila* exposes its protagonist's awkward presence in an uncomfortable narrative and phenomenological world. The structure of the novel reflects Lila's experience of existential anxiety by constantly revisiting her detachment from the lived world of the novel. The protagonists of *Housekeeping* and *Gilead* inhabit the everyday self-consciously, transforming the ordinary into a form of numinous presence; Lila's self-conscious perception, on the other hand, continually returns her to an uncomfortable presence amplified by shame. Rather than fostering the illusion of access, the novel adopts a more radical stance, replacing the narrative construction of Lila's interiority with the disrupted rhythm of an everyday world that remains flat and inaccessible. The aesthetic choices that some critics decry thus mirror the structure of Lila's anxiety. Using the frames of everyday studies and narrative theory, as well as sociological, phenomenological, and psychological studies of trauma and anxiety, this chapter explores why and how *Lila* refuses to lend the reader the intimate access to character or the heightened acts of perception that many critics see as characteristic of Robinson's fiction.

Whereas the lyrical voices of *Housekeeping* and *Gilead* collaborate with the work of their narrators to rewrite loss, *Home* and *Lila* document the expulsion of their protagonists from the dynamics of ordinary life on which their more naturalistic narratives appear to dwell. Although the novels focus closely on the particulars of daily life, the foregrounding of the everyday overwhelms characters crowded out by their own futile attempts to embody cultural norms. In contrast, the protagonist of Robinson's most recent novel struggles with an experience of marginalization not explained by the dynamics of gender, class, or upbringing. Through its focus on an interracial relationship in St. Louis after the Second World War, *Jack* interrogates the imaginative privilege of a white character whose seeming transcendence of the ordinary occurs at the expense of the black woman he romances. Robinson's protagonist consistently frames his lived experience in literary and symbolic terms that situate him in a representational realm devoid of empirical effect; at the same time, he seeks objective correlatives for a consistent feeling of alienation that contradicts his apparent privilege. By setting the romance central to the novel in a time and space where quotidian divisions of geography and law exaggerate the policing of the black body, Chapter 6 argues, the novel raises the stakes of Jack's decision to locate himself outside the conventions of ordinary life. Jack's aesthetic sensibility immobilizes and isolates him in an imaginative landscape; his desire to have Della accompany him there, however, implicates him in the literal destruction of her everyday world. Even as their unsanctioned marriage objectifies and exacerbates Jack's existential challenge, rendering their combined existence illegal, it threatens Della's home, her safety, and her livelihood. This chapter uses phenomenological race theory and everyday life studies to highlight the way that the historical, material, and political pressures of the period, including the threat of eminent domain that looms over the abstracted landscape of the novel, disrupt Jack's literary and symbolic rendering of this love story. By inviting the reader to pursue Jack's imaginative interests, the novel constructs an uncomfortable romance troubled by the encroachments of the wider world it would exclude.

Existing in a heightened state linked to the perception of loss, the protagonists of Robinson's fiction find themselves expelled from the realm of the
ordinary. Her characters inhabit a defamiliarized landscape that demands
the rigid maintenance of aesthetic, existential, or social self-consciousness.
Robinson's novels situate their protagonists in a representational relationship
to reality that renders the habitual, embodied dynamics of ordinary life
elusive. Habits of literary reading that consign the everyday to the background
facilitate perceptual shifts that endorse the symbolic and stylistic recuperation
of loss, contributing to the tendency of Robinson scholarship to focus on the
resignifying power of the novels' religious, aesthetic, or perceptual frames. The
withdrawal of the consolations of literary form in her recent fiction, however,
exposes the strained facsimile of the everyday that serves as the backdrop for
all her novels. Shifting critical attention to the awkward positioning of her
characters in the everyday illuminates the void around which Robinson's
fiction takes shape, revealing the way in which loss registers not only in the
realm of the tragic and the sublime but in the labored performance required
to maintain the "taken-for-granted backdrop" that is the ordinary (Felski,
"Invention" 80).

2

Housekeeping and the Phantom Ordinary

Although the plot of *Housekeeping* centers on a series of deaths, desertions, and losses, its lyrical beauty offers stylistic reinforcement of a first-person narrative that seeks consolation in immaterial forms. Paul Tyndall and Fred Ribkoff describe the speculative mode of *Housekeeping* as a narrative and stylistic device Ruth employs "to come to terms with grief and loneliness, and ultimately to transcend the pain and alienation of everyday life" (88). Tracing religion's role in the aesthetics of Robinson's fiction, Ray Horton explores the way that the novel initiates a process of "transfiguring and renewing the familiar objects of perception" (130). Ruth's narrative, Mary Esteve argues, "ends by reveling in a surfeit of fictitiousness, effectively bidding farewell to the actual" (241). Although they acknowledge the tension between Ruth's experience of traumatic loss and her attempts at narrative compensation, critics tend to follow the novel's lead in dwelling on the consolation of image and aesthetic form.[1] As a narrator whose poetic descriptions of the ordinary often obtain the power to mesmerize, Ruth conspires with such readings by continually redirecting focus away from the lived world that she inhabits uncomfortably. Even as it lends form to her abstract imaginings, however, the novel disrupts the illusions she creates to return us to the quotidian. In the argument that follows, I will use the frame of the everyday to push back against the powerful aesthetic force of Ruth's imaginings and Robinson's writing to highlight the significance of the uncomfortable ordinary. In doing so, I hope not to resolve the tensions of the novel but to restore its disequilibrium, an imbalance rooted in its disclosure of Ruth's inability to transcend the ordinary or settle comfortably into the everyday.

---

[1] Stefan Mattessich, for example, highlights the way that the formal properties of the text negotiate trauma by overlaying the miraculous over naturalistic description; the abstracted perspective that results, he argues, results in a productive self-consciousness, "the equilibrium of the schizoid self in the volatile space of its worldly implication."

The Elusive Everyday in the Fiction of Marilynne Robinson. Laura E. Tanner, Oxford University Press (2021).
© Laura E. Tanner. DOI: 10.1093/oso/9780192896360.003.0002

Housekeeping is filled with violent and cataclysmic losses that, in combination, undermine the protagonist's grounding in home, family, community, and identity. For Ruth, the spectacular suicide of her mother, the discovery of the dead body of her grandmother, the desertion of her sister, all contribute to what Cathy Caruth describes as "the fundamental dislocation implied by traumatic experience" (9). A number of critics have traced the way in which *Housekeeping* can be read as a trauma narrative.[2] My interest lies in the way in which the dynamics of traumatic loss that shape the form of *Housekeeping* unfold in the dark interstices of the ordinary. Ruth's exquisitely textured images of her mother testify to an embodied absence the significance of which she consistently disavows. Critical focus on the transfigured ordinary and its aesthetic compensations tends to substantiate rather than interrogate the project of Ruth, focusing on the vibrancy and vitality of the images that she conjures rather than her terrifying expulsion from the everyday. The romantic resignification of her escape from the domestic world ignores the way in which Ruth's retreat into representational space reenacts the gesture with which the novel begins: the suicide of her mother. Shifting critical attention to the awkward positioning of Robinson's protagonist in the everyday illuminates the void around which the novel takes shape, revealing the way in which loss registers not only in the realm of the tragic and the sublime but in the labored performance required to maintain what Rita Felski terms the "taken-for-granted backdrop" that is the ordinary ("Invention" 17). *Housekeeping* subtly but powerfully interrogates Ruth's substitution of aesthetic images for ordinary presence in a way that anticipates the dramatic collapse of aesthetic consolation in Robinson's later fiction.

*   *   *

The novel locates the effects of trauma and loss in the realm of the everyday. In doing so, however, it complicates understandings of the everyday as the tacit background of existence, the habits, motions, gestures that we enact without conscious thought or reflection. Unlike the stabilizing platform of routine posited by most everyday theorists, the everyday of *Housekeeping* is characterized by disrupted rhythms, self-conscious acts, and disabled experiences. By revealing the way that consciousness and emotion encroach

---

[2] See Christine Caver,"Nothing Left to Lose: *Housekeeping*'s Strange Freedoms." Tace Hedrick, "'The Perimeters of Our Wandering Are Nowhere': Breaching the Domestic in *Housekeeping*," Sinead McDermott, "Future-Perfect: Gender, Nostalgia, and the Not Yet Presented in Marilynne Robinson's *Housekeeping*," and Martha Ravits, "Extending the American Range: Marilynne Robinson's Housekeeping."

upon the parameters of even the most mundane lived experiences, the novel traces the collapse of the distinction between foreground and background that Felski's model of the everyday posits. *Housekeeping*'s repeated references to the "ordinary" only emphasize the elusiveness of that realm; the novel documents Ruth's conscious and continual search for a form of daily lived experience that is routine in its predictability.

In his work on the phenomenology of trauma and everyday life, Robert D. Stolorow explores the way that trauma shatters the "horizons of normal everydayness" ("Phenomenology of Trauma" 467). Psychological trauma manifests not only in a relationship to a single jarring event or events, but in an altered relationship to a lived world the most basic parameters of which can no longer be taken for granted. Insofar as the assumptions of stability and predictability that we associate with ordinary life allow us to function on a daily basis, the perceived absence of safety and continuity expels the traumatized person from the comfort of the everyday. "Stripped of its sheltering illusions," Stolorow concludes, "the everyday world loses its significance, and the traumatized person ... feels anxious and uncanny—no longer safely at home in the everyday world" ("Identity" 207).

If, as Stolorow argues, "trauma shatters the absolutisms of everyday life" that serve as the scaffolding of the daily, *Housekeeping* explores the way that such a shattering renders even the most ordinary acts strange and unfamiliar ("Existential Anxiety, Finitude, and Trauma" 44). Held at bay by her psychological and narrative strategies, the world-shattering effects of Ruth's repeated experiences of loss emerge only gradually in the novel. Even in the more detached early sections of her narrative, however, Ruth foregrounds the everyday by illuminating it as the stage on which trauma is enacted. Her narrative rendering emphasizes how the train accident that devastates her grandmother—and the community of Fingerbone—penetrates and revises the conventions of the everyday: "One day my grandmother must have carried out a basket of sheets to hang in the spring sunlight, wearing her widow's black, performing the rituals of the ordinary as an act of faith" (16). The "performance" of the ordinary represents a failed attempt to reinstate the taken-for-granted quality that defines the everyday in the wake of sudden and traumatic loss:

And she whited shoes and braided hair and turned back bed clothes as if reenacting the commonplace would make it merely commonplace again, or as if she could find the chink, the flaw, in her serenely orderly and ordinary life ... she was aware of too many things, having no principle for selecting the more from the less important, and that her awareness could never be diminished, since it was among the things she had thought of as familiar that this disaster had taken shape.   (25)

For those left behind, the "disaster" that causes husbands and fathers to vanish into the lake without warning creates a disturbance that plays out not just in the mind but in daily experience, rendering the most habitual motions alien and the most ordinary acts unfamiliar. Catastrophe dislodges and denaturalizes the conventions of domesticity, rendering the grand-mother's relationship to her "orderly and ordinary life" oddly self-conscious and contingent.[3] "No longer safely at home in the everyday world," the grandmother experiences a form of psychic dislocation that permeates her forced attempts to renegotiate a once familiar landscape. Like Sylvie, the homeless wanderer who "undertook the most ordinary things with an arch, tense, tentative good will that made them seem difficult and remarkable" (187), Ruth's grandmother performs the smooth motions of housekeeping with a self-consciousness that renders even her practiced motions awkward.

For most of *Housekeeping*, Ruth details the way in which those around her are expelled from the ordinary without acknowledging her own presence in that disrupted landscape. Describing the train accident that widows several members of the community as an assault on "the dear ordinary," Ruth observes, "That event had troubled the very medium of their lives. Time and air and sunlight bore wave and wave of shock, until all the shock was spent, and time and space and light grew still again and nothing seemed to tremble, and nothing seemed to lean" (15). The trembling and leaning of time and space testify to the way in which trauma disrupts not only the habitual motions of ordinary life but the very structures that orient and locate the self; the spectacular derailment cannot be contained as event but instead dissipates, troubling "the very medium" of the lives of the survivors who absorb its impact. The Fingerbone community responds to the experi-ence of such "fundamental dislocation" (Caruth 9) by attempting to locate the source and thus confine the effects of their trauma:

> They began to speculate that this was not after all the place where the train
> left the bridge. There were questions about how the train would move

---

[3] Kristin Imre argues persuasively for considering the shift in Ruth's relationship to the everyday through the lens of attention rather than action; Ruth's heightened attentiveness to routine acts, as Imre explores, renders even the most ordinary gestures or activities unfamiliar.

through the water. Would it sink like a stone despite its speed, or slide like an eel despite its weight? If it did leave the tracks here, perhaps it came to rest a hundred feet ahead. Or again it might have rolled or slid when it struck bottom, since the bridge pilings were set in the crest of a chain of flooded hills, which on one side formed the wall of a broad valley (there was another chain of hills twenty miles north, some of them islands) and on the other side fell away in cliffs. Apparently these hills were the bank of still another lake, and were made of some brittle stone which had been mined by the water and fallen sheerly away. If the train had gone over on the south side (the testimony of the porter and the waiter was that it had, but by this time they were credited very little) and had slid or rolled once or twice, it might have fallen again, farther and much longer.   (7)

The focus here on pinning down the trajectory of the derailed train, although presumably in the service of locating its inhabitants, also betrays a desire to respond to the dislocation of trauma by situating this inexplicable accident within precise referential systems of direction, angle, and quantifiable measurement. Instead of shoring up a familiar landscape that, in the wake of catastrophe, has begun to tremble and lean, however, the geographical mapping collapses into the undifferentiated; hills and valleys, solid and liquid, dissolve without regard for borders or boundaries, as even stone is "mined" by water and "fall[s] sheerly away." As the narrative piles question upon question and theory upon speculation, the breathless motion of accumulating conditionals betrays the limits of a quest for objectification and precision meant to keep the dislocation of trauma at bay.

Although Ruth holds herself distant from the experience of disequilibrium she narrates, her own estrangement from the everyday manifests itself in the form of a heightened awareness that prohibits her from relaxing into the lived world she reports on. The everyday is often defined not only by its content but by its form; daily rituals and routine acts emerge as everyday not merely because they are habitual and repeated but because they are undertaken in what Ella Ophir describes as an "inattentive" mode ("Modernist Fiction" 15). Everyday life, Felski argues, "simply is the routine act of conducting one's day to day existence without making it an object of conscious attention" ("Invention" 27). Everyday attention, Bryony Randall argues, "would be characterized by its lack of attention" (47). Even as its title directs us toward the everyday and its descriptions render the quotidian detail luminous, *Housekeeping* thematizes the cost of pulling the "taken-for-granted backdrop of the ordinary" (Felski, "Invention" 17) into the spotlight.

A childhood defined by repeated catastrophic loss renders Ruthie unable to relax into the comfort of habit or routine. Instead, she remarks, "We had spent our lives watching and listening with the constant sharp attention of children lost in the dark. It seemed that we were bewilderingly lost in a landscape that, with any light at all, would be wholly familiar" (130).

The novel marks Ruth's expulsion from the assumption of a lived world into a continuous mode of heightened attentiveness. The sudden and inexplicable suicide of her mother, coupled with the death of her grandmother, leads Ruth into a state of constant alert that manifests in her continual anticipation of imminent catastrophe. Like her widowed grandmother, whose "awareness could never be diminished, since it was among the things she had thought of as familiar that...disaster had taken shape," Ruth's only routine is sustained hypervigilance (25). Her everyday life with Sylvie is punctuated by panicked attention to potential clues of her aunt's desertion or death. Seeing Sylvie with her coat on the morning after she arrives, Ruth and her sister immediately assume that Sylvie is abandoning them, rather than planning to take a walk. At several points in the novel when her aunt fails to answer Ruth's call, Ruth panics, racing through the house and shouting Sylvie's name repeatedly. When the sisters glimpse Sylvie on the railroad bridge, they immediately assume that she has gone there to jump. Although Sylvie reassures them,

> We were very upset, all the same, for reasons too numerous to mention. Clearly our aunt was not a stable person. At the time we did not put this thought into words. It existed between us as a sort of undifferentiated attentiveness to all the details of her appearance and behavior. At first this took the form of sudden awakening in the middle of the night, though how the sounds that woke us were to be interpreted we were never sure. Sometimes they occurred in our heads, or in the woods...one's own dread is always mirrored upon the dread that inheres in things. (82–3)

Citing the unusual vigilance that often follows trauma, Kai Erikson charts the way that trauma not only assaults the stability of subjectivity but alters processes of perception and interpretation: "[Trauma survivors] evaluate the data of life differently, read signs differently, see omens that the rest of us are for the most part spared" (195). In the wake of catastrophe, Ruth's "undifferentiated attentiveness" to quotidian detail continually disrupts any attempt to relax into the routine of the everyday (82). Even sleep, which promises a relaxation from hyperconsciousness, affords her no respite; she remains constantly on guard for signs of imagined danger. Although Sylvie's instability provides a resting place for Ruth's anxiety, the threats Ruth reacts to come from within as well as from without.

Sylvie's sleeping posture originates in the pragmatic vigilance of a transient with no roof over her head: "when Sylvie lay down there was nothing of crouch or sprawl. Even when she slept, her body retained the formality of posture one learns when one sleeps on park benches" (138); Ruth's tense sleep, however, responds to a threat of a different kind, one much more difficult to isolate and defuse. For the trauma survivor, Gretchen Schmelzer observes, "Any thoughts of the future are imagined to be as dangerous as the trauma that was experienced, so any planning for the future is to protect yourself from what already happened" (38). Without present referent or the promise of future respite, the hypervigilance associated with trauma cannot be assuaged. Ruth's inability to relax into the comfort of sleep manifests not only outside, where, she remarks, we "fell uneasily asleep, never forgetting that we must keep our heels against our buttocks, always aware of the mites and flies in the sand" (115), but in the familiar space of her own home, by the warmth of the fire: "I slept precariously upright, aware of my bare feet, hearing the wood in the stove crackle" (118). *Housekeeping*'s aesthetic intensity is thus enacted at the expense of a protagonist who patrols the margins of the ordinary with unceasing vigilance; Ruth's capacity to be dazzled by the commonplace marks less her immersion in the textured details of the everyday than her expulsion from its comfortable realm. "That most moments were substantially the same," as Ruth observes, "did not detract at all from the possibility that the next moment might be utterly different. And so the ordinary demanded unblinking attention. Any tedious hour might be the last of its kind" (166).

* * *

Although Ruth is clearly located in the storyworld of the novel, she rarely registers her felt presence there or acknowledges the traumatic impact of the repeated losses she suffers. The first-person narrative of *Housekeeping* is consistently descriptive and often poetic; in the first three-quarters of the novel, however, Ruth's struggle for detachment manifests in a carefully legislated narrative voice that struggles to contain her subjective presence within disciplined form. Early on, the event of her grandmother's death is buried in the detached formality of a subordinate clause: "When, after almost five years, my grandmother one winter morning eschewed awakening, Lily and Nona were fetched from Spokane and took up housekeeping in Fingerbone" (29). The logistical detailing that follows distracts from Ruth's unwillingness to linger over the death of her grandmother, her closest relative and sole guardian after the suicide of her mother. The significance of that understatement is revealed only later in the novel, when Ruth gestures toward the traumatic impact of this moment by belatedly acknowledging her own physical location in the scene of her grandmother's death: "Lucille and I had found her crouched on her side with her feet braced against the rumble of bed clothes, her arms flung up, her head flung back, her pigtail trailing across the pillows" (164). The defensive posture of her grandmother's contracted body and braced feet belies the gentle passivity of the earlier narrative of her death, in which Ruth's grandmother simply and decorously "eschewed awakening." The disjointed image of a corpse with its arms flung up and head flung back occupying her grandmother's bed reflects the violent way in which, for a young girl, the familiar is rendered suddenly and alarmingly alien. Ruth's narrative return to the scene of her grandmother's death functions as the unbidden structural repetition of a traumatic event in which, despite her efforts at narrative dissociation, she remains intimately located.

Try though she does to contain it, the trauma of catastrophic loss results in a dynamic of dislocation that seeps from Ruth's experience as character into the forms of her narration. In her description of Fingerbone's response to the sudden deaths of the train passengers that plunged into the lake, Ruth charts the community's obsessive attempt to map the physical trajectory of the train in order to geographically locate their traumatic loss. Although Ruth has no part in the search committees that send divers into the lake or the forensic professionals that speculate on the train's angle of entry and distance traveled, her actions as narrator perform on a narrative plane a similar task of managing trauma. For much of the novel, Ruth's immersion in her narrative function manifests in a proliferation of details, directions, and categorizations that render the dislocation of loss in geographic terms.

Despite *Housekeeping*'s well-deserved reputation as a model of lyrical fiction, Ruth's motion through the landscape of the novel often adopts a quantitative, mathematical, and concrete language inversely proportional to the amorphous form of her overwhelming grief. The language of geometric space, as Stolorow explores more broadly, functions as one way to locate the emotional experience of trauma, "transform[ing] the vulnerable, context-dependent, and evanescent experience of mineness into the stability and clarity of geometric space" ("Phenomenology of Language" 5). Ruth's struggle to orient herself in a world defamiliarized by grief manifests in the construction of a narrative that employs surprisingly specific enumerative pauses ("all the windows—there were five altogether, and a door with five rows of small panes"), the terms of geometry ("the hall from the kitchen to the front door sloped rather sharply, though the angle was eased somewhat by a single step midway"), and the language of the compass ("we walked north, with the lake on our right hand") (20, 44, 112). Her narrative mapping extends to a rendering of her mother's suicide that lurches back and forth between what a child can name and know and all that cannot be grasped:

> Helen took us through the mountains and across the desert and into the mountains again, and at last to the lake and over the bridge into town, left at the light on to Sycamore Street and straight for six blocks. She put our suitcases in the screened porch, which was populated by a cat and a matronly washing machine, and told us to wait quietly. Then she went back to the car and drove North almost to Tyler, where she sailed in Bernice's Ford from the top of a cliff named Whiskey Rock into the blackest depth of the lake.   (22)

As the "blackest depth" of Ruth's loss resists articulation and form, she names what she is able to identify, whether it be the broad forms of a shifting landscape, the numbers of blocks after an intersection, or the assorted objects she inventories in a room. Her telling responds to the dissolution of the taken-for-granted with the labored performance of a narrative that would erect structure and routine through enumeration and observation. Contrasting the everyday experience of space with the "imaginary totalizations" of geographical systems that represent landscape, de Certeau describes the everyday as what escapes mapping, "the practices that are foreign to the 'geometrical' or 'geographical' space of visual, panoptic, or theoretical constructions" (93). Commenting on ways of abstracting space that order and contain, he observes, "the geographical system [may] transform action into legibility, but in doing so it causes a way of being in the world to be forgotten" (97). Ruth's geometrical mapping of her mother's suicide route functions both to stabilize her apprehension of the tilting world and to disavow an intimate experience of it that she labors to forget.

Ruth's attempt to anchor herself in a world turned upside down by trauma assumes corporeal form as she attempts, in the wake of her mother's absence, to ground herself in relation to Sylvie. Working from the outside in, Ruth wills her body to assume the habits and posture that would signify the innate maternal connection that she has lost. Racing to catch up with an aunt whose maternal presence she can never assume, Ruth mimics Sylvie's confident stance and relaxed demeanor in a series of discrete bodily postures and movements:

> Finally, Sylvie was in front of me, and I put my hands in my pockets, and tilted my head, and strode, as she did, and it was as if I were her shadow, and moved after her only because she moved and not because I willed this pace, this pocketing of the hands, this tilt of the head.   (145)

Ruth responds to the dislocation of trauma by attempting to reconstruct a severed bond on a step-by-step basis, concentrating with determination on performing a sequence of corporeal motions that would naturalize her connection with Sylvie. The articulation and repetition of the discrete components of the supposedly effortless stance she adopts, however, expose Ruth's disjointed experience of being in the world, undermining her claim that "following [Sylvie] required neither will nor effort" (145). Treating her body as a system that she can control and legislate through the force of her own determination, Ruth emphasizes the very alienation from the ordinary that she seeks to address.

Under the discursive cover of her function as a first-person narrator, Ruth's diegetic performance reveals a similarly detached relationship to the everyday world of the novel. Her status as storyteller disguises, at least to some degree, her estrangement from the relaxed and inattentive mode of the everyday. The conventions of a first-person narrative that relies on description to situate the reader in any scene often obscure Ruth's forced attempt to orient herself in a landscape that should be intimately familiar. Her use of narrative strategies to artificially locate herself in what should be an ordered and ordinary world becomes most visible in moments of the novel that thematize the process of orientation they simultaneously enact:

> We felt small in the landscape, and out of place. We usually walked up a little sheltered beach where there had once been a dock, and there were still six pilings, upon which, typically, perched five gulls. At intervals the gull on the northernmost piling departed with four cries, and all the other gulls fluttered northward by one piling. Then the sojourner would return and alight on the southernmost piling. This sequence was repeated again and again, with only clumsy and accidental variations. We sat on the beach just above the place where the water wet it and sorted stones (Fingerbone had at the best a rim or lip of sand three or four feet wide—its beaches were mostly edged with little Pebbles half the size of peas).   (79–80)

Ruth's elaborate breakdown of the habitual into a series of micro-steps testifies to a type of forced attentiveness that belies the inattentive, taken-for-granted quality that theorists associate with the everyday. Ruth testifies to routine in a hypervigilant fashion that contests the everyday mode of attention and the naturalized sequence of ordinary acts. Couched in the service of what Roland Barthes describes as "the reality effect," the prolifer-ation of fictional details that sustain referential illusion (148), Ruth uses her status as narrator to situate herself reassuringly in a world in which she feels "out of place." Insofar as the conventions of description demand the artic-ulation of even the most familiar settings a character inhabits, Ruth's status as narrator allows her to deemphasize her estrangement from the ordinary even as she attempts to recuperate it in narrative terms. Ruth's breakdown of the habitual into a series of cataloged steps—a strategy that governs her description of the gulls on the pier as well as her attempt to mimic Sylvie's walk—undercuts in its attentiveness the taken-for-granted status of an everyday world in which Ruth struggles to immerse herself unself-consciously.[4]

As the everyday world eludes her, Ruth uses narrative technique—enumeration, repetition, directional location, measurement—to create a structure that would hold the trembling, leaning world in place.[5] In "Naming the Indescribable," Dora Zhang juxtaposes "the felt qualities of our everyday experience" with the mediation of language, highlighting the limits of description and the difficulty of translating the warmth and inti-macy of everyday knowing into the abstract forms of representation (59). *Housekeeping* traces the same tension from an opposite perspective. Inverting the dynamics of representation Zhang outlines, Ruth uses descrip-tion not to capture but to create a place for herself in the everyday world:

> The shore drifted in a long, slow curve, outward to a point, beyond which three steep islands of diminishing size continued the sweep of the land towards the depths of the lake, tentatively, like an ellipsis. The point was high and stony, crested with fir trees. At its foot a narrow margin of brown sand abstracted its crude shape into one pure curve of calligraphic delicacy, sweeping, again, toward the lake. We crossed the point at its base, climbing

---

[4] As narrator, she performs that connection in a different way, offering multiple images and metaphors of pregnancy and childbirth that would naturalize her embodied relationship to Sylvie in the same scene: "I crawled under her body and out between her legs" (146), "I lay like a seed in a husk" (162), "I swelled and swelled until I burst Sylvie's coat" (162).

[5] See Maurice Merleau-Ponty's *Phenomenology of Perception* for a discussion of the interplay of body and space that creates the structure of habit.

down its farther side to the shore of the little bay where the perch bit. A quarter of a mile beyond, a massive peninsula foreshortened the horizon. (113)

Working backward from description, Ruth works to locate herself in what Henri Lefebvre describes as the "irrefutable concreteness" of the everyday world (55). In attempting to anchor herself in the everyday by mapping her surroundings, however, Ruth situates herself in the domain of "'geometrical' or 'geographical' space" that de Certeau opposes to the practice of the everyday (93). Largely absent from the first half of the novel, the felt qualities of everyday experience that Zhang describes as primary are replaced by the built world of narrative; Ruth materializes only as a figure dwarfed by the landscape she represents. Even as she uses familiar strategies of enumeration, measurement, and geometry to counter the displacement of trauma, Ruth's first-person narrative continually detaches itself from the intimacy of everyday engagement. Her mapping of the landscape slips into a panoramic perspective locating Ruth and her sister at a coordinate at the base of a point situated against a curve.

The novel highlights this tension in the passage above by documenting the slippage of Ruth's empirical description into forced abstraction. Through an analogy that compares the sweep of land with "an ellipsis" and a metaphor that describes the "margin of sand" that "abstracted its crude shape into one curve of calligraphic delicacy," the novel connects Ruth's "geometrical" view of space, which de Certeau links with visual, panoptical, or theoretical construction, with the act of writing. Ruth uses her status as narrator to enforce her location in a landscape that, unlike the images in her mind, "had weight and took up space" (163); even as she uses description to enumerate and solidify, however, the ties she attempts to create to her surroundings continually slip into abstraction, marking the failure of her efforts to write herself into a lifeworld that remains stubbornly and persistently "strange."

Ruth's narrative choices are partially obscured by conventions of first-person narration that justify a detailed description of even a character's most familiar surroundings. The narrating act, it might be said, provides aesthetic cover for Ruth's estrangement from the ordinary. Artistic representation, as Arto Haapala explores, typically reflects a perceptual acuity that he contrasts with an everyday relationship to space. Ruth's estranged relationship with the ordinary bears close resemblance to what Haapala terms "the outsider's gaze": "strangeness creates a suitable setting for aesthetic considerations.

Our senses are more on alert in a strange milieu than in our home region" (44). Insofar as the dynamics of aesthetic defamiliarization resist an everyday way of apprehending place, Ruth's discursive role in the novel seemingly justifies her hypervigilance by situating it on a narrative plane. Ultimately, however, the novel reveals the limits of its protagonist's forced attempt to evacuate the landscape of the storyworld. Arguing that "we are in the world in such a way that we create familiarity around ourselves," Haapala emphasizes that "strangeness ... cannot be a continual state": "While we are living in the lifeworld, doing and making things ... we create ties to our surroundings, and in this way familiarize ourselves with it. We make the environment 'our own'" (40, 44–5). Ruth's attempt to use description as a response to the dynamics of traumatic dislocation only highlights her continual inability to make the environment her own; lacking what Zhang describes as "the inexorable, irreducible way in which we know our own experience," she begins with linguistic representation and tries to work her way back to the primacy of felt experience (59).

In her work on trauma and everyday life, Carola Kaplan extends Stolorow's theories of traumatic dissociation to encompass a category she terms "traumatic spatiality" (470). Highlighting the way that the ordinary physical world looms as a threat to a traumatized person, she observes, "If, to an untraumatized person, daily life is like a walk that stretches smoothly and safely ahead, to a traumatized person the pavement may at any moment crack open, revealing a sudden hole in space, an unbridgeable chasm into which the walker may fall and disappear" (470). In such a state, the border between physical and psychic vulnerability dissolves, destabilizing the ground beneath literally as well as figuratively. Trauma results in an experience of hypervigilance that refuses to be contained within the symbolic realm. Infiltrating ordinary acts in measurable terms of heart rate and systemic arousal, trauma "renders impossible the comfortable, inattentive navigation of daily life" (Ophir 15). In *Housekeeping*, the lake that is the site of trauma is notable not only for the many dead bodies it holds but for how it works its way daily into the somatosensory experience of the survivors. The widows of the town "said they could no longer live by the lake. They said the wind smelled of it, and they could taste it in the drinking water, and they could not abide the smell, the taste, or the sight of it" (8–9).

Ruth's experience of traumatic spatiality is reflected not only in her struggle to quantify, systematize, and orient, but in her description of Fingerbone as a place where the borders between solid and liquid, self and other, inside and outside continually collapse. In contrast to what Ruth describes as "the lake of charts and photographs," carefully mapped and possessing a clearly demarcated "stony, earthy bottom," the lake of lived experience in Fingerbone has a liquid foundation and a tendency to seep everywhere (9). *Housekeeping* reframes what de Certeau celebrates as the everyday experience of space—"a second, poetic geography on top of the geography of the literal" (105)—in terms that render the unstructured flow of lived world interaction diffuse and uncanny:

> It is true that one is always aware of the lake in Fingerbone, or the deeps of the lake, the lightless, airless waters below. When the ground is plowed in the spring, cut and laid open, what exhales from the furrows but that same, sharp, watery smell. The wind is watery, and all the pumps and creeks and ditches smell of water unalloyed by any other element. At the foundation is the old lake, which is smothered and nameless and altogether black.   (9)

Searching for the foundation of the lake, one finds only another lake: dark, undifferentiated, unnameable. Rather than functioning as an anomaly, the flood that fills the Foster house with thigh-deep water merely exposes the way in which the geography of the literal is undermined throughout the novel. Remarking that "the house flowed around us" (64), Ruth testifies to the collapse of the familiar. Neither natural landmarks nor human structures provide a frame of reference:

Lucille said, "I don't think Simmons's house is where it used to be."

Sylvie went to the door and peered down the street at a blackened roof. "It's so hard to tell."

"Those bushes used to be on the other side."

"Maybe the bushes have moved." (65)

Indeed, the novel undercuts the very source of location in the human body that, as Sara Ahmed argues following Merleau-Ponty, functions as the referent for understanding space: "The body provides us with a perspective: the body is 'here' as a point from which we begin, and from which the world unfolds, as being more or less over there" (8). For Ruth, in contrast, the dislocation of the physical environment seeps into and emerges from an unstable experience of embodiment that dissolves the illusion of spatial orientation:

When we did not move or speak, there was no proof that we were there at all. The wind and the water brought sounds intact from any imaginable distance. Deprived of all perspective and horizon, I found myself reduced to an intuition, and my sister and my aunt to something less than that. I was afraid to put out my hand, for fear it would touch nothing, or to speak, for fear no one would answer.   (70)

Stripped of its location in a point of origin or a medium of perception, the grounding of sensory experience is itself rendered unreliable. The watery landscape of the novel continually disrupts Ruth's narrative efforts to enumerate, chart, and measure, demonstrating not only the intangibility of the material environment but the unreliability of corporeal touchstones. The chiasmic intertwining of body and world that, in Merleau-Ponty's terms, underlies the exchange of touch here threatens to unravel. Unreciprocated, Ruth's prospective gesture reflects back to render her, like the fluid landscape that surrounds her, a mutable phantom presence. As sound travels "intact from any imaginable distance," empirical reference dissolves to emphasize Ruth's experience of dislocation: "Apart from the steady shimmering of the lake and the rush of the woods, there were singular, isolated lake sounds, placeless and disembodied, and very near my ears, like sounds in a dream" (115).

The watery landscape of *Housekeeping* emphasizes the twofold nature of what Kaplan describes as the "feeling of radical displacement" associated with trauma (470). Even as a sense of traumatic dislocation prohibits Ruth's immersion in an everyday landscape, separating her from the lived world she inhabits, trauma dissolves the assurances of everyday life that would function as a protective barrier. The traumatized person, Stolorow asserts, "cannot help but perceive aspects of existence that lie well outside the absolutized horizons of normal everydayness" ("Phenomenology of Trauma" 467). Ruth finds herself caught up in a landscape of intimate alienation in which trauma infuses commonplace acts and redefines the horizons of the ordinary, disrupting the illusion of "normal everydayness." The dislocation of trauma renders even the embodied grounding of daily experience illusory: "I was appalled by the sheer liquidity of the water beneath us. If I stepped over the side, where would my foot rest? Water is almost nothing, after all" (164).

When, as narrator, Ruth shifts her focus from a panoramic view of the landscape that surrounds her to her own embodied efforts to navigate that landscape, her detachment from the lifeworld manifests in an oddly distanced representation of her own experience:

> We walked along the shore more quickly than we had walked by daylight. Our backs were stiff and our ears hummed. Both of us fell repeatedly. As we were easing our way past a mass of rocks that jutted into the lake, my feet slipped on a silty face of submerged stone and I slid full-length into the water, bruising my knee and my rib and my cheek. Lucille pulled me up by the hair.   (117)

Although Ruth is positioned in the setting she describes, she lacks what Michael Sheringham describes in *Everyday Life* as the kind of "participation" in the lived world that marks our everyday engagement with space: "What needs 'factoring in' if one is to apprehend the everyday street is . . . our lived experience of it, our participation and immersion in its fields, the ways in which we make it part of our world and recognize it as such" (386). Even as she navigates this landscape, Ruth's disconnection from the everyday extends to detachment from her own bodily experience. Collapsing the distinction between her intimate sensations and those of her sister, she provides a succinct but unsituated bodily inventory: "Our backs were stiff and our ears hummed." Figuring her own body as a shape in a field of shapes, a mass easing past a mass of rocks, she renders her fall—"I slid full-length into the water"—in broad strokes that, combined with her description of Lucille pulling her up by the hair, render her lived experience of the scene elusively cartoonish. Her description of the "silty face of submerged stone" that she slips on registers in less detached terms than her catalog of her own injuries: bruised knee, rib, cheek. In passages such as this one, Ruth's narrative distills what Henri Lefebvre describes as "the murky thickness of everyday life" into outlines of bodies and acts, emptying out the texture of her own experience (66).

Shortly before this scene, Ruth describes herself as "invisible—incompletely and minimally existent, in fact" (105). Although her character goes through the motions of everyday life, her narration reflects—even as it attempts to recuperate—an alienation from the everyday that renders her "minimally existent." If the everyday is conceived as "a level of reality" (Lefebvre 47), Ruth's retreat into her status as narrator represents a failed attempt to ground or transcend her own awkwardly embodied presence: "It seemed to me that I made no impact on the world, and that in exchange I was privileged to watch it unawares. But my allusion to this feeling of ghostliness sounded peculiar, and sweat started all over my body, convicting me on the spot of gross corporeality" (105–6). Straddling the line between narrator and character, Ruth traverses the landscape of the novel unable either to anchor or to dematerialize her presence in the everyday world.

*   *   *

Critics of *Housekeeping* often refer to a shift in the novel's narrative voice, describing that evolution in varying terms. Katherine Weese discusses the way that Ruth's first-person narration assumes omniscience. Stefan Mattessich cites a change from a "naturalist" to a "miraculous" point of view (63), while Kristin King juxtaposes the gawky female narrator of the early novel with the self-assured narrator of the ending, who displays "resounding omniscience and authorial confidence" (569). None of these critics locate the transformation in narrative voice at a particular moment in the novel, or explain how the narration of the early novel relates to that of the ending. Using the intersection of trauma and the ordinary as a focus, I will argue that that change of voice represents the adoption of a new narrative strategy that correlates with Ruth's surrender to her alienation from the everyday. Whereas the restrained, logistical narrative impulse of the early novel represents an attempt to stabilize herself in the wake of traumatic dislocation, the trigger of an additional desertion prompts an experience of defensive dissociation that manifests in Ruth's expulsion from the storyworld of the narrative. At the end of the novel, she willfully vacates her position in the everyday in favor of a discursive presence that critics have aligned with the novel's increasingly omniscient and didactic narrative voice.

In his *Critique of Everyday Life*, Henri Lefebvre charts the accepted theoretical opposition between the "lower depths" of the everyday and the "upper sphere" against which it is posited.

> In the "lower depths," time and space are limited, and these limits must be endured; and yet individuals and groups have an environment; they find something compact and (relatively) solid around them and under their feet. It is a zone of sweaty, suffocating heat, of intimacy, where the temperature maintains an organic warmth…In the "upper sphere," space and time…open out indefinitely in the icy air of higher realms… People move and act amid formal and conventional abstractions, or more precisely, amid signs and signals.   (53)

Defining the everyday as "existence and the 'lived,' revealed as they are before speculative thought has transcribed them," Lefebvre emphasizes that the separation of these two spheres is possible only in theoretical terms (47).

Although Lefebvre's Marxist focus shifts his analysis to political and economic structures that perpetuate alienation, his critique highlights a continuing assumption of the everyday as "a level of reality" (47); situated "below" the spheres of consciousness and creativity that define the human, the lower level "has its compensation: the vitality and direct, immediate character of the 'lived,' a sort of irrefutable concreteness" (55). In *Housekeeping*, I will argue, Ruth's quest to anchor herself in the relative solidity of the everyday after her mother's suicide is continually frustrated by the way that thought and feeling infiltrate even the most mundane acts and habitual gestures of lived experience. The images of "organic warmth" and "icy air" that Lefebvre associates with the everyday and its abstract counterpart emerge with frequency in *Housekeeping*, a novel that figures its protagonist's struggle to inhabit the lived world in repeated images of her attempt to warm herself in an inhospitable landscape and, when that fails, to abandon that "level" of experience and embrace what Lefebvre describes as "the icy air of higher realms" (53).

The failure of Ruth's attempt to orient herself in an everyday landscape comes to a head in the scene where Sylvie leads Ruth into the fantastical landscape inhabited by imaginary children. Although the early part of this scene maintains a characteristic tension between Ruth's experience of dislocation and her efforts to ground herself in the everyday, the section culminates in Ruth's decision to abandon all efforts to ground herself in the empirical world of sensation and the assurance of the ordinary. The opening of this scene, in which Sylvie rouses Ruth to head out into the damp, cold darkness, emphasizes Ruth's forced expulsion from the everyday (145). As Maria Moss points out, Ruth agrees to this weekday expedition only because Sylvie craves it; Ruth herself prefers the structure and routine of school, despite its many negatives. Running behind Sylvie before dawn with her shoes untied, her coat undone, gripping a piece of bread that Sylvie tells her to eat while she walks, Ruth observes, "There was nothing out there—no smell of wood smoke or oatmeal—to hint at human comfort . . . I had given up all sensation to the discomforts of cold and haste and hunger, and crouched far inside myself" (144). As narrator, Ruth uses analogy to suture together this disarticulated experience of being in the world. Using "like" and "as if" as discursive springboards, she attempts to stabilize her location in an environment saturated not only with sensory discomfort but with the trauma of her mother's suicide: "I walked after Sylvie down the shore, all at peace, and at ease, and I thought, We are the same. She could as well be my mother. I crouched and slept in her very shape like an unborn child" (145).

Extending the manipulation of bodily posture into the realm of narrative, Ruth uses metaphor to "crouch and sleep," attempting to restore a lost maternal connection in surprisingly tangible terms even as she abstracts Sylvie's presence into an unspecified shape. The repetition of the verb "crouch" in these adjacent passages emphasizes the metaphorical sleight of hand; narratively, Ruth converts the posture signifying withdrawal and discomfort—"I had given up all sensation to the discomforts of cold and haste and hunger, and crouched far inside myself"—into a womb-like image that would lend material force to Ruth's symbolic attempt to heal her cold and orphan status. The dislocation of trauma plays out in the intermingling of psychic loss and physical discomfort, both of which Ruth struggles to dismiss; proclaiming that she is "all at peace, and at ease," she labors to construct a way of being at home in a world rendered strange by the experience of traumatic grief.

Despite her claim of being "at ease," the scene that follows is punctuated by Ruth's continual attempts to restore what she describes earlier as an "orderly and ordinary" world of warmth and nourishment that she can no longer take for granted:

> [Sylvie] was unperturbed by our bare escape and by her drenched loafers and the soggy skirts of her coat. I found myself wondering if this was why she came home with fish in her pockets.
>
> "Aren't you cold, Sylvie?"
>
> "The sun's coming up," she said. The sky above Fingerbone was a floral yellow. A few spindled clouds smoldered and glowed a most unfiery pink... In an hour it would be the ordinary sun, spreading modest and impersonal light on an ordinary world, and that thought relieved me.   (147)

Even as Ruth's narrative voice relies on image and metaphor to frame this setting, her telling disrupts a purely aesthetic frame by emphasizing the lived experience of this inhospitable landscape; although the sky glows "a most unfiery pink," its beauty holds no warmth. Returning repeatedly to the experience of overwhelming cold, Ruth consistently longs for the restoration of "an ordinary world":

> "Well, let's not wait here, though. It's too cold."
>
> Sylvie glanced at me, a little surprised. "But you'll want to watch for the children." ...

"Yes, but it's too cold here." ...

After a while I said, "Sylvie?"

She smiled. "Shhh."

"Where's our lunch?" (151)

Repeatedly voicing her need for the structure and safety of routine—food, warmth, a day punctuated by the assurance of meal time, school time, bed time—Ruth seeks out what Lefebvre describes as the solidity and "organic warmth" of the everyday (53). In opposition to Ruth's quest for ordinary warmth, Sylvie offers the beauty of a frozen landscape:

We walked up it along the deep, pebbly bed left by the runoff in the rain, and there we came upon the place Sylvie had told me about, stunted orchard and lilacs and stone doorstep and fallen house, all white with a brine of frost. Sylvie smiled at me. "Pretty, isn't it?"

"It's pretty, but I don't know how anyone could have wanted to *live* here." (151)

Stone and stunted, this deserted landscape with its brine of frost crystallizes the breath of lived experience, its brilliant sheen brittle and uninhabitable.

It is here that Ruth's quest to resituate herself in the ordinary world, to find warmth and sustenance, collapses, forcing her to find another form of comfort entirely. Ruth's short relationship with Sylvie has been punctuated from the beginning by a heightened vigilance born of her fear of imminent desertion. Abandoned by Sylvie without warning in this ice orchard— "Sylvie was gone. She had left without a word, or a sound" (153)—Ruth consciously surrenders her tenuous tie to the everyday:

I sat down on the grass, which was stiff with the cold ... and let the chills run in ripples, like breezy water ... up my neck. I let the numbing grass touch my ankles. I thought, Sylvie is nowhere, and sometime it will be dark. I thought, Let them come unhouse me of this flesh, and pry this house apart. It was no shelter now, it only kept me here alone, and I would rather be with them, if only to see them, even if they turned away from me.

(159–60)

Beneath the pressure of this final abandonment, the disciplined forms of narrative orientation give way, unleashing a grief for which the ordinary world has no answer. Ruth's imperative, "Let them come unhouse me of this flesh," represents a violent dissociation not only from her body but from the backdrop of the everyday that constitutes a platform for lived experience and realistic narrative. If, as Stolorow argues, the traumatized person "lives in another kind of reality, an experiential world felt to be incommensurable with those of others," the collapse of Ruth's location in an everyday world marks what he terms the defensive dissociation of traumatic shattering ("Phenomenological-Contextual" 133). Rendering her own embodied existence in ghostly terms, Ruth breaks with the conventions of empirical reference within which she has struggled to orient herself.

Willfully attempting to break her hold on the lived world of the novel, Robinson's character situates herself in a phantom ordinary. Acknowledging that her mother is "lost to all sense," Ruth writes herself out of the sensory world and into the spectral landscape in which her mother continues to exist:

> If I could see my mother, it would not have to be her eyes, her hair. I would not need to touch her sleeve. There was no more the stoop of her high shoulders. The lake had taken that, I knew. It was so very long since the dark had swum her hair, and there was nothing more to dream of, but often she almost slipped through any door I saw from the side of my eye, and it was she, and not changed, and not perished. She was a music I no longer heard, that rang in my mind, itself and nothing else, lost to all sense, but not perished, not perished. (159–60)

Her narrative continually replays images that come to constitute what Ruth describes as the mind's "music," an aesthetic image of consciousness echoed in the lyrical rhythms of Robinson's prose. Once again, Ruth's writerly status conspires with her narrative attempts to heal the dislocation of trauma. Highlighting the "force field of linguistic... effect," Garrett Stewart argues in *The Value of Style in Fiction* that "the momentum of prose has its own kind of generative structure" (27). For the reader, the compensations of lyrical language and textured image formally and stylistically supply, at the level of narrative discourse, support for Ruth's claim of her mother's absent presence. The rhythmical, repetitive flow of these lines—"She was a music I no longer heard, that rang in my mind, itself and nothing else, lost to all sense, but not perished, not perished"—lends sensory presence to an otherwise inaccessible form. The conventions of fiction predispose the reader to assent to a disavowal of the everyday in favor of a kind of lyrical or imagistic compensation that is, as readers, *our* only form of sensory immersion in the novel's world. Building on Peter Boxall's work on the dialectic between bodies and the immateriality of the texts that conjure them, Garrett Stewart observes,

> One way in which style takes part in manifesting this interchange between "mere" writing and embodiment is when it makes palpable in reading— makes all but tangible—the phonic basis of verbal production in the silent but no less material enunciation (somaticized by readers themselves) of lexical forms and syntactic rhythms. In this way, the active engagement of our sensorium brings us closer to the imagined corporeal energy of fictional characters—across the conduit of style.   (*Value* 2)

In this case, style creates a form of sensory presence that substantiates Helen's dematerialized form; the conventions of reading render Ruth's body and its ghostly counterpart similarly palpable. The beauty of Robinson's words rings in the reader's mind, a lingering affirmation of Ruth's claim that what cannot be touched may still be present.

Initially, Ruth observes of the icy landscape in which Sylvie abandons her, "The lilacs rattled. The stone step was too cold to be set upon. It seemed at first that there was no comfort for me here at all" (155). Unable to make herself comfortable on those cold stone steps, Ruth increasingly moves out of the storyworld into diegetic space, so that her presence as character becomes steadily overwhelmed by her narrative function. From the beginning of the novel, the duality of Ruth's position in the text as actor and teller creates a tension: "It was a source of both terror and comfort to me then that I often seemed invisible—incompletely and minimally existent, in fact. It seemed to me that I made no impact on the world, and that in exchange I was privileged to watch it unawares. But my allusion to this feeling of ghostliness sounded peculiar, and sweat started all over my body, convincing me on the spot of gross corporeality" (105–6). Ruth's process of evacuating corporeal presence culminates in the staged suicide of the novel's conclusion, which allows her to begin a sentence with the casual phrase, "Since we are dead" (217). Ruth's first-person narrative, dependent as it is on her location within the storyworld, dissolves along with her embodied presence into an unmoored, abstracted narrative voice; "breaking the tethers of need one by one," she willfully begins to erase her location in the novel (204). In her place emerges a more philosophical narrative voice that subsumes her presence within larger cultural narratives of loss and longing.

Imagine a Carthage sown with salt, and all the sowers gone, and the seeds lain however long in the earth, till there rose finally in vegetable profusion leaves and trees of rime and brine. What flowering would there be in such a garden? Light would force each salt calyx to open in prisms, and to fruit heavily with bright globes of water.   (152)

Like the bright prismed landscape of light Ruth describes as "fruiting" with water, the beauty of this description threatens to obscure the empty content. The flow of the passage—"leaves and trees of rime and brine"—is facilitated by a slant rhyme that, in aural terms, smooths over the tension between form and content, rhyme and rime. Lyrical passages such as this one enact what Karsten Harries describes in "Metaphor and Transcendence" as a process of poetic collusion that "decompose[s] familiar reality": "This collusion, which has its ground not so much in a real similarity of the referents as in the flow and texture of the words themselves...lets us accept the poet's broken metaphors" (81). Even as Ruth resignifies the inhospitable landscape in which she finds herself abandoned, however, the narrative word choice emphasizes Ruth's sleight of hand; growing "in vegetable profusion," the rime leaves and brine trees Ruth describes are narratively situated in the realm of everyday sustenance that Ruth attempts to disavow.

Religious references in this section of the novel hold the same tension. As Ruth's evolving narrative voice labors to dissolve her personal loss into biblical archetype, the aesthetic force of her prose lightens the dark outlines of choices that threaten to disrupt their stabilizing function in the narrative: "If there had been snow I would have made a statue, a woman to stand along the path, among the trees. The children would have come close, to look at her. Lot's wife was salt and barren, because she was full of loss and mourning, and looked back" (153). Even as she would subsume her own story within stabilizing biblical precedent, Ruth's focus on Lot's wife—like her reference to Noah's wife at the end of the novel—demonstrates her attraction to marginalized characters and disruptive moments in the Bible. Whereas the biblical story presents Lot's wife as a disobedient minor character whose punishment reiterates the grandeur of God and his judgment of Sodom and Gomorrah, Ruth's representation reframes her "looking back" as an intimate act of turning away from the orphan children who surround her:

But here rare flowers would gleam in her hair, and on her breast, and in her hands, and there would be children all around her, to love and marvel at

her for her beauty, and to laugh at her extravagant adornments, as if they
had set the flowers in her hair and thrown down the flowers at her feet, and
they would forgive her, eagerly and lavishly, for turning away, though she
never asked to be forgiven. Though her hands were ice and did not touch
them, she would be more than mother to them, she so calm, so still, and
they such wild and orphan things.   (153)

The maternal figure that Ruth imagines is cloaked in floral adornments that
parallel the beauty of Ruth's narrative voice. Like the barren and beautiful
landscape in which she is situated, however, this unresponsive maternal
figure offers a beauty that is decidedly cold. In its rhythmic enumeration of
the statue's components—"here rare flowers would gleam in her hair, and on
her breast, and in her hands"—the passage enacts the beauty it attributes to
her, even as it lingers sensually on the elements of a female body that might
but do not nurture. Despite its mythic appropriations and its "extravagant
adornments," Ruth's narrative fails to animate the unresponsive presence at
its core.

Arguing that Ruth's symbolically powerful and increasingly confident
authorial voice "undermines the narrative of plain fact it purports to be
tracking" (572), Kristin King reads this scene as a testimony to female
sovereignty:

> "More than mother" suggests the possibility of other roles beyond mother-
> ing. But it also suggests new constructions of mothering in which women
> are not punished for looking in other directions, for expressing desire:
> "they would forgive her, eagerly and lavishly, for turning away." Ruth's
> enjambment with these ghost children ... suggests that she too can mother
> herself through desire. Like the transformation of the icy valley when the
> slant of new light "coax[es] a flowering from the frost, which before seemed
> barren and parched as salt" (p. 152), the myth of female desire/defiance
> made immobile and mute for turning against the word of God is given a
> new slant in the image of lovable and shimmering extravagance that
> mothers these strange children.   (573–4)

Accepting Ruth's observations at face value, King parallels this image with
the "flowering" of the ice valley. In both cases, however, the novel reveals
that beauty is achieved at the cost of sensory and human warmth. The
subordinate clause at the end of a lyrical sentence divided by ten com-
mas—"though she never asked to be forgiven"—betrays a lingering

resentment reiterated in the subordinate clause tucked at the beginning of the next: "though her hands were ice and did not touch them, she would be more than mother to them." These references to frigidity and intangibility bracket the phrase "more than mother," emphasizing even as they dismiss the quotidian impact of a maternal figure that "turn[s] away."

Once again, the everyday impact of her mother's suicide reverberates beneath Ruth's claims of aesthetic or symbolic compensation, disrupting the beauty of her figurations. The ice hands of this figure situate her in the landscape of cold stone and rattling lilacs of which Ruth declares earlier, "It's pretty, but I don't know how anyone could have wanted to *live* here." Robin Vogelzang describes Robinson's view of metaphor as "both powerfully connective—linking writer and reader, word and reality—and profoundly, even constructively, limited by human inability to fully integrate its parts" (748). As Robinson herself makes clear, the "dazzling" face of metaphor masks its necessary imperfection: "You can create an absolutely dazzling metaphor that seems to be resolving things and pulling things together and reconciling things and making sense of things, and then you can collapse the metaphor, and what you're left with is an understanding that's larger than you had before, but finally it is a legitimate understanding because you know it's wrong or you know it's imperfectly partial" (Interview, 240–1).

The maternal figures that Ruth's imagination fashions, whether they be ghostly images or women made of snow, illuminate the void that they are meant to fill; they are all marked by a frigidity or aloofness that manifests the unrequited desire for physical connection that Robinson's protagonist desperately seeks to repress. The more heightened these figures become, the more inaccessible they are; Ruth's narrative crafts images that project an aesthetic integrity inversely proportional to their tangibility. Although her philosophical ruminations and aesthetic constructions would pull her into the icy realm of the abstract where, in Lefebvre's terms, consciousness and creativity reside, the trauma of abandonment returns her again and again to what the symbolic cannot reach: the dark, gaping holes that have swallowed up the familiar quotidian landmarks of the everyday. Not surprisingly, then, Ruth's turn to cultural and religious narrative to shore up the dislocation of trauma often falters. Ruth refigures the story of Christ's death, for example, in intimately singular and oddly mundane terms that resist transcendence or abstraction:

And when He did die it was sad—such a young man, so full of promise, and His mother wept and His friends could not believe the loss, and the

story spread everywhere and the mourning would not be comforted, until
He was so sharply lacked and so powerfully remembered that his friends
felt Him beside them as they walked along the road, and saw someone
cooking fish on the shore and knew it to be Him, and sat down to supper
with Him, all wounded as He was.   (194)

Ruth focuses on the grounded, everyday aspects of Christ's rising from the
dead, never mentioning his ascension into a heavenly sphere. The symbolic
aspects of Christian theology are, for Ruth, less important than their material referents; this powerfully signifying narrative is resituated in the realm of
the ordinary, where the trauma of Ruth's loss settles. Rejecting the allure of
otherworldliness, she dwells on the everyday acts that follow Christ's resurrection: walking along the road with friends, cooking, sitting down to
supper. In this scenario, Christ's wounding testifies to the immediacy of a
tangible presence that Ruth contrasts with the "subtle and miscible" images
of consciousness.

Even as she struggles to hold the trauma of her mother's suicide at a
distance, Ruth's hope that "memory will fulfill itself, and become flesh"
underlies her response to her own loss (195). Reflecting at the end of the
novel on the narrative of her mother's death, Ruth highlights the opposition
between ordinary presence and its heightened, aestheticized, and symbolic
counterpart in the wake of tragedy. Returning to the scene of their final
journey together, Ruth acknowledges the way that memory renders her
mother's ordinary presence profound and apocalyptic, as what was once
taken for granted comes to bear the weight and significance of impending loss:

It seemed to me that in all this there was the hush and solemnity of
incipient transfiguration ... For it seems to me that we were recalled
again and again to a sense of her calm. It seems that her quiet startled us,
though she was always quiet ... I remember her, grave with the peace of the
destined, the summoned, and she seems almost an apparition.

But if she had simply brought us home again to the high frame apartment
building with the scaffolding of stairs, I would not remember her that way.
Her eccentricities might have irked and embarrassed us when we grew
older. We might have forgotten her birthday, and teased her to buy a car or
to change her hair. We would have left her finally ... Then we would
telephone her out of guilt and nostalgia, and laugh bitterly afterward
because she asked us nothing, and told us nothing, and fell silent from
time to time, and was glad to get off the phone.   (197)

Loss plays out in the evacuation of the everyday, displacing the quotidian incidentals of hair styles and birthdays and phone calls—as well as the petty frictions and ambivalent emotions accompanying them—with memories that assume retrospective import. Ruth's grief-stricken consciousness transforms inconsequential or routine details into signs that resonate with significance, rendering ordinary presence simultaneously portentous and apparitional.

In her provocative discussion of the fictional versus the actual in *Housekeeping*, Mary Esteve argues,

> And Ruth clearly prefers her "miracle" of transfigured memory to this what-if scenario. The transfiguration renders her mother one of Ruth's revered personae who reiterate a nearly infinite series of losses, abandonments, and sorrows, stretching back to Cain and Abel...The effect of Ruth's transfiguration is...to fix her in a fictitious destiny of apparition that has little or nothing to do with her once-living personhood. (244–5)

Although I observe the same tension between the fictional and the actual that Esteve cites, I am reluctant to dismiss the vision of the everyday that Ruth offers as the poor cousin of transfigured memory. Remarking on "the blitheness with which Ruth negates her conjecture" of everyday life with her mother, Esteve concludes, "While we like to think that people aspire to quality, not quantity, of life, we might also expect a daughter to prefer being 'irked and embarrassed' by her mother's lengthy, suicide-free life than to transfigure and marvel over her terrible demise" (244). In fact, I would suggest, Ruth's meditation on the nature of loss exposes the "marvel" of her mother's transfigured presence as a hollow construct; it is exactly the loss of her mother's "once-living personhood" that Ruth laments, linked here with the irk and embarrassment of everyday squabbles that would testify to the routine dynamics of ordinary presence.

Even as imagination positions her mother in the realm of image and archetype, transfiguring her ordinary presence in a way that locates her alongside Cain, Abel, and other mythical figures, it renders her apparitional and elusive. Ruth's imagining of ordinary interactions highlights the taken-for-granted quality of an everyday maternal presence that stretches over the course of days and years, a fixture of family life that, even as it reflects the embarrassment of adolescence or the obligation of adulthood, can always be assumed. Charting the way that grief interferes with ongoing lives and projects, Bob Plant observes, "The phenomenological and psychological fact is that an absence can be more poignant, more noticeable, more obsessive, than any presence" (332). Memory simultaneously heightens and empties out, creating a form of absent presence that transcends what Lefebvre terms "the murky thickness of everyday life" at the cost of immersion in a textured world (66). As Ruth makes clear right before the passage Esteve references, the transfiguration of memory results in a form of presence simultaneously intensified and diminished:

> Sylvie did not want to lose me. She did not want me to grow gigantic and multiple, so that I seemed to fill the whole house, and she did not wish me to turn subtle and miscible, so that I could pass through the membranes that separate dream and dream. She did not wish to remember me. She much preferred my simple, ordinary presence, silent and ungainly though I might be.   (195)

Although *Housekeeping*'s imagistic and stylistic frames often redirect focus away from "simple, ordinary presence," the novel continually calls attention to what Esteve describes as Ruth's "logic of compensatory equivalence" (241). Passages such as this one thematize the limits of the compensations Ruth's narrative would enact. Tracing Ruth's negotiation between a world of sensation and its transformation through language and image, Stefan Mattessich argues, "The structural unconscious indicated by this negotiation depends, rather paradoxically perhaps, on the formal properties of her text, which balances a quest for the extraordinary (redemption) in the ordinary with the unsettling prospect of its ideality or false perfection" (65). Reading the novel through the lens of the diminished ordinary exposes, even as it fails to resolve, this sustaining tension.

Unable to rescue her mother from the intangible realms of memory and image, Ruth does the next best thing. Severing her relationship with the ordinary, she attempts to move from the lived world of the story into the space of representation her mother inhabits, a space she describes as one of "images and simulacra" (183). "By crossing into a space whose curvature is no longer that of the real," Baudrillard observes, "simulation is inaugurated by a liquidation of all referentials—worse: with their artificial resurrection in the system of signs, a material more malleable than meaning, in that it lends itself to all systems of equivalences" (95). In such a spectral landscape, it is impossible to distinguish "the real from its artificial resurrection, as everything is already dead and resurrected in advance" (95). Unable to resurrect her mother, Ruth unrealizes herself, imaging herself as a ghost moving through an intangible landscape. The townspeople, she observes, had reason to feel...that soon I would be lost to ordinary society. I would be a ghost, and their food would not answer to my hunger, and my hands could pass through their down quilts and tatted pillow covers and never feel them or find comfort in them. Like a soul released, I would find here only the images and simulacra of the things needed to sustain me.   (183)

Assigning the realm of the ordinary to townsfolk who inhabit a mundane world of down quilts and tatted pillow covers, Ruth figures herself as transcending the conventions of the everyday. Moving quickly away from how others perceive her, however, Ruth lingers instead on what she herself can neither feel nor perceive; although she describes herself as a soul released, she emphasizes not her transcendence of everyday needs but the failure of the ordinary world to satisfy her continuing hunger, offer her the comfort of sleep, or lend her the reciprocity of touch.

Although Sylvie's abandonment of Ruth turns out to be temporary, Ruth's experience of that final trauma sets in motion a process of withdrawal from the everyday world that culminates in her presumed death. After Ruth and Sylvie return home, the novel revisits the scene of Sylvie abandoning Ruth in the cold orchard. This time, however, it is Ruth who turns away from her own house to run out into the orchard and embrace the cold: "I learned an important thing in the orchard that night, which was that if you do not resist the cold, but simply relax and accept it, you no longer feel the cold as discomfort...I was hungry enough to begin to learn that hunger has its pleasures, and I was happily at ease in the dark, and in general, I could feel that I was breaking the tethers of need, one by one" (204). Through a process of rhetorical inversion, Ruth turns the ordinary inside out. Like the imaginary children in the first orchard scene, Ruth's location in the story-world dissolves into immateriality. If, as Carola Kaplan asserts, trauma creates "a feeling of radical displacement, of belonging nowhere, of being irremediably homeless" (470), Ruth responds to that feeling by attempting to sever the "tethers of need" that would bind her to domestic life.

Locked out of a familiar house that she now views only from a distance, Ruth consciously embraces her radical displacement by adopting what Haapala describes more broadly as "the outsider's gaze" (44); abandoning the ontological level of the everyday for the "strangeness" of the aesthetic (Haapala 44), Ruth enters her house only imaginatively, through her function as storyteller. In the fairytale universe she creates, the cold of the orchard blankets while the trappings of the everyday world encumber; as narrator, Ruth effects a genre shift that dismisses "coarse" materiality in favor of metaphor. Describing the house, which "stood out beyond the orchard with every one of its windows lighted," as "large, and foreign" (203), Ruth observes,

> I could not imagine going into it. Once there was a young girl strolling at night in an orchard. She came to a house she had never seen before, all alight so that through any window she could see curious ornaments and marvelous comforts. A door stood open, so she walked inside. It would be that kind of story, a very melancholy story. Her hair, which was as black as the sky and so long that it swept after her, a wind in the grass... Her fingers, which were sky black and so fine and slender that they were only cold touch, like drops of rain... Her step, which was so silent that people were surprised when they even thought they heard it.
>
> (203–4, all ellipses in original text)

Ruth's turn from the storyworld into the realm of narrative discourse is marked here by the phrase, "Once there was," and by the reiterated reminder that Ruth is imagining rather than perceiving. Description here calls attention to the disruption of the everyday world that anchors realistic narrative, highlighting the silent step and "cold touch" of a young girl for whom the comforts of the domestic are "marvelous" and the décor of this familiar home "curious." Although Ruth and the character she creates are both located in the orchard in the dark, the text highlights the split not only through Ruth's third-person reference ("She came," "her hair," "her fingers") but by ellipses that emphasize the textual space available for imaginative construction.

In that narrative space, as she imagines the character she creates forced to enter an unfamiliar domestic world of warmth and plenty, Ruth reverses the process of forced narrative orientation that governed the beginning of the novel—the quest to quantify, locate, enumerate, map—by resignifying the everyday as a weight rather than a ballast. The traumatic dissociation that Stolorow conceptualizes as "the keeping apart of incommensurable emotional worlds" does not hold, however, as the fact of Ruth's trauma disrupts the coherence of the fiction she spins to distance herself from it ("Phenomenological-Contextual" 132):

> [The girl] would be transformed by the gross light into a mortal child. And when she stood at the bright window, she would find that the world was gone, the orchard was gone, her mother and grandmother and aunts were gone. Like Noah's wife on the 10th or 15th night of rain, she would stand in

the window and realize that the world was really lost... Before, she had
been fleshed in air and clothed in nakedness and mantled in cold... she
could walk into the lake without ripple or displacement and sail up the air
as invisibly as heat. And now, lost to her kind, she would almost forget
them, and she would feed coarse food to her coarse flesh, and be almost
satisfied. (204)

Despite Ruth's attempt to transcend the limits of the actual, the trauma of
loss forces its way past the mantle of cold she lends her fictional counterpart,
returning the character she creates to an everyday world of coarse food and
coarse flesh. Through the displacement of the fantastical story she narrates,
Ruth articulates the enormity of her very personal loss. Without introduction or narrative context, the specific reference to her mother, grandmother,
aunts, all gone, disrupts the fairytale fiction Ruth spins, calling attention to
her awkward position in the narrative. Rather than shoring up her narrative
through mythic allusion, her biblical analogy also destabilizes. Even as she
alludes to a famous biblical story, Ruth renders the fact that "the world was
really lost" in intimate terms; bypassing the trope of Noah's ark, she introduces instead the poignant, solitary image of his wife, an unnamed minor
character, standing at the window looking out on an empty landscape after
days and days of rain. This moment of disorientation, marked by the
simultaneous location and dislocation of Noah's wife in space, time, and
weather, shifts the story of loss from biblical exemplum to personal
unworlding.

As Ruth's response to traumatic dislocation shifts from attempting to
situate herself in the everyday world through a process of narrative quanti-
fication and orientation to renouncing her embodied presence in a world of
lived experience, her narrative voice becomes increasingly abstract and
didactic. By the end of the novel, Ruth frames her conception as an act of
violence and her materialization as an expulsion from the comfort of "reach-
less oblivion" (214): "But this I have in common with all my kind. By some
bleak alchemy what had been mere unbeing becomes death when life is
mingled with it" (215). Ruth attempts to resituate her personal trauma by
relocating the traumatic shattering that haunts and isolates her in the shared
condition of human existence. In doing so, she collapses the distinction
between loss and absence, terms that Dominick LaCapra uses to address the
problem of specificity in trauma. LaCapra highlights the need to differentiate
the specificity of actual, historical events of trauma—such as acts of violence
or the death of loved ones—from the broader metaphysical or ontological

claim that every human existence is constituted by a lack of wholeness, which he describes as a structural trauma. Almost as if she is aware of this critique, Ruth follows her discourse about the nature of human existence and mortality with an acknowledgment of her personal trauma:

> Then there is the matter of my mother's abandonment of me. Again, this is the common experience. They walk ahead of us, and walk too fast, and forget us, they are so lost in thoughts of their own, and soon or late they disappear. The only mystery is that we expect it to be otherwise.   (215)

Collapsing the distinction between her mother's suicide and the everyday acts or routine developmental shifts of "common experience," Ruth attempts to absorb the trauma of her life within a universalizing narrative. In *Contemporary American Trauma Narratives*, Alan Gibbs identifies this as a strategy used by trauma victims to diminish their emotional pain: "Indeed, since LaCapra concedes that the conflation of absence and loss is most likely to occur in a post-traumatic condition, this conversion may be comprehended as one method through which victims begin to process their trauma, by de-actualising, universalising, and thus humanising and diminishing their condition's exceptional and overwhelming status" (206). Turning away from the shattering impact of her mother's self-inflicted death, Ruth normalizes and universalizes her singular experience. She invokes the commonplace—"They walk ahead of us, and walk too fast, and forget us"—in a strained effort to collapse the difference between absentminded inattention and suicide, attempting to force her catastrophic trauma into the realm of the ordinary.

*   *   *

Ruth's migration out of the parameters of the storyworld culminates in an inevitable expulsion from the world of Fingerbone—and the plot of the novel—into a kind of narrative omniscience; her self-imposed exile entails a series of events in the plot—deus ex machina—that begins with a literal burning down of the house in which her character dwells. Presumed dead, Ruth and Sylvie are liberated from the realm of coarse food and coarse flesh to wander, ghostlike. Although the novel makes some effort to place them in their displacement, to reference the route of their travels or the practical means by which they survive, the narrative in its final pages also "breaks the tethers of need one by one" (204). Even as it references Ruth's occasional work as a waitress or a clerk, *Housekeeping* abandons the reference points of realism to document her expulsion from the ordinary. As the novel's grounding in plot dissolves, it traces the way that Ruth's performance in the storyworld becomes less and less convincing:

> But finally the imposture becomes burdensome, and obvious. Customers begin to react to my smile as if it were a grimace...they begin to suspect me, and it is as if I put a chill on the coffee by serving it. What have I to do with these ceremonies of sustenance, of nurturing? They begin to ask why I do not eat anything myself...Once they begin to look at me like that, it is best that I leave. (214)

As Ruth finds in the ordinary world "only the images and simulacra of things needed to sustain" her (183), she responds to her expulsion from the ordinary by withdrawing into narrative space. A ghost, she unrealizes herself in the mimetic landscape of the novel to attain a kind of narrative omniscience marked by the absence of location. Describing the way in which the image of ghostliness that Ruth employs throughout the novel becomes more literal by the novel's end, Katherine Weese highlights the collision of the factual and the fantastic, a collision marked both in plot events that challenge a realistic framework and in a narrative voice that moves toward what Susan Lanser describes as the "superhuman privileges" of an omniscient narrator (Weese 72; Lanser 19).

The novel ends with Ruth imagining Lucille imagining Ruth and Sylvie. In the restaurant in Boston where she locates Lucille, the vivid detailing of her narration situates Ruth in the space of the "not there" shared by all those who have died:

> Sylvie and I do not flounce in through the door, smoothing the skirts of our oversized coats and combing our hair back with our fingers. We do not sit down at the table next to hers and empty our pockets in a small damp heap...My mother, likewise, is not there, and my grandmother in her house slippers with her pigtail wagging, and my grandfather, with his hair combed flat against his brow, does not examine the menu with studious interest. We are nowhere in Boston. However Lucille may look, she will never find us there, or any trace or sign. We pause nowhere in Boston, even to admire a store window, and the perimeters of our wandering are nowhere. No one watching this woman smear her initials in the steam on her water glass with her first finger, or slip cellophane packets of oyster crackers into her handbag for the sea gulls, could know how her thoughts are thronged by our absence, or know how she does not

watch, does not listen, does not wait, does not hope, and always for me and Sylvie.   (218–19)

Imagining herself as lost to someone else whom she imagines imagining her, Ruth uses the power of narrative description to establish absent presence in vibrant terms, "leaving the reader wondering," as Weese observes, "what really does take place at the novel's end, and on what ontological plane" (72). As narrator, she creates a world by detailing its absence, summoning into being for the reader what is not there. Situating herself, along with her mother, grandmother, and grandfather, in an everyday scene built on the foundation of quotidian detail, Ruth uses the act of telling to restore what she describes earlier as "simple, ordinary presence" (195). Rescuing herself, along with her mother and grandparents, from an image realm defined by simultaneous heightening and intangibility, she uses her powers as story- teller to summon presence through an act of mimesis that belies the con- tinued assertion of absence. Ruth's narrative takes what begins as an admission of physical displacement from the scene—"We are nowhere in Boston," "We pause nowhere in Boston"—and turns it inside out; in its transgression of ontological planes, the narrative adopts a strategy of affirm- ation through negation, enacting her claim that "the perimeters of our wandering are nowhere."

If Ruth's strategies as character and narrator—first to orient herself in an unstable landscape and then to remove herself from it by severing her ties with the everyday—represent unacknowledged attempts to process the death of her mother and the loss of a world, in the motion between referentiality and abstraction, enumeration and lyricism, occasional moments of less guarded expression break through. At the end of the novel, in the matter of a few pages, Ruth tells and retells the story of the dangerous journey over the railroad bridge that she and Sylvie must make in order to substantiate the illusion of their deaths. In both cases, she empha- sizes the terrifying darkness, the sound of the water below, her fear of the bridge; one telling, however, frames the passage as a symbolic act of tran- scendence, while the other transports Ruth back to the grounded sensory experience of an actual everyday interaction. In the one case, immediately after dismissing her mother's abandonment as "the common experience," Ruth's rendering situates the scene in an abstract, symbolic, and elusive frame:

Something happened, something so memorable that when I think back to the crossing of the bridge, one moment bulges like the belly of a lens...

Was it only that the wind rose suddenly, so that we had to cower and lean against it like blind women groping their way along a wall? Or did we really hear some sound too loud to be heard, some word so true we did not understand it, but merely felt it pour through our nerves like darkness or water?   (215)

In this rendering, the "something" that happens during the bridge crossing remains intangible, its source located only in the symbolic, in a signifying realm that bypasses the senses entirely. Reversing the dynamic of representation that Zhang describes, Ruth replaces the "warmth and intimacy" of "the felt qualities of everyday experience" with the primacy and immediacy of the word (59).

In Ruth's alternate representation of the bridge crossing, however, that "something" is a literal noise that invokes a specific experience of her mother notable for its textured immediacy and the way that it is framed in the actual, rather than the conditional. The creaking of the bridge beneath her recalls Ruth to the immediacy of an embodied childhood experience she locates with surprising exactitude:

But I could hear the bridge. It was wooden, and it creaked. The slow creaking made me think of a park by the water where my mother used to take Lucille and me. It had a swing built of wood, as high as a scaffold and loose in all its joints, and when my mother pushed me the scaffold leaned after me, and creaked. That was where she sat me on her shoulders so that I could paddle my hands in the chestnut leaves, so cool, and that was the day we bought hamburgers at a white cart for supper and sat on a green bench by the seawall feeding all the bread to the sea gulls.   (212)

This memory, anchored in all five senses, interrupts the narrative of Ruth's symbolic escape from Fingerbone with vibrant detail that conjures the "felt qualities of everyday experience" with her mother for the first time in the novel (Zhang 59). Situated in place and time—"That was where...that was the day"—it evokes Ruth's location in a world of ordinary acts and everyday sensations. In so doing, it not only restores focus on the referential but reveals that the imagistic and abstract conditionals of the novel are grounded in the actual. Throughout *Housekeeping*, Ruth's narration consistently defaults into a speculative or theoretical mode that disrupts placement in an empirical world; forty-four times, she prefaces individual sentences with the phrase, "Say that." The specificity of this memory not only returns the reader to Ruth's location in the storyworld but authenticates one of those conditionals (introduced a hundred pages earlier in the novel) in the realm of the concrete. This passage anchors the speculative language of the earlier conjecture—"Say that my mother was as tall as a man, and that she sometimes set me on her shoulders, so that I could splash my hands in the cold leaves above our heads" (116)—in time and space: "That was where she sat me on her shoulders so that I could paddle my hands in the chestnut leaves, so cool."

Even this momentary revisiting of her mother's everyday presence, however, returns Ruth to a trauma more deeply situated than she has acknowledged. Briefly, for a few sentences, the mantle of style slips as her narrative voice slows and simplifies:

> My mother was happy that day, we did not know why. And if she was sad the next, we did not know why. And if she was gone the next, we did not know why. It was as if she righted herself continually against some current that never ceased to pull. She swayed continuously, like a thing in water, and it was graceful, a slow dance, a sad and heady dance.   (213)

In the pause before the lyrical recuperation of metaphors that figure her mother as swimming against the current or swaying in a slow dance, Ruth exposes the unstable foundation of ordinary life *before* her mother's death. Three sentences in a row collapse into a childlike admission of confusion: "we did not know why." As Ruth reveals here, the world of loss she inhabits preceded her mother's suicide, infiltrating day after day in which her mother's depression threatened the taken-for-granted background of the ordinary.

If one of trauma's defining characteristics involves the continued intrusion of a past event into the present, resulting in the disruption and dislocation of the everyday, Ruth's tentative return to everyday life with her mother erodes the perimeters defining her loss. The spectacular event of her mother's suicide, she reveals here, extends rather than initiates an uncomfortable ordinary; her trauma emerges as an ongoing, everyday experience that resists localization in an event or containment within the parameters of catastrophe. Early in the novel, Ruth provides a description of her childhood home that renders in painstaking detail the arrangement of furniture, the angle of light, the list of possessions, but offers very little insight into her mother's presence in that domestic space. Following that list, Ruth observes, "Helen put lengths of clothesline through our belts and fastened them to the doorknob, an arrangement that nerved us to look over the side of the porch, even when the wind was strong" (21). If *Housekeeping* follows the trajectory of Ruth as, one by one, she breaks the tethers of need to disavow her location in a diminished everyday, the image of the clothesline tether that ties her to home renders the trauma that Ruth cannot speak deeper and more amorphous, unveiling her tenuous grounding in a child-hood ordinary situating her precariously even in the familiar space of home.

3

Living Dying in *Gilead*

In the final weeks of his life, John Ames, the elderly and critically ill protagonist of Marilynne Robinson's *Gilead* (2004), finds himself caught between the urgent experience of painful embodiment and the psychic negotiation of anticipated absence; he comes increasingly to experience a world he cannot fully inhabit. The novel takes the form of a journal written by Ames to his young son, a journal that becomes both a narrative of Ames's inevitable movement toward absence and a collection of images and memories that would resist such progress by rendering the temporal form of narrative spatial and countering embodied absence with representational presence. Confronted with the knowledge of his imminent death, Robinson's protagonist writes to his son, "I'm trying to make the best of our situation. That is, I'm trying to tell you things I might never have thought to tell you if I had brought you up myself, father and son, in the usual companionable way. When things are taking their ordinary course, it is hard to remember what matters" (102). Haunted by a past of uncommunicative fathers and emotionally damaged sons, Ames turns from the world to the pen in an attempt to salvage "what matters" for his little boy through a journal filled with history, reflection, and knowledge.[1] Even as he opposes the process of "telling" with the "usual companionable" forms of everyday experience, however, Ames's representations return his stream of consciousness narrative again and again to its origins in embodied sensory perception.

Acknowledging that fact, critics who have read *Gilead* as a celebration of the force of human consciousness in the face of death locate the novel's power not just in its philosophical and religious vision but in its immersion in the sensory details of ordinary life. Highlighting the beauty and power of

---

[1] Of course, Ames's written attempt to capture and preserve his identity for his son ultimately implicates him in rather than releases him from that lineage of faulty bonds. If, as Merleau-Ponty observes, "A pure essence which would not be at all contaminated and confused with the facts...would require a spectator himself without secrets" (111), Ames's narrative gradually reveals the way that he is implicated in the secrets that he's kept.

The Elusive Everyday in the Fiction of Marilynne Robinson. Laura E. Tanner, Oxford University Press (2021).
© Laura E. Tanner. DOI: 10.1093/oso/9780192896360.003.0003

Ames's celebration of commonplace objects and quotidian experiences, for example, Christopher Leise argues, "I offer that Gilead promotes the kind of aesthetic attention to the world that Ames exhibits...as a vehicle to an experience of the divine in the immediate and the immanent: an experience that stops short of knowing through reason and is content with simply living the experience of the miraculous in the everyday" (349). In highlighting the "miraculous" power associated with the narrator's heightened perception of the moment, however, critics risk ignoring the novel's inquiry into how the anticipation of "looking back from the grave" (*Gilead* 141) disrupts Ames's somatosensory experience in the narrative present. Readings of the novel that focus on aesthetic or religious compensations for loss tend to accept at face value the transcendent vision of everyday experience that Robinson's narrator labors to maintain.[2] "Ames's quiet is based in joy," Rachel Sykes observes, "and *Gilead* is the quietest of Robinson's novels because, as a narrator, Ames is largely unconcerned with the noise of the world and is happy with the quiet of his own life" (112). In a recent essay, Robert Chodat acknowledges the "rapturous entries" that Ames "devote[s] to identifying beauty in the most ordinary things" (346), but qualifies Sykes's assessment of Ames's state of quotidian contentment. Provocatively suggesting that "Ames acknowledges a certain portion of an unwelcome reality but minimizes its significance and ignores its full implications," Chodat identifies but does not fully explore what he describes as the narrator's "psychological evasiveness" (345). Beneath its lyrical rendering of quotidian wonder, I will argue, Robinson's novel registers a disquieting dynamic that unsettles Ames's location in the everyday world he celebrates. The cultural force of

---

[2] David James's discussion of *Gilead* in *Discrepant Solace* offers a notable exception. James acknowledges the tensions that fuel the novel but argues that Ames's writing and Robinson's style provide their own solace: "Ames might be existentially defenceless, in other words, but the novel stylistically isn't. To be sure, acquiescence often sabotages his moments of wonder... However, if describing the exceptionality of what he sees escalates Ames's anticipation of losing it, then anticipation's sorrow is itself consoled by his foreknowledge of passing his descriptions on. In this respect, Robinson's style...also hews from Ames's monologue, chaperoned as it is by grief, an alternative kind of inheritance, one that's less concerned with lessons on life than with preserving in limpid descriptions the solace of ordinary moments" (132). James beautifully captures the affective power of Robinson's prose and gestures toward the complex relationship of style and content in *Gilead*. Describing Ames's journal entries as "aching, elegiac, ardent," he argues, "descriptions of Ames's embrace of the inscrutable, 'cataract' world of everyday life call attention to Robinson's sensuous, gently reparative manipulation of diction and syntactic rhythm, as much as they intensify our pathetic response to what's dramatically occurring in the text" (140). Although I agree with his conclusion that "There's no reason why these alternative reactions can't go hand in hand" (140), James's argument raises the question of how we, as readers and critics, might disentangle Robinson's perspective and stylistic choices from those of Ames in the text's first-person narrative.

Robinson's text stems from its powerful unveiling of how dying complicates the sensory and psychological dynamics of human perception, expelling Ames from the ordinary world his prose illuminates. In fact, I will argue, *Gilead* localizes Ames's psychic struggle with his own imminent death in acts of perceptual processing that it both depicts and thematizes. The novel pushes existential concerns back into the realm of the everyday to explore the way that the lived experience of dying traps Ames uncomfortably in the collapsing space between perception and representation.

*   *   *

Neuroscientist Antonio Damasio is well known for his cogent articulations of current scientific understandings of the neurobiology of consciousness. His descriptions of the process of how perception operates locate the way that perspective is constructed through a variety of sources, including not only the perceptual apparatus (such as vision or hearing) and consequent adjustments in the muscular and vestibular systems of the perceiver, but also signals derived from the observer's emotional responses to a particular object (*Feeling* 146). Depending on the object, that emotional component may assume greater or lesser significance, but it is always present, belying the notion that there is any "such thing as a pure perception of an object in a sensory channel" (*Feeling* 147). Instead, in the model that Damasio develops, "Consciousness begins as the feeling of what happens when we see or hear or touch . . . It is a feeling that accompanies the making of any kind of image . . . The feeling marks those images as ours" (*Feeling* 26). Breaking down what Damasio describes as "the multidimensional, space-and-time integrated image" (*Feeling* 322) we experience in perception thus returns us—in scientific as well as humanistic terms—to the situatedness of perspective not only in the body but in the emotions of the perceiver.

In Ames's memory, heightened moments of interaction between father and son mark the intermingling of emotion and perception. Ames's images of such moments render significance not merely through but in the sensory details of shared experience: his father feeding him bread from an ash-covered hand, he and his father standing damp and dirty in an empty graveyard, his father and grandfather silently shelling walnuts on the porch side by side. As Ames describes the first of these childhood memories—his father, hands and face blackened with ash, kneeling in the rain to feed his son a piece of bread—the spiritual significance of the moment remains inextricable from its emotional and perceptual immediacy. In rendering his father an "old martyr," the food he holds "the bread of affliction," and the process of conveying it to his son an act of "communion," Ames's first-person narrative situates his memory firmly within a series of religious frames that render it symbolically meaningful (102).

Rather than subsuming the specificity of embodied experience solely within the symbolic realm, however, the narrative simultaneously returns the reader to the textured details of memory that continue to escape the text's symbolic hold. Memory, as Damasio observes, not only *proceeds from* emotion and sensory perception, but remains inextricable from them:

> The records we hold of the objects and events that we once perceived include the motor adjustments we made to obtain the perception in the first place and also include the emotional reactions we had then ... We tend to reconstruct memories not just of a shape or a color but also of the perceptual engagement the object required and of the accompanying emotional reactions. (147–8)

In Ames's journalistic recollections, the narrator's typological rendering of the image's significance continually rubs up against the textured immediacy of a young boy's embodied apprehension of the moment:

> I remember my father down on his heels in the rain, water dripping from his hat, feeding me biscuit from his scorched hand, with that old blackened wreck of a church behind him and steam rising where the rain fell on embers, the rain falling in gusts and the women singing "The Old Rugged Cross" while they saw to things, moving so gently, as if they were dancing to the hymn, almost. In those days, no grown woman ever let herself be seen with her hair undone, but that day even the grand old women had their hair falling down their backs like schoolgirls. It was so joyful and so sad. I mention it again because it seems to me much of my life was comprehended in that moment. (95)

What emerges from Ames's repeated representation of memory is not merely an essence that represents the distillation of experience but an emotional truth that emerges in and through the heightened rendering of everyday sensations: Ames's recollection of joy and sadness is immersed in the feel of rain, the sight of steam rising against the blackened church, the sound of women's voices, and, most importantly, the touch of his father's body on his own preserved in the transfer of a biscuit blackened by his father's "scorched hand." As Ames the narrator circles round and round his childhood memory, the emotional impact of the experience he recalls remains inextricable from his sensory apprehension of the moment.[3] The image's intelligibility can be traced not only to Ames's ability to "comprehend" its symbolic meaning but to a different sort of comprehensiveness: the narrative's gathering up of multiple strands of intercorporeal experience, its testimony to memory's stubborn situatedness in the realm of the textured particular. Even as he pushes the bread his father feeds him towards the spiritual realm of the communion wafer, it is the body of the symbol—the hands that present that communion, the bread covered with ash, the food offered from his father's side—that Ames would leave his son;[4] his attempt to exchange essence for experience only returns him to moments that render "the usual companionable way" of father and son rare and holy.

The impact of *Gilead* stems in part from its poignant rendering of Ames's attempts to recuperate the enormity of anticipated loss through the intensity of his focus and the power of his perception. Even as Ames's faith in the afterlife assures him of continuing spiritual presence, he struggles to come to terms with his inevitable expulsion from a transitory world of everyday experience. "I know this is all mere human apparition compared to what awaits us," Ames observes, "but it is only lovelier for that. There is a human beauty in it. And I can't believe that, when we have all been changed and put on incorruptibility, we will forget our fantastic condition of mortality and impermanence" (57). Robinson's protagonist recognizes the tension between physical and sacramental vision without subsuming one within the other. His theological perspective, as revealed in the novel, embraces rather than recoils from the tension between human embodiment and religious transcendence;[5] in his own sermons, and through his invocation

---

[3] Building on an earlier version of this argument, Emily C. Nacol highlights the significance of memory as she explores how "*Gilead* reveals a complicated story of growing old" (122). Ames, she argues, "considers his own body as a storied material object," "a source of memory and identity, and a reminder of the mysteries of a life lived in earthly time" (122).

[4] Edward Casey describes the particularity of images in bodily terms, noting their "quasi-corporealization, their imaginal embodiment as sensible concreta of soul" (305).

[5] Ames's imagination of greeting his family members in the afterlife functions as one means through which the novel explores the tension between the centrality of embodiment in lived experience and a Christian understanding of the body as "a suit of old clothes the spirit doesn't want anymore" (13). For dialogue about the significance of religion in *Gilead* and the tensions between religious and secular frameworks the novel invokes, see, for example, Douglas Christopher, "Christian Multiculturalism and Unlearned History in Marilynne Robinson's 'Gilead,'" Andrew Stout, "A Little Willingness to See": Sacramental Vision in Marilynne Robinson's *Housekeeping* and *Gilead*," and Kevin Seidel, "A Secular for Literary Studies."

of the humanistic theology of Ludwig Feuerbach,[6] Ames emphasizes the significance of what he describes in a sermon as "the gift of physical particularity and how blessing and sacrament are mediated through it" (69). Ames's belief that death is a bridge to another—and ultimately better—form of life thus does not preclude his grief at having to leave this world behind. Midway through the novel, Ames observes explicitly, "The fact is, I don't want to be old. And I certainly don't want to be dead" (141). His spirituality manifests itself not in the disavowal of ordinary experience but in the appropriation of that experience as a treasured dimension of human life. Although Ames's belief in a spiritual existence after death mitigates, to some extent, the tragedy of mortality, it also contributes to his tendency to anticipate his embodied absence; the assurance of his sustained existence in another form lends form and credence to the imaginative work of "looking back from the grave," anticipating a world without him in it. Addressing his son, Ames observes, "I want your dear perishable self to live long and to love this dear perishable world, which I somehow cannot imagine not missing bitterly" (53).

*   *   *

Ames's almost sacramental attention to "the gift of physical particularity" lends his narrative an extraordinary attention to texture and detail. As Jeffrey Hart observes in the *National Review*, Robinson's protagonist "achieves a concentration of mind that enables him to see, hear, reflect, his senses so alive to profound experience . . . As existence becomes conscious of itself it reaches its own edges, sees the world with greater clarity, and wonders about its is-ness"[7] (46). Ames's ability to represent the textured immediacy of experience—what Damasio describes as its "somatosensory modality"—emerges from his heightened capacity to inhabit the perceptual moment and to break down "the multidimensional, space-and-time

---

[6] Ames defends Feuerbach despite the fact that he is an atheist because "he is about as good on the joyful aspects of religion as anybody, and he loves the world" (24). Although Ames distinguishes his own position from Feuerbach's by describing the philosopher's view that "religion should just stand out of the way and let joy exist pure and undisguised" as his one "significant" error, he affirms Feuerbach's "wonderful" celebration of the natural as significant in and of itself and not merely as an expression of the divine.

[7] Hart cites several examples from the novel that highlight Ames's sensitivity to what he sees, hears, and touches, including a passage where Ames describes "a feeling of the weight of light" as "a pressing the damp out of the grass and pressing the smell of sour old sap out of the boards on the porch floor" (51) and a passage where Ames recounts walking into the church sanctuary at dawn: "I loved the sound of the latch lifting. The building has settled into itself so that when you walk down the aisle, you can hear it yielding to the burden of your weight. It's a pleasanter sound than an echo would be, an obliging accommodating sound" (70).

integrated image we are experiencing this very moment" into its constitutive parts (Damasio *Feeling* 322). Ames dwells in the space of the image long enough to gesture toward not just its origins in the perceiver's body but its attendant emotions and its effects. Although Ames's sensibility clearly accounts in part for his attentiveness to the world, the journal that he creates in *Gilead* also reflects the heightened self-consciousness of an aging, ailing individual whose awareness of his imminent death shapes both consciousness and perception. Even as the novel traces Ames' unique outlook, its representation of his end of life experience reflects perceptual and psychological dynamics often associated with aging. In "Toward More Human Meanings of Aging," Berg and Gadow observe,

> With age we realize time has the dimension of depth as well as duration ... We slow ourselves down to explore experiences, not in their linear pattern of succeeding one another, but ... to let their possibilities, their rich density emerge. We continue moving through time, but we also move into time, allowing it to expand in depth for us though its objective duration diminishes. (85–6)

Ames's location at the margin between this world and the next exaggerates the intensity of his embodied experience and the "rich density" of his narrative. "One of the pleasures of these days," Ames observes, "is that I notice them all, minute by minute" (93).

In aging studies, science's focus on "the feeling of what happens" has led recently to an awareness of the way that perception varies according to age, experience, *and* state of mind. Studies documenting the heightened intensity of perception for the elderly and the terminally ill tend to address the physiological and psychic experience of those close to mortality as a form of compensation for loss. The well-documented deterioration of sight and hearing capacity in aging subjects, for example, is offset at least to some degree by older observers' capacity to focus on visual fields with increased intensity. Recent scientific studies conclude that focused attention accounts for older adults' ability to perceive objects at a performance level similar to that of younger adults. In their study of sensory and attentional factors in aging and visual masking, Paul Atchley and Lesa Hoffman conclude that "older observers were probably using attention to increase the strength of a representation that was impoverished relative to their younger counterparts, resulting in a decrease in performance when the attentional gradient became less focused" (57). In order to compensate for a decline in perceptual efficiency, another study documents, older adults maintain a higher level of neural activation within simple visual processing tasks (Madden et al.). Acknowledging that "the most consistent changes noted in psychophysiologic studies of aging are temporal," Samuel Atkin et al. challenge the idea that the slowing of processes with aging always represents a deficit, arguing instead that "In some situations, 'slowing down' may actually improve the nervous system's information-handling capabilities" (13). Working in a similar vein, Carstensen et al. use socioemotional selectivity theory to suggest that the knowledge that time is limited has direct effects on older adults, including heightened awareness of immediate surroundings, goal setting, and associated effects on cognitive functioning. The cognitive theories cited here, ranging from the physiological to the psychological, chart the relationship between advanced age or illness and intensity of perception. In all these cases, the biology of aging and/or the knowledge of limited time contribute to increased focus and heightened awareness; the intensity of each act of perception emerges as compensation for the diminished ability or opportunity to perceive.

Testifying to the novel's power to unsettle narrative time by "noticing" and inhabiting the possibilities of each minute, critics of *Gilead* tend to deemphasize the novel's anticipation of loss by focusing on the compensation of an intensified participation in the narrative present. "Gradually," James Wood argues in his *New York Times* review, "Robinson's novel teaches us how to read it, suggests how we might slow down to walk at its own processional pace, and how we might learn to coddle its many fine details" (1). In initiating the reader into a form of heightened perception experienced by its protagonist, Wood concludes, the novel responds to the threat of death by undoing the force of temporality for both reader and protagonist:

> Robinson's book ends...as a dying man daily pictures Paradise but also learns how to prolong every day—to extend time, even on earth, into a serene imitation of eternity: "Light is constant, we just turn over in it. So every day is in fact the selfsame evening and morning." (1)

In drawing attention to the recuperative power of Ames's heightened perception, Wood and other critics in his wake reinforce cognitive paradigms which stress the intensity of perception as a form of compensation for loss. In *Gilead*, however, the intermingling of perception and consciousness, what Damasio would term "the feeling of what happens," unsettles and disrupts what Wood describes as Ames's "serene" experience of the present. If the intensity of Ames's perception penetrates the moment to forestall the approach of death, the expansiveness of the present also opens to accommodate the anticipation of future absence. Even as he attempts to hold death at bay, Ames lends his future absence sensory presence through a process of anticipation that manifests itself in perceptual as well as imaginative terms, gradually allowing Ames the intense experience of a world without him in it.

Ames's journal offers a series of achingly beautiful images of a world soon to be lost to a man whose awareness of his impending death heightens the powers of his perception and renders his every sensation an emotional and aesthetic composition:

> I saw a bubble float past my window, fat and wobbly and ripening toward that dragonfly blue they turn just before they burst. So I looked down at the yard and there you were, you and your mother, blowing bubbles at the cat, such a barrage of them that the poor beast was beside herself... Some of the bubbles drifted up through the branches, even above the trees. You two were too intent on the cat to see the celestial consequences of your worldly endeavors. They were very lovely. Your mother is wearing her blue dress and you are wearing your red shirt and you were kneeling on the ground together with Soapy between and the effulgence of bubbles rising, and so much laughter. Ah, this life, this world.   (9)

Ames's position at the window marks both the power and the limits of his liminal status.[8] Weakened by his heart condition and his advancing age,

---

[8] Robinson's use of the window in this scene to highlight Ames's location in such a liminal space recalls her representations of windows in *Housekeeping*, where the window emerges as a porous boundary that both marks and dissolves the space between inside and outside, consciousness and body, self and other. Robinson's interest in staging issues of absence and presence continually returns her fiction to questions about boundaries and the (im)possibility of transgressing them: "When one looks from inside at a lighted window, or looks from above at the lake, one sees the image of oneself in a lighted room, the image of oneself among trees and sky—the deception is obvious, but flattering all the same. When one looks from the darkness into the light, however, one sees all the difference between here and there, this and that" (*Housekeeping* 157–8). Robinson's use of the window as a double-edged boundary that alternately extends and delimits the margins of subjectivity functions, both in *Housekeeping* and in *Gilead*, to uncover dynamics of embodied accessibility associated with loss. As Ruth, the protagonist of Robinson's first novel, struggles with representation's role in sustaining her deceased mother's presence, the taunting images of memory—figured often through representations of windows, water, mirrors, and other reflective surfaces—seem to imply access to an embodied form that never materializes. Situated within a series of reflective surfaces, the image constructs an illusion of presence that collapses into the painful reiteration of intangibility: "The images are the worst of it. It would be terrible to stand outside in the dark and watch a woman in

he can watch but not participate in a scene made all the lovelier by virtue of his distance from it. Relegated now to the role of observer, the narrator finds compensation for his exclusion from ordinary experience as he claims the omniscience of a "celestial" perspective that holds the motions of his wife and child in an aesthetic, atemporal frame. As "were" merges with "are," Ames's past-tense rendering of their actions flows seamlessly into the presence of a representation that steadies before the reader's gaze, capturing the "loveliness" of color and form in an image that penetrates the motion of time to inhabit its interstices. Edward Casey locates the image in just such a shift from diachronic time to the space of synchronicity:

> Where diachronic time tends to "disperse subsistence" ... by emphasizing possibilities of decay and replacement—think only of how each "now" takes the place of its immediate predecessor, shoving the latter into oblivion—synchronic space allows for the retaining of the subsistent in the face of time's dispersal itself. (131)

With the shift from past to present tense in this passage, Ames responds to the threat of "oblivion" by gathering up the multiplicity of experience to usher it into the space of representation. Throughout the novel, Ames's way of looking supplements his autobiographical goal of preserving identity in the face of embodied absence; the pressure of mortality serves as the lens through which his vision distills the sensory data of experience into the essence of the image. As Damasio observes, not all images are made conscious: "There are simply too many images being generated and too much competition for the relatively small window of mind in which ... images are accompanied by a sense that we are apprehending them, and that, as a consequence, are properly attended" (*Feeling* 319). Damasio links different emotional states to different modes of cognitive processing; the feeling of elation, for example, "permits the rapid generation of multiple images such that the associative process is richer and associations are made to a larger variety of cues available in the images under scrutiny" (*Descartes' Error*

---

a lighted room studying her face in a window, and to throw a stone at her, shattering the glass, and then to watch the window knit itself up again and the bright bits of lip and throat and hair piece themselves seamlessly again into that unknown, indifferent woman" (162–3). In the context of Ruth's grief, the image that might appear to function as consolation merely aggravates the experience of loss, just as the "celestial" perspective that Ames claims at the window marks his exclusion from—as much as his unlimited access to—the world his family inhabits so casually below. For a fuller discussion of absent presence in *Housekeeping*, see the fourth chapter of my book, *Lost Bodies: Inhabiting the Borders of Life and Death*.

163–4). Insofar as the knowledge of his impending mortality shapes the "window of mind" through which Ames perceives, he "attends" to the images he processes with an unusual self-consciousness linked—at least in part—to his anticipation of embodied absence. Combining physiological and psychological approaches to age studies, Ihsan Kapkin suggests that the psychic experience of time has implications for the way that terminally ill and aging subjects both perceive and process information:

> It appears to me that the concept of "Time" and its use is redefined in the aged. This new valuation of time is somewhat similar to that noticed among alert, articulate, terminally ill patients. While short-term memory and certain cognitive changes are somewhat troublesome among the elderly, when speed is not required intellectual performance reportedly is refined... I believe that in healthy aging our data processor (the cerebrum) may have mastered its data management ability by adding more power to its phenomenal capacity.   (128)

In apprehending the world through the lens of his impending mortality, Ames compensates for the loss of future time through an increased "phenomenal capacity" to apprehend the present. As the act of representation pushes backward into the very dynamics of perception, the intensity of Ames's look affords him a way of holding what he will soon be unable to touch. Locating himself above and beyond his family, on the other side of the window, Ames would distill their interaction into an image to be pulled back into the space of representation he would occupy.

Insofar as Ames's narrative testifies to a material (dis)location it would rewrite as imaginative autonomy, it returns the reader to the impossibility of maintaining what Merleau-Ponty describes as the "transparency of the imaginary" (111). Tracing the way that every "essence" emerges from "a space of existence" (111), Merleau-Ponty replaces theories of transcendent knowledge with a reciprocal model of embodied perception that he figures as a chiasm, an intertwining of the embodied subject and the world. Insofar as the human subject always approaches the world through the locatedness of the body, Merleau-Ponty argues, perception must be understood as a dynamic, interactive process in which the subject can see and touch only insofar as it is seen and touched by the surrounding world. The embodied subject sees the solidity of things not "from the depths of nothingness," as "a pure object which the mind soars over," but from within a shared world: "What makes the weight, the thickness, the flesh of each color, of each sound, of each tactile texture, of the present, and of the world is the fact that he who grasps them feels himself emerge from them by a sort of coiling up or redoubling, fundamentally homogenous with them" (114). Merleau-Ponty's focus on the immersion of the sentient observer in the world highlights the origin of sense in the body and the impossibility of extricating perception from the dynamics of space, time, color, sound, and texture that the viewer not only observes but inhabits. Given what Merleau-Ponty describes as the viewer's chiasmic implication in the "thickness" of a world, Ames's "celestial" perspective must return us to his spatial and temporal location; the open window through which he views the world functions as a permeable boundary, a porous margin of perceptual interface that limits but does not preclude exchange.

Even as Merleau-Ponty's phenomenological framework usefully locates Ames's vision in his ailing, aging body, however, *Gilead* revises the chiasmic model Merleau-Ponty develops as a paradigm for perception. The "space of existence" that Ames inhabits is defined not just by spatial location but by the physical limitations of illness and age and the psychic consciousness of his own impending mortality. If our human doubleness, our status as what Merleau-Ponty describes as "sensible-sentients" (116), renders us incapable of reducing our experience to essence, Ames's failed attempt to do so speaks not only to the way his aesthetic vision is located in the realm of the corporeal but to the way that his literal perception is shaped by the consciousness of mortality.

The anticipation of embodied absence both filters Ames's apprehension of the everyday world and unravels his chiasmic relationship to it, altering the fundamental dynamics of the way that he sees and is seen. Insofar as we are "within life," Merleau-Ponty argues, we not only possess the visible, but are "filled" and "occupied" by it (116, 134, 143). His tactile description of vision as a "palpation with the look" emphasizes what he describes as the "intimacy" of the looker and the object, the inscription of both in the same order of being (134). "He who looks," Merleau-Ponty observes, "must not himself be foreign to the world he looks at" (134). Insofar as Ames's imaginative anticipation of his death belies the stability of his literal location in the world, consciousness places him in a different relation to time and space than those for whom mortality is less immediate. Advancing age, as Joseph Esposito argues, constitutes "a state of being-toward-death different from the abstract being-toward-death that all who are alive must confront" (65). As the abstraction of death gains increasing immediacy, embodied subjectivity may shift to accommodate newly defined borders of the self.

Physiological limitations of illness and advancing age emerge as inextricable from the psychic pressures associated with a corresponding loss of autonomy; Ames's frustration at his inability to negotiate the stairs in his home, for example, points to a contraction of world and time far more exaggerated than his physical restrictions would seem to warrant. In *The Fate of Place*, Edward S. Casey explores the intertwining of human motion and the space it animates to argue that motion functions not merely as a means to an end but as the opportunity "to constitute myself as one coherent organism": "My body, then, is a body—a sheerly physical entity—as well as a source of intentionality and projects, correlations and orientations" (224, 227). Even as the body's limitations may circumscribe an individual's ability to function independently, such physical constraints emerge as inseparable from the subject's frustrated desire for psychic stability and control.[9] In Robert Coles's *Old and On Their Own*, a collection of interviews conducted with adults over the age of seventy-five, one interviewee after another describes how the imminence of death brackets lived experience on a daily basis. Coles's subjects document the stresses of a life interrupted not only by loss of physical function and difficulty of movement but by the impossibility of escaping the heightened self-consciousness that frames every act and thought, disrupting what Rita Felski describes as the "taken for granted backdrop" of the everyday. Everyday life, Felski argues,

> comprises not just an array of behaviors and activities but also distinctive attitudes or forms of consciousness. It is often equated with a habitual, distracted, mode of perception...We act without being fully cognizant of what we are doing, moving through the world with the uncanny assurance of sleep-walkers or automatons. Everyday life thus epitomizes the quintessential quality of taken-for-grantedness. (607–8)

Unable to take for granted not only their projected existence in the future but their steady location in the present, Coles's subjects lose physical and psychical access to an everyday experience often assumed to be a shared human phenomenon.

Severe arthritis makes it impossible for one of Coles's subjects to stand unassisted; even with the help of a specially designed chair, the simple act of sitting demands careful planning and negotiation. As a result, she observes,

---

[9] I discuss this idea at more length in Chapter 3 of *Lost Bodies*.

I'm always on the alert; I'm ready to go...I don't get settled in, because if
I do, that's it. I only half-sit! That way, I can stand up when I want to—I
never put myself into this chair without thinking, at the same time,
whether I'll be able to get out of it.   (9)

The breakdown of the body necessitates the supplement of a vigilant consciousness; the weakening of physical structures that support the simplest of
motions demands that an inversely powerful stream of thoughts be formulated and directed toward actions formerly governed by reflex. As consciousness engulfs even her simplest acts, the breakdown of the body raises
questions of autonomy and identity that she articulates in her dialogue
with Coles: "I remember how my arms and legs used to work, and that is
the standard [of what should be], and I fall further and further short, and so
I am left to wonder: am I *really* me, still?" (11). Another housebound
individual in Coles's study observes,

> You know, for me 'life' is being here, in this chair, in this room, and
> thinking about leaving! I guess it's every day, now, that I do it...I'll be
> thinking to myself: you're here now, but it's near the end of your being
> here, and maybe this is it, the big day: when you stop being here, and that
> will be that.   (56)

For this speaker, the literal inability to negotiate space parallels a psychic
experience in which the world contracts, locking the speaker into an endless
present pressured by the inevitability of its loss.

Merleau-Ponty defines experiences as "thoughts that feel behind themselves the weight of the space, the time, the very Being they think" (115);
Ames's perception of the world, on the other hand, is framed by thoughts
that feel ahead of themselves the weightlessness of space and expulsion from
time. If, for the subject Merleau-Ponty describes, "The space, the time of the
things are shreds of himself, of his own spatialization, of his own tempor-
alization" (114), for Ames, perception enacts an opposite dynamic; his
apprehension of the world functions not to confirm his extension into
space and time but to "shred" his sense of self over and over again, reinfor-
cing his exclusion from the chiasmic experience of an everyday world he
comes to inhabit only contingently. Looking, Ames remains "foreign to the
world he looks at" (Merleau-Ponty 134); the fundamental homogeneity of
flesh and world that Merleau-Ponty describes unravels painfully in each act
of perception.

As important as what *Gilead* reveals about the productive intensity of heightened perception, then, is the way it calls attention to the weight of consciousness carried by those who experience the world simultaneously from within and without. The price we pay for consciousness, as Damasio observes, "is not just the price of risk and danger and pain. It is the price of knowing risk, danger, and pain . . . The feeling of what happens is the answer to a question we never asked" (316). In *Gilead*, Ames's perception exaggerates rather than resists his forced retreat into a position of observing a quotidian landscape in which he gradually ceases to exist. As he inhabits the boundaries between life and death, Ames sees the world without being seen by it. Even as his dying body comes increasingly to assert its claims, Ames's embodied presence in the scenes he documents collapses into the diminished role of observer rather than participant. Imaginatively anticipating his own disembodiment, Ames brings the full power of consciousness to a material world he seems unable to transcend or to impact. The journal that would serve as a stay against absence both represents and enacts the way that old age propels Ames into the margins of the lived world, positioning him as an observer or, in his words, a "spy" who watches and records from a position of embodied invisibility a kind of voyeuristic experience of his own anticipated loss.

The novel figures the tensions of dying as the collapse of chiasmic experience into a series of distanced perceptions that reflect the aging subject's liminal location in a culture of autonomy. The anticipation of absence not only heightens sensory perception, locking diachronic experience into the synchronicity of the image, but renders Ames's every act and every thought self-conscious. Harkening back to a youthful experience unmarked by the tensions of embodied subjectivity, Ames recalls the grace and ease of acts performed without the knowledge of mechanism or agency. What he describes as "that wonderful collaboration of the whole body with itself" (115) functions to implicate the subject in the world so thoroughly that the boundaries of the self and the awareness of agency disappear, as in the line drive Ames recalls that occurs "when you're so young that your body almost doesn't know about effort" (142). "To be young," Jean Amery observes in *On Aging*, "is to throw one's body out into a time that is no time at all, but life, world, and space" (15). In contrast, world and space "withdraw," in Amery's terms, from the elderly, as their sense of the future contracts into what he describes as the "density" of lived time (23). If, as Amery contends, "lived time manifest[s] itself with a much greater density" for the aged, the synchronic experience of what one of Coles's interviewees describes as "slow time" is bracketed by the threat of the ultimate narrative denouement: "It's the slow dragging down of me toward the grave," this seventy-five year old with heart disease reports. "It's slow time—around and around the hand goes, and suddenly: boom!" (89).

Even as age and infirmity limit Ames's autonomy, the imaginative anticipation of absence dissolves the "wonderful collaboration" he associates with youth into a painful unraveling of his chiasmic relationship with the ordinary world, time, and space. The distance that Ames would appropriate to sustain "celestial" vision turns against him at other moments in the text to reveal the difficulty of inhabiting a gaze capable of perceiving the world without him in it. Jeffrey Hart, like most of Robinson's reviewers, locates the balm of *Gilead* in the intensity of Ames's perception:

> The Rev. John Ames...perceives the empirical world so sharply that around the edges of his words we hear the "noises"...These do not resemble the terror we sense around Hemingway's equally hard edges...
> In Robinson's prose the presences are much more benign, because of the way Ames apprehends the world.   (47)

If Ames's vision is benign, however, it is also terrible. The intensity of his perception reflects the workings of a consciousness that infiltrates the dynamics of his every sensory experience, yielding torment as well as compensation. Describing life lived in the context of illness and an overwhelming awareness of death, another of Coles's subjects observes,

> You've got this life of yours, and it's in danger, and you try to keep going, but you know that something is wrong...So you hold your breath, and you talk to yourself, and try to keep yourself going, through the day—but, I'll tell you, it keeps coming back to your mind...Being old and being sick... You're at the edge of life; you're hurting; you never do know if you'll see another day, so you never do relax and just live, the way other folks do.
> (82, 85)

The heightened perception of every moment depends upon the denaturalization of what Felski describes as the "taken-for-granted" conventions of everyday experience; the intensity that Hart documents thus bears the cost of psychic expulsion from familiar realms of time and space. Unable to "relax and just live," Ames finds himself, like Coles's subject, inhabiting a prolonged present shadowed by the consciousness of loss.

*   *   *

Several moments in *Gilead* thematize the way that the psychic experience of finitude infiltrates the dynamics of perception to locate Ames "at the edge of life." As Ames preaches one of his final sermons, the power of manipulating words falters beneath the acuteness of a vision that reveals his exclusion from the very world he is forced to perceive. Ames looks down on the congregation below to see Jack Boughton, the younger man he fears will displace him after his death, casually slide into the pew beside his young wife and son; the sight of the three of them together crystallizes in an image that haunts Ames for much of the novel. Locked behind the lectern in a space that yields vision of all he does not want to see—a world without him in it— Ames observes, "The truth is, as I stood there in the pulpit, looking down on the three of you, you looked to me like a handsome young family...And I felt as if I were looking back from the grave" (141). Ames's synaesthetic immersion in the world—what Merleau-Ponty describes as the "intimacy" between the seer and the seen—collapses into an experience of intimate detachment as he is forced to perceive a world in which he is located but denied participation, to observe what he will soon be unable to manipulate with his touch. The unity of the image which haunts Ames—the three individuals combining to form "a handsome young family"—documents his anticipated dispossession. Caught between the powerlessness of pro-jected absence and the conscious burden of subjective presence, Ames images himself—"looking back from the grave"—as subject to the painful experience of his exclusion from a world in which he is forced to participate without agency. As the congregation's leader, Ames occupies the pulpit; his authorization to speak parallels his position above and beyond the group of bodies below. In this instance, however, Ames's "celestial" perspective turns against him to emphasize his exclusion from the everyday world that unfolds beneath him. Once again, his gaze locks on the image and holds steady; this time, however, the act of perception subjects Ames to a sustained encounter with a tableau he can neither enter experientially nor release back into the dispersal of diachronic time.

All sensory images, as Damasio records, are realized through the inter-action of an individual's core consciousness in a particular relationship with an object; the images in the consciousness narrative, Damasio explains, "flow like shadows along with the images of the object for which they are providing an unwitting, unsolicited comment" (171). In this case, the image Ames perceives from the pulpit is shadowed by his anticipation of his own loss. In Damasio's model of perception, consciousness functions as "the umbrella term for the mental phenomena that permit the strange confection of you as observer or knower of the things observed, of you as owner of thoughts formed in your perspective, of you as the potential agent on the scene" (127). Insofar as Ames's consciousness of his impending death disrupts his faith in himself as "potential agent on the scene," the image he processes charts his own absence as well as Boughton's presence. The form as well as the substance of Ames's cognitive process reflects the way his relationship to time constructs the image before him. His consciousness narrative disrupts the dynamics of cognitive processing, undoing conventions which typically dictate that the formation of a neural pattern "automatically" results in the recognition "that the now-salient image of the object is formed in your perspective, belongs to you, and that you can even act on it" (126). In contrast, Ames's anticipation of his own loss of agency results in the agonized perception of an ordinary world that, no matter how intently he directs his gaze upon it, no longer belongs to him.

If, in Amery's terms, "To be young is to throw one's body out into a time that is no time at all, but life, world, and space," Ames's retreat into language during this scene documents his inability to "throw [his] body" out into the lived world he is forced to observe from the pulpit. Sending words out into an otherwise inaccessible space, Ames writes his response to young Boughton's occupation of his family pew in an extemporaneous sermon directed at his rival. The rhetorical efficacy of the sermon, however, fails to answer to the quotidian details that reverberate behind the image of the "handsome young family" that Ames perceives. In contrast to the lyrical language and heightened aesthetic quality of the bubble-blowing image, Ames's narrative rendering of the sequence of actions he observes from a distance here traces his pain to its origin in the offhand way the individuals beneath him inhabit "life, world and space":

> Then young Boughton came to the service. That was nothing I would have expected. You saw him and waved and patted the pew next to you, and he came down the aisle and sat with you. Your mother looked at him to say good morning, and then she did not look at him again. Not once.   (128)

If Ames's distance from his family lends him a powerful perspective in the earlier scene, his forced exclusion from a world he cannot access from the pulpit reverberates beneath every word of this understated representation. The quotidian dimension of the series of embodied motions and simple gestures he reports locates his son and wife, with Boughton, in the temporality of a landscape Ames can observe but cannot inhabit; the represented absence of a significant look highlights not only Ames's anxious attentiveness to the scene before him but the unself-conscious ordinariness of the way it unfolds in time and space. It is not the abstraction of mortality that torments Ames, but this intimate glimpse into the casual way in which, after his death, his family continues to inhabit the everyday world he once shared with them.

The representational perspective that would render vision as image to preserve presence against the onslaught of time here turns itself inside out, trapping Ames in the anticipation of his absence and forcing him to conceive of himself as the "immediate predecessor" of a "now" in which he participates only insofar as he is rendered obsolete. In the face of his own death, Ames's status as "sensible-sentient" locks him into the apprehension of a loss he is forced not only to imagine but to perceive; "looking back from the grave," he enters the space and time of the present only in imaginative terms that position him outside the realm of corporeal agency. Despite the presence of his increasingly diminished, progressively overwhelming body in all of the scenes he documents, Ames figures himself as hauntingly disincarnated, rendered insubstantial by the assured presence of others who carry on around and in front of him as if he is already gone; he watches himself inhabiting a world that he can no longer seem to affect.

Although Ames's faith in the continuity of life after death functions at one level to mitigate the threat of mortality, his belief that he will exist in another form after death also exaggerates the psychic dynamics of loss associated with dying. In his reflections on the fear of death, Derrida highlights the way that human consciousness remains unable to envision its own loss; more frightening than death itself, he argues, is the imagination of a future in which the subject is forced to witness its own absence in the everyday world:

> What is scarier is the fantasy...that we are going to be present at and in attendance at this non-world, at our own death. We will continue to be dead, that is, absent, while attending the actual world, being deprived of sharing the life of the survivors...What is absolutely scary is the idea of being dead while being quasi-dead, while looking at things from above, from beyond. (216)

The impossibility of imagining his own absence leads Ames to conceptualize his future status as a form of presence without agency; his repeated image of "looking back from the grave" figures life after death as a type of conscious paralysis. Describing a sleepless night just prior to the pulpit scene, Ames observes, "I just lay there, helplessly subject to my anxieties...I had to endure a kind of dull paralysis. To struggle within paralysis is a strange thing" (128). In the face of his illness, the embodied subjectivity that once functioned as a source of self-expression and chiasmic intercorporeality functions instead to immerse Ames in the textured experience of loss. Ames's figure of struggling within paralysis recalls the image of "holding my breath" used by the elderly interviewee who described in detail his failed attempt to protect himself against "the knowing, the thinking, the expecting the worst."

If Ames imagines death as continued sensory immersion in a world he is powerless to penetrate, those around him reinforce that experience of dislocation by anticipating the limits of his participation in the world. "I feel as if I am being left out," Ames observes, "as though I'm some straggler and people can't quite remember to stay back for me" (142). He follows that observation with an anecdote:

> This morning you came to me with a picture you had made that you wanted me to admire. I was just at the end of a magazine article, just finishing the last paragraph, so I didn't look up right away. Your mother said, in the kindest, saddest voice, "He doesn't hear you." Not "He didn't" but "He doesn't."   (142)

Rather than empowering him, Ames's location in the space of representation—this time as reader rather than writer—marks his exclusion from rather than transcendence of the particulars of sensory participation. As Ames's wife extends his unresponsiveness from the specific frame of a single moment into the universality of an ontological state, the shift of tense that rendered experience continuously present in the bubble-blowing scene renders Ames prematurely absent. Jean Amery relates the difficulty of negotiating impending mortality to the struggle of the elderly and the ill to

> come to terms with the fact that they are now present in space and time but, on a certain day getting nearer and nearer they will no longer be there...The human beings who give themselves up to this dismay...have in any case already partly left the space in which they can remain a bit longer...And more and more they are becoming strangers to the others.   (Amery 26)

The odd spatial metaphor Amery uses to describe those who have "already partly left" a space they continue to occupy is one taken up not only in *Gilead* but in numerous accounts of those close to the end of their lives. In "On Being Old (A Psychoanalyst's New World)," Samuel Atkin describes the split between the self that inhabits space and the self that observes and anticipates its own absence:

> I set myself the task of viewing what is transpiring. It is as if my dying is on stage, with myself the audience as well as the actor. I am in the grip of, yet lost to, the flow and rhythm of surrounding life. In yet out of it... The fish out of water.   (14)

Ames's status as a "fish out of water," a "stranger" to those around him and to the world he will soon leave, also manifests itself in the way he both perceives and is perceived in the pivotal scene where his wife and Jack Boughton interact in his presence. Jack happens along the road in front of Ames's house on a warm early autumn evening when Ames and his wife, Lila, are curled up in a quilt on the porch swing in the dark, listening to the quiet. At the invitation of Lila, Jack joins them on the porch. After a while, Ames reports, "I believe they thought I had nodded off, as I do with fair frequency, I know. They began to talk" (199). Speaking in "a lowered voice," Ames's wife engages in a conversation with the younger man that Ames reports word for word (199). Ames's objective narration belies the intimacy of his embodied presence in the scene he represents; despite the fact that Ames sits next to his wife on the porch swing and close enough to Jack to smell the smoke of the cigarette he lights, the scene consists almost entirely of dialogue transcription and straightforward description: "He said..." "After a moment, she said..." "Another silence." "She laughed." "They laughed" (199–200). Although Ames renders this understated yet oddly intimate dialogue—the only extended communication between Jack and his wife reported in the novel—largely without commentary, the reader's acute awareness of Ames's embodied presence in the scene that unfolds beside, beneath, and around him heightens the reader's sensitivity to any hint of impropriety, forcing us to listen harder, to probe the flatness of the unembellished dialogue for signs of inflection or pierce the darkness to perceive the telltale gesture that Ames cannot see. The content of the scene thus rests not only in the interaction it represents but in the process of representation it enacts as it situates Ames uncomfortably in the space of representation, tracing his status as narrator to its painful origin in the sustained dynamics of embodied subjectivity. Ames's conscious, objectified perspective in this scene points less to the impossibility of objective representation—what Merleau-Ponty describes as the illusion of a pure idea formed outside a "space of existence"—than to the simultaneous materialization and dispossession of Ames's place in the world (111). Oblivious to his conscious presence, Jack and his wife talk over and around Ames's body in a scene that renders him fully present to the experience of his own absence. If here, as in the earlier scene where he glimpses the younger Boughton joining his family from the pulpit, Ames struggles within paralysis, that struggle is visible only to the reader, who views it from an extradiegetic as well as an intradiegetic level. Although the scene offers no evidence of infidelity or betrayal, it ends with an exchange where Ames's wife whispers, in a "very gentle" tone, "Well, Jack, bless your heart," and he replies, "Why, I thank you for that, Lila" (200). In voicing the proper name of Ames's wife for the first and only time in the novel, Jack speaks to and of her with a youthful intimacy that reverberates against the formality of Ames's journalistic voice, implicating the reader in a process of displacement that renders the disease of Ames's narrative authority.

Even as the reader struggles to penetrate the veneer of representation that limits access to the full import of what develops, Ames finds himself immersed, unobserved, in the midst of the very interaction he has fearfully anticipated. In this case, his status as a "stranger" to the world expresses itself not in the dislocation of distance but in his location within an intimate, textured space where he is forced to apprehend with sensory immediacy an interaction that assumes and anticipates his absence. When Jack asks Lila whether Ames has warned her to stay away from him, Ames's narrative reports not only the exchange that unfolds in his presence but his own unspoken response:

> She found my hand and took it between her two warm hands. "He don't speak unkindly. He never does."
>
> There was a silence. I was fairly uncomfortable with myself, as you can imagine, and I was about to show some sign of stirring, just to extricate myself from this discreditable situation I had put myself into, which seemed almost to be spying. (200)

Conscious but unacknowledged, present but not participating, Ames becomes a "spy," a pleasureless voyeur granted invisibility by the process of dissolution that accompanies illness and age. The unconscious, effortless ease of youth that Ames remembers as the whole body's "collaboration" with itself unravels; Ames's chiasmic being fragments into an object body reduced to a physical entity occupying space and a perceiving consciousness forced to absorb in agonizing detail its uncomfortable exclusion from an everyday world that it can apprehend but no longer impact. In the terms formulated by Atkin, Ames experiences himself as both actor and audience, "in the grip of, yet lost to, the flow and rhythm of surrounding life." Even as Ames concludes that "We participate in being without remainder," the experience of approaching death unsettles his claim that "No breath, no thought, no wart or whisker, is not as sunk in Being as it could be" (178). Like the critically ill subject Robert Coles interviews who describes life in the context of death as "hold[ing] your breath," or an elderly woman in the same study who lives every day, as she puts it, "hovering" near her death (19), Ames experiences himself as above or outside everyday existence even as he is caught within it. As his wife takes his hand "between her two warm hands," Ames registers tactility and temperature only in relation to the textured world that surrounds his own, lending him temporary warmth even as it threatens withdrawal.

For Ames, the anticipation of his own absence renders him incapable of dwelling in the present with ease; his position both within and without undercuts his attempts—perceptual and representational—to steady his hold on experience. As Ames propels himself forward into a future he will not inhabit, he also pulls the anticipated experience of loss back into the present, where it disrupts his ability to cohabit a world with others in "the usual companionable way." At one point in his journal, addressing a grown child he will never see, Ames observes, "At this very moment I feel a kind of loving grief for you as you read this, because I do not know you, and because you have grown up fatherless, you poor child, lying on your belly now with Soapy asleep on the small of your back" (104). Imagination's power to counter future absence here rebounds to over-whelm the present with anticipated loss, rendering grief Ames's immediate companion. The autobiographical self that attends each moment of con-sciousness, Damasio argues, reflects not only "the remodeling of the lived past that takes place consciously and unconsciously, but also... the laying down and remodeling of the anticipated future" (*Feeling* 224–5). Ames's perception of the child on the floor beside him is "remodeled" by an "anticipated future" that renders every detail of sensory particularity—his son's familiar belly-down posture, the sleeping cat, the curve of the little boy's back—an image of painful inaccessibility rather than companionable presence. The reach of imagination, then, not only extends but contracts the scope of the body's touch; the intensity of heightened perception in the face of loss may swell the moment only to exclude the observer from participation in it.

Harkening back to a youthful memory of moving through the world with his father at his side, Ames describes the intermingling of sensation with sense, motion with emotion. "I can't tell you, though, how I felt," Ames writes to his own son, "walking along beside him that night, along that rutted road, through that empty world—what a sweet strength I felt, in him, and in myself, and all around us...What a power you have to experience beyond anything you might ever actually need" (49). In penetrating the moment and stockpiling images of the perceptible world, the aging and ailing Ames attempts to appropriate the seemingly limitless power to experience within an economy of loss. Even as his heightened perception yields some compensation for abbreviated opportunity, however, the surplus intensity of Ames's experience cannot be banked against the inevitable loss of embodied presence. In tracing experience to its origins in both the physiological operation of perception and the psychic dynamics of participation in the lived world, *Gilead* reveals that perception and consciousness are neither separable nor interchangeable. The "unneeded" intensity of Ames's power to apprehend the world not only resists its conversion into increased temporal opportunity but heightens his experience of anticipated loss. In *Gilead*, the "power you have to experience beyond anything you might ever actually need" remains both overwhelming and insufficient; the novel acknowledges that the reach of consciousness extends past the borders of mortality into the intimate experience of an absence the imagination is powerless to forestall.

*   *   *

Attempting to convey the challenge of communicating the embodied psychological dynamics of aging to others, one of Robert Coles's subjects uses a metaphor of dislocation to describe both the experience of social marginalization and the difficulty of conveying that experience. "Years ago," Coles observes, "she spoke, and others spoke, and as she poignantly put it, 'we were all in the same room'" (21). As *Gilead* represents and thematizes the perceptual processes through which its protagonist struggles to create meaning, the novel allows the reader not just to comprehend Ames's vision but to inhabit his experience of seeing, to occupy not only the porch, the prairie, and the pulpit but the psychic space of displacement. Given the tremendous range of physical and psychical experiences associated with the processes of aging and illness, imaginative access to Ames's narrative offers only one point of entry to broader cultural dialogues about these issues.

In breaking down the walls between our living rooms and the space just past where others lie dying, however, *Gilead* not only exposes the isolating dynamics of aging but imaginatively unsettles them by positioning the reader, along with Ames, at the margins of everyday life. "Before the essence as before the fact," Merleau-Ponty observes, "all we must do is situate ourselves within the being we are dealing with, instead of looking at it from outside...what we have to do is put it back into the fabric of our life" (117–18). As it pulls us into a heightened experience of the present, *Gilead* also pushes us to acknowledge the interweaving of life and death in the fabric of our own daily lives, to claim a relationship not just to its protagonist but to the inevitability of a shared loss situated within us. Defining the knowledge of that inevitable loss as "the inherent tragedy of conscious existence," Damasio warns against perpetuating simple Cartesian categories of mind and body. "Versions of Descartes's error," Damasio observes,

> obscure the roots of the human mind in a biologically complex but fragile, finite, and unique organism; they obscure the tragedy implicit in the knowledge of that fragility, finiteness, and uniqueness. And where humans fail to see the inherent tragedy of conscious existence, they feel far less called upon to do something about minimizing it." (*Descartes' Error* 251)

In lending Ames's voice texture, dimension, and location, Robinson achieves a vision that celebrates the power to inhabit the moment without denying the tensions implicit in the uncanny experience of "looking back from the grave." For the reader imaginatively situated in the spaces of the novel, anticipating absence may lead not only to a heightened appreciation of the present but to the ability to move toward a reimagined future in which individual attitudes, social spaces, and cultural boundaries mitigate rather than exaggerate the burdens of dying, clearing a space for aging and ailing subjects to continue inhabiting the realm of the everyday even at the margins of life.

4

The Uninhabitable Space of *Home*

The third-person narrative of *Home* unravels through the focalizing consciousness of Glory, the grown daughter who returns to her family of origin to keep house for her aged father and her alcoholic brother. Glory's presence mediates experience in and of the novel; at the level of the plot, she sustains the men around her by cooking and cleaning, while at the level of narration her perceptions anchor the reader's response to the elusive presence of her brother, Jack, and to the sometimes unintelligible hopes and dreams of her dying father. The structure of the novel, however, positions Glory as background, relegating her personal history and emotion to the margins of the text. *Home*, unlike Robinson's first two novels, has no first-person narrator. As the keeper of the house and the focalizing consciousness of the narrative, Glory facilitates the construction of a space in which her voice is often muted. Both *Housekeeping* and *Gilead* are famous for their lyrical, first-person stream of consciousness narratives, which locate the extraordinary in the ordinary through the power of observation and the force of language. Arguing that those novels depend on their speakers to "build drama from the transfigurative moments of a unique perception," Siobhan Phillips observes of Robinson's third novel, a companion piece to *Gilead*, "*Home* is told in the third person—a frustrating choice for Robinson's fiction" ("Merit" 167). Although reviewers of *Home* sometimes focus on the novel's spare plot, limited cast of characters, narrowly confined setting, and achingly slow pace to describe a reading experience several describe as "claustrophobic," the novel shares many of those characteristics with *Gilead* (see Kakutani, "Family"; MacDonald; Gwinn; and Ihara). In building on Phillips' observation, I would suggest instead that the absence of a "transfigurative" narrative voice in *Home* functions to reinforce Glory's experience of the limiting parameters of the domestic everyday.

By locating the reader uncomfortably within its circumscribed fictional world, *Home* highlights the confining cultural, historical, and narrative structures through which the dynamics of family are experienced and represented. The novel situates the contemporary reader in a household

The Elusive Everyday in the Fiction of Marilynne Robinson. Laura E. Tanner, Oxford University Press (2021).

setting it never fully naturalizes to expose the uneasy way in which Glory occupies domestic and narrative space. Glory's role in sustaining the symbolic story of the family necessitates the disavowal of her embodied presence and the masking of her voice; the narrative, however, gradually exposes the flimsy props through which that drama is staged, complicating the simple designation of Glory as "a reserved person" (Montgomery-Fate, "Back at Home"), "a straightforwardly saintly woman" (Baker 24). *Home* disrupts the story Glory's supporting role would facilitate to expose the unworkable fixtures of everyday domestic life and the forced conventions of narrative upon which that story depends.

In describing the process of reading, Alice Munro observes, "I don't take up a story and follow it as if it were a road . . . I go into it, and move back and forth and settle here and there, and stay in it for a while. It's more like a house" (1707). Munro's metaphor emphasizes the spatial and experiential rather than the temporal dynamics of narrative, suggesting an alternative to the process Peter Brooks describes as "reading for the plot." Munro's revised map of reading is particularly relevant to representations of home in contemporary women's fiction; as such fiction enacts the process of inhabiting space in narrative *and* thematic terms, it raises questions about what it means for readers as well as characters to "settle" in the domestic realm. Early feminist criticism consistently highlights the painfully limiting gender and power dynamics of social narratives of domesticity. Sandra Gilbert and Susan Gubar's critique of women's entrapment in "the architecture of patriarchy" (85) encompasses a history of the novel inhabited, in Susan Fraiman's words, by "women burdened by a stifling or terrifying domesticity" (341). Second-wave feminism rejects the bounds of domesticity (Hollows) in favor of what Susan Stanford Friedman terms "a poetics of dislocation" that enables speech and writing (205); recently, however, Friedman and others, including Kathy Mezei and Chiara Brigante, have begun to document the dangers of a binary or essentialist way of thinking that reduces feminist history to the choice of naming ourselves as insiders or outsiders to "the family romance" (Heller 220). Munro's description of inhabiting the rooms of a fictional house suggests one means of complicating binary models of reading domestic fiction; because the literary text functions both as a theoretical platform for representation and as a lived space, naming ourselves as insiders *and* outsiders demands attention to our status as participants in as well as critics of imaginative worlds. The novel, like the home, engages us not just theoretically but experientially. Extending contemporary feminism's critique of socially constructed norms to the category of the experiential highlights the intertwining of domestic, familial, and representational forms, revealing the complexity of cultural and narrative structures that encourage us to "settle" into particular domestic stories.

As an account of life in a rural Midwestern town in the late 1950s, *Home* (2008) is situated before second-wave feminism. Although the novel echoes what Dana Heller describes as contemporary feminism's focus on the family as a social construction (222), it does not approach that critique through the lens of feminist rebellion. Instead, *Home* represents the force of domestic ideals through a more subtle process that gradually denaturalizes the ideology of mid-twentieth-century domesticity and disrupts the conventions of narrative that situate the contemporary reader comfortably in the text. Feminist readings of Robinson's first novel, *Housekeeping*, often frame the protagonists' escape from the confines of domestic space as a liberation from the ideology of patriarchal family structures embodied in the house left behind in flames (Geyh 109). Whereas the dramatic plot turns of *Housekeeping*'s conclusion highlight the female characters' rejection of traditional domesticity, Glory's decision at the end of *Home* to sacrifice her freedom in order to preserve her father's dark and cluttered house has troubled contemporary feminist critics. Unable to define themselves definitively as insiders or outsiders to Robinson's family romance, many denounce "the disturbing gender politics of the ending" (Phillips, "Merit" 169) even as they attempt to resuscitate meaning by framing Glory's decision in highly symbolic terms (e.g., Holberg; Phillips, "Merit"). Such mixed responses testify to the way that *Home* captures the force of hegemonic narratives in formal as well as thematic terms, revealing that domestication, as Rachel Bowlby argues, "is not such a firmly fixed, univocal concept in the first place" (89). The narrative structures of the novel complicate the assumptions of a theoretical, third-wave feminist perspective by locating the reader firmly within the walls of one mid-century, Midwestern household, enforcing the equivocal, experiential apprehension of what it might mean to "settle here and there, and stay in it for a while" (Munro 1707).

Through a focus on the tyranny of memory and the performativity of family dynamics, the first two sections of this chapter explore the intertwined aspects of domestic ideology that continually mediate the Boughtons' lived experience of home. The third section explores the way that *Home* enacts Glory's sense of domestic entrapment formally as well as thematically by denaturalizing the conventions of narrative that render the experience of reading comfortable. The novel's unsettling conclusion, which lends Glory voice only to articulate her continued entrapment within the patriarchal structures of her father's home, resists the critical impulse to read the novel in binary feminist terms. By frustrating the desire to locate Glory, and the reader, as insiders *or* outsiders in this domestic story, Robinson's novel returns us, instead, to the representational and cultural structures of mediation the novel exposes and enacts.

* * *

Glory's inability to inhabit the space of the domestic comfortably points to the tension *Home* exposes between lived experiences of domesticity and the symbolic demand that the home should embody familial identity, both past and present. Even as it participates in the genre of domestic fiction, Robinson's novel continually exposes the space between Glory's everyday experience of keeping house and the symbolic/cultural work that the home she tends is asked to perform. Although much of the novel is taken up with depictions of daily routines and ordinary acts, the experiential present of the novel is often subsumed within nostalgic images of an ideal family based on a sequence of staged performances of domestic life. *Home*, then, continually directs the reader away from the rhythms of daily life that the domestic novel would represent into the space of representation in which the family dwells.

His wife dead and his children gone, Robert Boughton occupies a house of memory in which objects, once prized for their use value, now function primarily to bolster the family narrative. "Empty" and "useless" in the phenomenological world, the family's property exists almost entirely in the realm of signification:

> Boughtons, who kept everything, had kept their land, their empty barn, their...horseless pasture. There on the immutable terrain of their childhood her brothers and sisters could...remember those years in great detail, their own memories, but more often the pooled memory they saw no special need to portion out among them.   (8)

The symbolic structures of nostalgia, Susan Stewart asserts in an argument responsible for initiating much contemporary dialogue on the topic, often operate by displacing "the lived relation of the body to the phenomenological world" with a "nostalgic myth of contact and presence" (*Longing* 133). As the "immutable" décor of the Boughton house assumes a primarily nostalgic function, its "big, crowding furniture" overwhelms the lived bodies of the present (52). Whereas *Gilead* immerses the reader in the textured details of Ames's sensory perceptions to lend surprising depth to the most quotidian experiences, *Home* highlights in narrative as well as thematic terms its characters' expulsion from the pleasures of the phenomenological present:

> When evening fell no lights were put on, and suppertime came and went unremarked. Her father stepped out of the dining room and saw her in the dark parlor. He said, "Yes, Glory," as if reminding himself of something, and went upstairs. She toasted two pieces of bread and ate them dry because she dreaded the sound she might make spreading butter on them. (58)

Glory finds herself inhabiting the dim recesses of an inhospitable symbolic landscape unilluminated for the reader by Robinson's characteristically poetic prose; in the dark parlor, her father's gaze reduces Glory's embodied presence to a mere "remind[er] ... of something." Ann Romines argues that the literature of domestic ritual engages the reader through its artistic representation of the "profoundly felt life" of domesticity (16). In *Home*, by contrast, Glory appears to lend herself as support for a nostalgic project that unrealizes her location in the lived present and often excludes the reader from immersion in the textured rhythms of domestic life. As the novel continues, however, Glory's consciousness of what Svetlana Boym describes as "nostalgia's mechanisms of seduction and manipulation" complicates her relegation to a supporting role in the Boughtons' domestic drama.

The text repeatedly traces Glory's invisibility to her gender status in the traditionalist ethos of mid-twentieth-century family and religious life:

> She seemed always to have known that, to their father's mind, the world's great work was the business of men ... They were the stewards of ultimate things. Women were creatures of a second rank, however pious, however beloved, however honored. This was not a thing her father would ever have said to her. (20)

Exploring the gendered dynamics underlying the emergence of family as "an object of worshipful contemplation" in the early twentieth century, John Gillis argues that women came to facilitate such worship not only through their housekeeping but through their effort to sustain symbolically "the family tableau," the "rituals, myths, and images on which the newly enchanted world of family had come to depend" (77). As Glory returns to her childhood home, the difficulty of caring for her aging father and her alcoholic brother pales beside the strain of upholding the myth of the family. Robinson's text unveils the invisible force of inscribed gender roles even as it exposes the connection between culturally maintained structures of gender, religion, and family. In locating the structural definitions of those categories outside the realm of articulation, Robinson encourages us to read the novel not only for what it represents but for what it fails to say.

Home can thus be contextualized within recent feminist attempts to complicate our understanding of space and identity. The realignment of spatial subjectivity, Dana Heller argues,

> is most powerfully... inscribed in contemporary fictional narratives that make use of the... dynamics of classical family romance precisely in order to redescribe [them] in light of recent skepticism concerning the usefulness of categories such as "identity," "family," and "genre." This skepticism implies a shift from an idealization of coherence... to a preoccupation with representational systems themselves... as constitutive of what the familially situated subject takes to be her "self." (220–1)

In *Home*, Glory upholds the family image at the expense of participating in a representational system that dismisses her own embodied and articulating presence. As internal focalizer of the text, Glory subtly renounces her phenomenological placement in a storyworld oriented by her perceptions. Her perspective, thoroughly embedded in the narrative, only intermittently announces the forced limits of its point of view. The success of Glory's labors as homemaker and focalizer is marked by the propagation of a coherent image of family that obscures what Pierre Bourdieu describes as the "constant and intense maintenance work" required to uphold it (*Logic* 63). As Glory reflects, "It seemed sometimes as if her father must have meant to preserve all this memory... so that when they came home... *there would be no need to say anything.* In the terms of the place, they would all always have known everything" (88). Glory's work to sustain not just the family home but its story often necessitates the erasure of her embodied and articulating presence. By highlighting that erasure, Robinson documents historical realities of mid-century family life even as she locates the "familially situated subject" within cultural and textual systems of representation.

Throughout *The Poetics of Space*, Gaston Bachelard elides the distinction between our psychic and physical location in the home to emphasize, instead, the way we "experience the house in its reality and in its virtuality, by means of thought and dreams" (5). *Home*, in contrast, situates the Boughton house in the space where reality and virtuality overlap in order to explore the tensions between these two means of apprehending experience: "The town seemed different to [Glory], now that she had returned there to live. She was thoroughly used to Gilead as the subject and scene of nostalgic memory" (7). Describing nostalgia as "a longing for a home that no longer exists or has never existed," Svetlana Boym highlights the tension between the fantasy of home and its experiential counterpart as the defining characteristic of nostalgia: "A cinematic image of nostalgia is a double exposure, or a superimposition of two images—of home and abroad, of past and present, of dream and everyday life. The moment we try to force it into a single image, it breaks the frame or burns the surface" (7). In the narrative of *Home*, the uncomfortable everyday testifies to the force required to sustain the singular image. Held in place as a tribute to the life of the family in its prime, the Boughton home subtly discourages the routine engagements that would constitute ordinary life in the present: "It was being home that made her remember . . . sitting beside the irksome radio trying to read the book she had chosen as possibly least unreadable among the hundreds of old books in the scores of shelves . . . that narrowed the overfurnished rooms" (19). Whereas the volumes Ames surrounds himself with in *Gilead* affirm the limitless scope of his mind, piles of "unreadable" old books trap the adult Glory within the contracting parameters of lived space.

For the Boughtons, then, holding onto the house of memory comes at the expense of agreeing to live in an overly cluttered and representational domestic space "overfurnished" to the point of becoming uninhabitable. The dining room table Glory sets for Jack's arrival is covered with dust by the time they sit down to it; descriptions of food in the novel emphasize the discarded and uneaten. Even when the house is filled at holiday time, the past overwhelms the present, reducing objects to their projected status as bearers of memory: "At Easter she and her sisters could still bring in armfuls of flowers, and their father's eyes would glitter with tears and he would say, 'Ah yes yes,' as if they had brought some memento, these flowers only a pleasant reminder of flowers" (4). The tangible materiality of things in the present continually dissolves beneath their function as signs capable of evoking a recollected past. Glory's attempt to enliven the present through entertaining visitors leads her guests to settle uncomfortably into "creaky chairs no one ever sat on. It had almost been forgotten that they were there not just to be dismally ornamental, chairs only in the sense that the lamp stand was a shepherdess" (179). When Jack's son visits his father's childhood home at the end of the novel, it is fitting that the memento Glory offers him is itself a representation. "Here," Siobhan Phillips observes in her review of *Home*, "the water that was a terrifying flood in *Housekeeping* and a mysterious sacrament in *Gilead* appears as a framed picture of a river: this safe arrest of elemental fluidity is what home and *Home* want to offer" ("Merit" 169).

*   *   *

If the Boughtons, in the narrative present, inhabit a symbolic landscape pointing to the lived experience of the past, revelations of the past expose the fact that "the old robust domestic life" is largely a construct. Even as children, the younger Boughtons found themselves on a stage, participating in the rituals of a family life lived under pressure of performativity. Insofar as *Home* serves as a meditation not just on family but on the creation of the family's story (63), it reveals the Boughtons' extraordinary investment in the construction of image. Boughton family life is defined from its origins by a level of self-consciousness that, when filtered through the lens of Glory's point of view, verges on theatricality:

> Her good, kind, and jovial siblings were good, kind and jovial consciously and visibly. Even as children they had been good in fact, but also in order to be seen as good. There was something disturbingly like hypocrisy about it all ... They were as happy as their father could wish, even happier. Such gaiety! And their father laughed at it all, danced with them to the Victrola ... Such a wonderful family they were!   (6–7)

The forced gaiety Glory recounts erupts in the strained exclamations that punctuate the representation of the family's seeming spontaneity. Like the rehearsed emotional outbursts that interrupt the carefully controlled narrative, these seemingly impulsive acts continually freeze into *tableau vivants* meant to signify the natural dynamics of family. The family, Bourdieu observes, "endows experience with a commonsensical or self-evident appearance, that is, the family appears as the most natural of social categories" (*Logic* 62). That the Boughton household requires reiterated performances to reinforce an insufficiently naturalized family identity exposes both the instability of their happy home and the pressure of the cultural categories that enforce the terms of family.

Although Glory casts the performativity of their family life as a necessary attempt "to compensate for Jack" (6), the novel complicates that explanation by situating the Boughtons' domestic self-consciousness within broader cultural narratives of gender, family, and religion. The uncomfortable furniture of the Boughton home testifies to the overlapping pragmatic and symbolic functions of domestic space. Furnishings, as Katherine Grier argues, "exist as fact, but...can also make rhetorical statements...meant to persuade others (and, it can be argued, also ourselves) that we actually are what our possessions claim us to be" (54). For the Boughtons, the intersecting frameworks of domesticity and religion exaggerate the need to signify the stability of their Christian family. The Boughtons' uncomfortable furniture exemplifies a Gothic revival style designed to reinforce the "image of the Christian home" (Clark 26). Their "cluttered" and "oppressive" décor thus supports a symbolic mission at the expense of the lived body; in dreaming of "a real home" for herself, Glory imagines it as "a home very different from this good and blessed and fustian and oppressive tabernacle of Boughton probity" (102).

Although John Gillis traces the twentieth-century family's representational focus to a crisis of faith in Victorian culture (72), Robinson's novel parallels the production of family with the ritualistic operation of religion. For the Boughtons, the heightened symbolic elements of Sunday worship penetrate even the everyday family practices enacted in the private spaces of the minister's home. Not surprisingly, the rituals of the Sabbath involve the uncomfortable experience of individual bodies made to accommodate themselves to the "orderliness" of preexisting forms: "The children restless in their church clothes, the dresses and jackets and shoes that child after child...put on, took off, as his or her turn came. Too large and too small, but never ever comfortable" (39). Forced to tolerate the shared dress clothing that fits them for participation in public worship, the Boughton children find themselves no more at ease in their private space. In Glory's memory, the domestic experience of the family itself emerges as constrained and performative. Given the frequency with which esteemed members of her father's congregation visit the Boughton home, even ordinary family meals are marked by the children's sense of an embodied presence increasingly crowded out by the demands of public ritual:

Eight of them...crowded at that table...practicing their manners— keeping their elbows to themselves, not swinging their legs...Waiting for the blessing...Waiting to speak until they were spoken to, until the meal was finished, out of respect to talk of creeds and synods.   (39)

The constant presence of unnamed and unfamiliar guests transforms the domestic domain into a public arena where the Boughton children must contract their bodies into an impossibly small space policed by "ecclesiastical" dignitaries intolerant of "childish behavior" (39). Denied the luxury of the "everyday inattentiveness" that critics like Rita Felski ("Introduction") associate with the repeated rhythms of ordinary life, Glory and her siblings struggle to make themselves at home in the midst of the most familiar daily routines. As the children of a clergyman, "their lives were lived so publicly" (18) that even the most everyday experiences were rendered self-conscious activities.

Arguing in his discussion of space that "Life is lived, not a pageant from which we stand aside and observe," Yi-Fu Tuan concludes, "The real is the familiar daily round, unobtrusive like breathing. The real involves our whole being, all our senses" (145–6). In contrast, the ritualistic and performative dimensions of the Boughton household lock Glory and her siblings out of the multisensory, embodied experience Tuan associates with the "familiar daily round" of childhood. Even in moments of apparent ease or celebration, Glory observes, "there was something strained about it all" (184). In the Boughton household, the genuflection to "creeds and synods" assumes its secular counterpart in the scripted production of a domestic tableau meant to testify to the coherence and stability of the family. In rendering Jack's "exile" from domestic life as the single challenge to their happy home, the Boughtons reinscribe the hegemonic force of a domestic ideal that the novel denaturalizes as it highlights the labor necessary to uphold the "ordinary world" in which the family story is set.

*   *   *

Of course, for the reader, the experience of the Boughton home as virtual rather than sensory reality is a given. We enter the space of any novel through and as representation; we access the characters' lives only through a series of literary conventions naturalized through imagination. The lived experience of a narrative is hopelessly entangled with conventions of representation that encourage us, as narratologist Monica Fludernik explores, to project "real-life" parameters into the reading process (440). Extending Fludernik's claim that narrative cannot be understood apart from the category of the experiential, David Herman argues that any full-fledged narrative must "register the pressure of events on an embodied human" (*Story Logic* 256); successful narrative thus represents not only a sequence of events that unfold within the storyworld but the lived experience of those events by a particular embodied subject. As Susan Stewart explores in *On Longing*, linguistic representation takes on the challenge of describing the world in such detail that it appears to materialize the absent presence that is its referent: the lived experience of the body. Description not only lends immediacy to fiction's constructions by invoking the embodied subject's immersion in a phenomenological world but, in doing so, often obscures the work of representation by immersing the reader in a textured experiential space.

In the case of *Home*, however, Glory's embodied presence continually returns the reader to her awkward situation in a symbolically laden domestic space that the novel never quite naturalizes. *Home*'s powerfully written and achingly poignant representation of family builds painstakingly toward a conclusion that left me, unexpectedly, in tears. Unlike *Housekeeping* or *Gilead*, however, this novel resists the bursts of lyrical epiphany and imagistic transcendence that structure the reading experience of Robinson's earlier novels, generating a different kind of affective power. Reviews of *Home* often highlight the struggle of negotiating a slow-moving reading experience that denies the reader the pleasure of imaginative immersion in a multisensory phenomenological experience. Trapped within the confines of what one *New York Times* critic describes as "a static, even suffocating narrative in which very little is dramatized" (Kakutani, "Family" E1), some readers come to apprehend the parameters of the novel's domestic spaces as perimeters circumscribing the work of the imagination rather than the foundation of an evolving fictional world. The lush description of *Housekeeping* and the luminous accounts of perception in *Gilead* give way to the dim setting and unembellished dialogue of *Home*; as Malcolm Jones observes,

> Samuel Beckett couldn't have made it much sparer: three characters... who talk, talk, talk for more than 300 pages and say pretty much the same things over and over. Almost all the action is contained in the kitchen, the garden and the barn of an old house in the little fictional town of Gilead, Iowa. (73)

For every reviewer who praises the novel's subtlety and emotional power, there is another who describes feeling trapped within the four walls of the Boughton home. One particularly cranky reader describes the novel as "static" and ends his review by saying,

Toward the end of the novel, Glory wonders why anyone would stay in Gilead. It's a good question, because if all the households are as claustro-phobic as the Boughton manse and the other inhabitants are gripped by the kind of psychic paralysis that prevails there, then Gilead could well be the most boring place on earth.   (Wilson)

Although I would disagree with the rendering of the Boughton household as "claustrophobic" and the narrative as "almost suffocating," such readings of *Home* highlight the power with which Robinson's representational choices challenge unspoken conventions of fiction; experiencing everyday life in the novel as a form of confinement unmitigated by dramatic turns of plot or the broadening scope of a fully accessible narrative consciousness, readers such as Kakutani ("Family") and Wilson testify to the way that *Home* renders domestic and narrative space equally uncomfortable. Instead of invoking literary conventions to naturalize the lived experiences of its characters, the novel stalls the reader in a domestic landscape inhabited awkwardly and self-consciously by its most intimate denizens. Whereas the Boughtons live their lives in a self-conscious relation to the past, perched on the edge of uncomfortable furniture, the reader's discomfort may stem from the novel's refusal to provide mechanisms of imaginative transcendence that would transport us out of their oppressive space or render it more hospitable.

Initially, the energy of the novel's plot is driven by the quest to uncover details of Jack's exploits; as emerging details of those incidents remain disconnected and inaccessible, however, narrative suspense dissipates into the expectation of forced quiescence. Indeed, Jack's own compulsive activity revolves around waiting—waiting and waiting for a letter from the outside world that seems never to come. Although the novel thus begins by invoking what D. A. Miller describes as "the suspense that constitutes the narratable" (265), its lack of action, revelation, and motion undercuts the process that Peter Brooks describes as "reading for the plot." Defining reading as "a form of desire that carries us forward, onward, through the text," Brooks argues that narration "arouses and sustains desire" ("Narrative" 136). By contrast, it might be argued, Robinson's novel slowly extinguishes desire by circum-scribing possibility to locate the reader in a setting Hugh MacDonald, like Frank Wilson, describes as "almost claustrophobic." Noting the "soporific tenor" of the household and the narrative (Morrissy), critic after critic echoes Katherine Govier's assessment that "the book is wonderfully written, and painfully slow" (19).

The experience of reading the novel thus parallels its thematic focus on the painful dynamics of being stalled in a representational world. Occasional references to newspaper and television accounts of a larger world in the text only emphasize the location of characters and readers in a circumscribed domestic arena: "[Glory] hadn't read a newspaper in days or turned on the television set or the radio, so she could not think of a way to bring up Eisenhower or Dulles or baseball or Egypt, the things that focused her father's attention, lured him out of his dreams" (292–3). Whereas the larger worlds of politics and sports possess the potential to unsettle the senior Boughton's retreat into imagination, the space of the home may lull the reader, like Glory, into an almost hypnotic state of suspension: "She had almost forgotten weather, between her father and her novels and her unaccountable insistence on reading them in the darkest room of the house" (95). Positioned tightly by Robinson's prose and the construction of the narrative in the dimmed spaces of the home and the novel, readers may gradually release their hold on a larger world.

The novel highlights Glory's limited status as focalizer of this "claustrophobic" narrative by revealing her unwillingness to acknowledge the deviation of her thoughts from cultural scripts. The selves of stories, as Shelley Sclater argues, are always "superficial covers for something that is much more deep, complex and threatening... The storied self, far from encapsulating the 'real' self... is something that *defends against* it" (2). Even in moments when the text begins to open up to the representation of tentative engagement with a phenomenological world, Glory's unwillingness to cede control seizes the narrative, resulting in what Phillips describes as its defining characteristic, "this safe arrest of elemental fluidity" ("Merit" 169):

There [Jack] was, washing up at the kitchen sink with a bar of laundry soap. The house had always been redolent of lavender and lye. She wondered if he remembered. He had hung his jacket and tie over the back of a chair and loosened his collar and was scrubbing his face and his neck with a tea towel, one of those on which their grandmother in her old age had embroidered the days of the week. No matter.   (33)

Although still tied up with nostalgic images of the family past, this paragraph begins to break through structures of containment that repress the lived experience of the domestic present and its representation. The narrative echo of Glory's curt response to Jack's messy embodiment in its abrupt conclusion, however, functions as a "superficial cover" for Glory at the expense of closing down the reader's access to the textured details of the phenomenological present. In structural terms, Glory's status as focalizing consciousness reflects the dynamics of her absent presence in the family home, highlighting the impossibility of disentangling the text's unwillingness to lend her first-person voice from her own internalization of gendered voicelessness.

Toward the conclusion of the novel, that voicelessness becomes more readily identifiable as the tension it creates erupts not only in the narrative but in the storyworld. "Although the scene in which Robert Boughton expresses his intent to leave Glory the house is rendered" through her focalizing consciousness, the narrative fails to acknowledge either her placement in the scene or her reaction to the news. When, pages later, Glory openly voices her horror at inheriting the home she has worked so hard to maintain, however, we are forced to confront the uneasy way in which she has unobtrusively occupied domestic and narrative space. Her eventual revelation to Jack about inheriting the house—"I don't want to sound ungrateful, but I'm—'horrified' is too strong a word, but it's one that comes to mind" (298)—is startling not only in its strength of emotion but in the tension it reveals between Glory's passionate utterance and the understated rendering of the earlier scene, which is revealed, in retrospect, as marked by inexplicable narrative restraint.

Glory's uncharacteristic outburst shines a powerful light on the dim recesses of the domestic space that the novel has naturalized as its backdrop, illuminating the symbolic construction of the Boughton home by reducing it to a theatrical set cluttered with unusable props. Designated as the housekeeper assigned to maintain the structures of memory that symbolically support the autonomous lives of her family members, Glory calls attention to her literal entrapment within the uncomfortable confines of a house through which the idea of the family is reiterated and staged.

> "This is a nightmare I've had a hundred times," she finally confesses. "The one where all the rest of you go off and begin your lives and I am left in an empty house full of ridiculous furniture and unreadable books, waiting for someone to notice I'm missing and come back for me." (298)

Glory's reaction to the gift of her inheritance returns the reader to the lived practices of housekeeping that support and ultimately expose what Bachelard defines as the home's symbolic function as a source of protection and a bearer of memory. Disrupting the conventions of staging that her own unacknowledged position in the narrative has helped to perpetuate, Glory now records her resistance to Jack's symbolic gaze in a sudden explosion of descriptive adjectives:

But he kept looking around at it, the table and sideboard with their leonine legs and belligerently clawed feet, like some ill-considered, doily-infested species of which they were the last survivors. The wall sconces that were lotus blossoms with lightbulbs where their stamens ought to have been. She thought, Dear Lord, he is missing it all in anticipation. She thought, As long as he is alive in the world, or as long as no one knows otherwise, I will probably have to keep all that sour, fierce, dreary black walnut. (299)

Glory's uncharacteristic deployment of accumulated, subjective adjectives in this passage functions to create a wedge between the thing and its appropriation within Jack's preemptive nostalgic fantasy, returning the objects around her to awkward materiality by exposing their representational claim to life as forced and even absurd. As she dwells upon the "sour, fierce, dreary black walnut" furnishings of her father's house, Glory stalls the narrative, her typically subdued voice intruding to denaturalize once familiar domestic space. Her focus on what Liesl Olson describes in *Modernism and the Ordinary* as "the diffuse and messy particularities of [daily] life" highlights the tensions that constitute restorative nostalgia (5; Boym 13). Spotlighting her embodied location in an austere domestic realm designed not for comfort but for signification of the universal values of home and family, Glory exposes the way that the family story traps her in an unlivable space.

As Glory emerges from the backdrop of the narrative to locate herself in the act of telling, the very process of describing the childhood home becomes a means of resisting its power. Bachelard observes, "For the real houses of memory...do not readily lend themselves to description. To describe them would be like showing them to visitors...The first, the oneirically definitive house, must retain its shadows" (13). In this case, description functions not, as Susan Stewart (*Longing*) argues, to naturalize the fictional approximation of a phenomenological world, but to burden the symbolic props facilitating the family's story with an unwieldy materiality. Forced to "live out her life in a place all the rest of them called home," Glory resists the charge of defending intimacy by opening the darkened rooms up to narrative view and showing them to the reader/visitor. Glory's exposure of the gap between image and everyday life "breaks the frame" of nostalgia (Boym 7) through acts of saying that expose the uncomfortable practice of inhabiting a home cluttered with "ridiculous" furniture that fails to accommodate the weight of the lived body.

The novel's final scene disrupts the experience of reading that the text has naturalized in similarly unexpected ways. Surrendering the process of reading for the plot, the reader of *Home* must gradually relinquish the narrative "desire that carries us forward, onward, through the text" (Brooks, "Narrative" 132). Having gradually assimilated the narrow parameters of the Boughtons' home as the limits of this representational landscape, the reader may come to apprehend the storyworld outside its walls as shadowy illusion. As one critic observes, events of the novel that have occurred off stage emerge as "fleeting and unreal. What is real is this house...the tree with branches too high to be climbed safely, the porch, the ridiculous knick-knacks" (Govier 19). Having been lulled into foreclosing experience of a larger world, we are shocked when that world—in the form of Jack's "other" family—unexpectedly intrudes into the space of the narrative.

Six pages before the novel ends, long after a desire for major plot developments has been dulled or even extinguished by a narrative that suspends us in a representational rhythm slowed to the pace of dream, Jack's wife and child suddenly drive into the space of home/*Home*. This unexpected disruption, which occurs after the reader, like Glory, "had become used to the idea that nothing more of consequence would happen" (312), promises a kindling of motion and emotion. Against the familiar small town backdrop, Della and her young son stand out not only for her "very urban" outfit, his bright red tie, and the color of their skin, but for the lingering, attentive representation of their presence in the text. The revelation that Della is an African-American woman highlights the way her surprise visit disrupts the conventions of the town and the narrative, jolting Glory out of the dreamlike state Bachelard associates with the childhood home and opening up multiple narrative possibilities for the reader. As Glory watches Jack's wife gaze upon the porch, the orchard, the trees, she speculates, "Maybe there were stories attached to every commonplace thing, other stories than she had heard, than any of them had heard" (320). Della's fresh perspective destabilizes the oppressive signification of a home heavy with the past, raising the possibility of breathing life into the static domestic and narrative landscape: "She knew it would have answered a longing of Jack's if he could even imagine that their spirits had passed through that strange old house...The place would seem changed, to him and to her...New love would transform all the old love and make its relics wonderful" (323). That promise of transformation speaks not only to the inhabitants of the Boughton home but to the readers of the novel; continually redirected away from the textured experience of the novel's present to an inaccessible past, we may greet the introduction of new characters and the energy of new emotion with a rekindling of narrative desire.

Glory suggests that the presence of these unexpected visitors carries with it the possibility of reanimating a static domestic landscape by offering narrative resolution or opening up the possibility of generating entirely new stories. Having stirred the reader's desire for narrative motion, however, the novel offers neither the closure of biblical fable promised by the story of the prodigal son nor the pleasure of action and revelation offered by the tantalizing presence of new characters. The novel denies its readers the pleasure of watching Jack's wife and child enter the home, or the drama of witnessing their encounter with the elder Boughton on his deathbed. Even as it justifies this denial by invoking the violent racial dynamics of the time, the text flaunts the refusal of our narrative desire: "*And they would not walk in the door. They had to hurry, to escape the dangers of nightfall*" (323). Offering neither resolution nor the fulfillment of plot-driven desire, the novel disrupts the static conventions it has normalized only to return the reader, newly agitated, to the suspended state of waiting. Della and her son emerge as elusive figures notable mostly for the empty space they leave behind; their sudden intrusion offers less a climax of plot than a reminder of how circumscribed the domestic and narrative spaces of the novel remain.

The novel does not end with the exit of Jack's family, however. In the final paragraph of *Home*, with the simple transition of "She thought," Glory's first-person voice emerges, only to articulate her decision to remain the keeper of her father's empty house:

> She thought, Maybe this Robert will come back someday ... And I will be almost old. I will see him standing in the road by the oak tree, and I will know him by his tall man's slouch, the hands on the hips ... He will talk to me a little while, too shy to tell me why he has come, and then he will thank me and leave, walking backward a few steps, thinking, Yes, the barn is still there, yes, the lilacs, even the pot of petunias. This was my father's house. And I will think, He is young. He cannot know that my whole life has come down to this moment. That he has answered his father's prayers. The Lord is wonderful. (324)

In this concluding paragraph, the narrative offers the reader its most direct access to Glory's consciousness; although "no reflector ever literally tells the narrative we are reading" (Herman, *Story Logic* 97), this passage not only acknowledges Glory's point of view as a narrative filter but highlights her potential claim to authorship by marking the creativity of her imaginings and the clear emergence of her distinctive voice. Even as she expresses her thinking in the first person, however, Glory not only fails to resist the patriarchal constraints of her father's house but extends the image of return that has governed textual and familial dynamics far into the future. If Glory's mediated presence in the narrative voice of *Home* functions as parallel to her domestic experience, her assumption of authorial voice in the novel's conclusion would, we might expect, reflect a decision to liberate herself from the bounds of patriarchal space.

Glory remains stalled, however, not only in the impossible recollection of the nostalgic past but in the imaginative anticipation of a tableau that would symbolically unite the contradictory strains of the family story only by erasing her own life narrative. Representing herself as a figure subsumed within the ritualistic return of parable, a mere vehicle facilitating a moment of imagined narrative closure, she sidelines herself in the very story she imagines; as Glory glosses over the twenty years of daily experience that cannot be appropriated within the culminating image of her narrative, she writes herself out of a life. In the parable of return she constructs, Glory's advanced age—"And I will be almost old"—renders the passing of the prime of her life a parenthetical aside; her commitment to sustaining the family tableau emerges at the expense of inhabiting her own life narrative.

Critics have successfully framed Glory's decision to maintain her father's house in religious and historical terms, persuasively arguing that her decision embodies the values of Christian faith and represents a chance to disrupt the inherited racism that plagues her community.[1] It is difficult to reconcile these affirmative readings, however, with what such critics acknowledge as the "disturbing gender politics" of the conclusion (Phillips, "Merit" 169). Readings that frame Glory's decision as a model of social change or religiously based altruism often find themselves falling into troubling echoes of patriarchal systems of representation. After documenting Glory's "sense of gendered inadequacy," for example, Jennifer Holberg unselfconsciously concludes that "The book seems to suggest that someday, through Glory's efforts in the old, odd house with its cumbersome furniture... both young Robert Boughtons... may return together to take up habituation in this land of their fathers" (18).

---

[1] See Holberg, who argues that Glory embodies Robinson's theology, and Phillips, who reads Glory's decision as a political act that resists the history of racism in Gilead.

Reading the novel's conclusion in the context of its historical period, I would argue, might suggest an alternative to readings that, alternately, dismiss the gender implications of Glory's choice or ignore its symbolic and narrative import. Caught as she is between her desire for an unfettered life as an individual, her internalization of traditional mid-century gender roles and the genuine concern she feels for her family, Glory uses a culturally sanctioned script of feminine self-sacrifice to clear a space for herself in her father's home. Under the cover of that script, she creates a story that authorizes a life of solitude rendered in the service of family. Even as she acknowledges the death of her dream to create her own family, Glory imaginatively constructs a future that positions her centrally in the home in which she often felt herself dispossessed. Although Glory here seems to buy into the nostalgic impulses that she critiques with increasing fervor throughout the novel, her self-consciousness aligns her with what Boym describes as a "reflective" nostalgia or what Outka identifies as "a calculated, self-conscious stance" capable of rendering nostalgia a useful tool (Boym 13; Outka 260); following in the footsteps of critics like Boym and Clewell, who move to depathologize nostalgic longing (Clewell 5), Outka argues that nostalgia "potentially becomes more useful, more powerful, and less dangerous, when it is wielded not as an overpowering longing but as a self-aware construction" (256). In the story she constructs at the end of the novel, Glory emerges as the embodiment of the thing worth returning to, the personification of home. Constituting her as a familial subject, Glory's story renders her presence the nucleus of family dynamics and disavows the significance of her own life narrative even as it clears a space for solitary subjectivity within the patriarchal structures she inhabits.

Although Glory's decision to embrace the role of keeper of her father's home seems to entail the sacrifice of her own vision of home, the novel lays the groundwork for understanding Glory's final decision through a more radical lens. The novel's back story traces Glory's susceptibility to a manipulative "fiancé" to her blinding desire to create her own family, a desire embodied in her reiterated imaginings of a modest, uncluttered home. Throughout the novel, however, Glory's ruminations offer conflicting narratives of her own desire. Although Glory consciously laments the loss of love and the absence of children, her presence as focalizer in the narrative emerges most vibrantly in descriptions of dream children and imagined romance that subtly highlight the rewards of authorial privilege. Glory takes unacknowledged pleasure in the fantasy status of her dynamically changing imaginative offspring. "[R]eal children," she acknowledges, would necessarily curtail her poetic license: "She had names for them, which drifted among them, and changed, as did certain of their attributes, ages, gender, number...In her fantasies she sang to them the ballad of lost children... She might have had doubts about dropping this tincture of sorrow into their hearts if they had been real children" (306). The tension between real and imagined domesticity emerges also in Glory's willingness to turn away from the embodied reality of her fiancé, a "robust" man with "red hair that crinkled against his scalp" (307), to privately embrace her own images of romance: "She gave him money so he would stop talking, maybe even so he would go away. He might have known this. He would go away and leave her with her thoughts of him" (312). Although Glory represses her desire to inhabit the felt life of the mind, the lived experience she mourns so intensely after her relationship ends is located, ironically, in the fruitful privation of *solitude*: "She could not let herself remember the lonely pleasures she found in living so simply, enjoying the renunciations and economies that would some time make possible—what?—ordinary happiness. The kind of happiness she saw in the luncheonette, passed in the street" (22). Although existing cultural logic cannot explain the "renunciation" of a rich domestic life in favor of the "lonely pleasures [of] living so simply" except as necessary sacrifice, Glory's forced denial of that remembered pleasure exposes it as more than a necessary means to a culturally sanctioned end. The question interposed in the narrative ("—what?—") that delays the naming of "ordinary happiness" creates a space for acknowledging the hesitation Glory exhibits as she renounces her economy of solitary pleasure in the name of cultural norms of desire. If "ordinary happiness" is tied up with traditionally gendered notions of the domestic, the "spare and functional" "modest" home that Glory continually associates with her dream of family accommodates that communal vision only with strain (22, 306, 306).

Glory's acknowledgment of the lonely pleasures of renunciation troubles her conventional reading of the modest, uncluttered home she imagines in the same way that her ability to embrace authorship of the novel's conclusion troubles her renunciation of her own lived experience. The shift to first person in the novel's conclusion opens up a space—however cramped and crowded—for Glory to begin to inhabit the phenomenological present that her parable-like story disavows. As Robinson herself points out, lived experience encompasses not only embodied apprehension and spatial location but what she terms "the felt life of the mind" (*Absence of Mind* 35). In interviews, she defends the creative potential of solitude, which she describes as "a lovely thing": "I'm kind of a solitary...I grew up with the confidence that the greatest privilege was to be alone and have all the time you wanted. That was the cream of existence" (Fay). In response to questions about Glory's loneliness at the end of *Home*, Robinson observes, "I think loneliness is the encounter with oneself—who can be great or terrible company, but who does ask all the essential questions. There is a tendency to think of loneliness as a symptom, a sign that life has gone wrong. But it is never only that. I sometimes think it is the one great prerequisite for depth, and for truthfulness" (Fay).

Although the conclusion of *Home* confines Glory to a solitary life in her father's house, what can be read as the sacrifice of her individual autonomy in the service of family, "it is never only that." *Home* acknowledges the pressure of normative categories that structure everyday experience even as it resists the simple binaries that recent feminist criticism has begun to dismantle. "Does representing feminist history in a post-feminist age," Dana Heller asks, "really come down to the choice...between naming ourselves as insiders or outsiders to the family romance?" (220). Situated in 1950s small town Midwestern life, *Home*'s setting predates that of *Housekeeping*; in suggesting the impossibility of fully liberating the gendered self from domestic structures, *Home*'s conclusion testifies simultaneously to the reality of historical constraints and to what contemporary feminists increasingly recognize as the theoretical impossibility of reifying the blurred border between inside and outside, individual and familial subjectivity. To that end, the shift to first person at the end of the novel by no means circumvents the representational and cultural structures of mediation the novel exposes. Glory's consciousness, even when we access it more directly in narrative terms, remains bound by the unspoken assumptions of history, family, gender, and culture. Earlier in the novel, Glory acknowledges the impossibility of escaping the structures that govern her own narrative of desire: "She used to ask herself, What more could I wish? But she always distrusted that question, because she knew there were limits to her experience that precluded her from knowing what there was to be wished" (20). In exposing the complexity of Glory's efforts to negotiate the "limits" of home, Robinson gestures toward the awkward ways in which we inhabit the cultural and narrative structures that support our material and imaginative constructs.

Robinson reconciles "the intensity of [her] attraction" to the life of the mind with her affirmation of "socially enmeshed existence" (Fay) by defining compassion and conscience as "two of the most potent and engrossing individual experiences" we can have (Montgomery-Fate, "Seeing"). Glory's ability to assume a voice at the end of the novel results from her ability to clear a space in the narrative and in her father's home that affirms her centrality in the family even as her sacrifice affords her what Robinson terms "the greatest privilege ... to be alone and to have all the time you wanted" (Fay). "Each of us lives intensely within herself or himself," Robinson argues in *Absence of Mind*, "continuously assimilating past and present experience to a narrative and vision ... And we all live in a great reef of collective experience ... that we receive and preserve and modify" (132). *Home* insists upon the simultaneous experience of individual and familial subjectivity even as its "narrative and vision" embody the strain of locating the mid-century female subject in domestic and narrative space. For many critics, the conclusion of the novel remains an awkward one; in forcing the contemporary reader to "settle" in the space of this unfamiliar home and "stay in it for a while," Robinson's fiction refuses to support the binary thinking that would either celebrate Glory's newfound voice or lament her continued entrapment within patriarchal structures. Although the idea of leaving home, as Ruth and Sylvie do at the end of *Housekeeping*, remains a fantasy for Glory, she finds a way, by the conclusion of the novel, to clear a place for herself in the midst of the uncomfortable furniture she inherits. As Robinson observes in a *Paris Review* interview, "The ancients are right: the dear old human experience is a singular, difficult, shadowed, brilliant experience that does not resolve into being comfortable in the world."

5

Anxiety and the Everyday in *Lila*

> She knew a little bit about existence. That was pretty well the
> only thing she knew about, and she had learned the word for it
> from him. It was like the United States of America—they had to
> call it something. The evening and the morning, sleeping and
> waking. Hunger and loneliness and weariness and still wanting
> more of it. Existence.
>
> (*Lila*, 74)

In titling the third novel of her recent trilogy *Lila*, Marilynne Robinson
extends the promise of accessing a character most notable, in the first two
books, for her inaccessibility. Although Lila's status as the narrator's wife
appears to lend her a central position in *Gilead*, she remains a surprisingly
elusive presence in that novel and in *Home*, the work that follows. In the
storyworld of these two novels, Lila's impoverished, itinerant upbringing
contributes to an uncomfortable reserve that marks her uneasiness in the
small-town, domestic landscape she enters when she marries Ames, an
elderly minister and lifelong community member. To some extent, the
reader of the trilogy *is* rewarded in *Lila* by the revelation of its protagonist's
back story and additional specifics about her early relationship with Ames.
The life history that the novel reveals—defined as it is by abuse and neglect,
childhood abandonment, murder, homelessness, and forced sex work—
possesses marked dramatic potential. As the narrative alternates between
a present in which Lila is married to Ames and a past marked by one
trauma after another, *Lila* incrementally fills in the outline of the character's
life story.

The novel's fractured structure and repetitive form, however, dull the
reader's apprehension of a series of plot events that might easily be sensa-
tionalized. The narrative of Lila's scandalous involvement with an older,
well-established clergyman is frequently interrupted by memories of the past
that push to the surface of the narrative discourse, dislodging the reader's
location in a romance story that spontaneously and repeatedly stalls at any
hint that Lila's feelings will be revealed. Although those memories often

The Elusive Everyday in the Fiction of Marilynne Robinson. Laura E. Tanner, Oxford University Press (2021).
© Laura E. Tanner. DOI: 10.1093/oso/9780192896360.003.0005

reference shocking events, the traumatic experiences of the past are revealed in fragmentary representations and seemingly tangential details often swallowed up by Lila's repetitive phrases and reiterated thoughts. Frustrating the reader's desire to experience the development of plot and character, the novel disrupts assumptions of depth and progression through structural and representational strategies that impede narrative progress even as they deny immersion in the richness of representational detail.

Despite the majority of positive reviews for *Lila*, some critics that praise it express an uneasiness about this "more knotty work" (Rahim 3) that "goes nowhere, slowly" (Power 1). When, towards the end of the novel, Lila contemplates confessing the bare facts of her life story to a stranger who gives her a ride, it is a story that appears surprisingly dramatic to a reader already familiar with its plot events:

> Lila could feel her wondering, and she almost said, I was working in a whorehouse because the woman who stole me when I was a child got blood all over my clothes when she came to my room after she killed my father in a knife fight. I've got her knife here in my garter. I was meaning to steal a child for myself, but I missed the chance and I couldn't stand the disappointment, so I got a job cleaning in a hotel. You can't say dang or go to movies, and look who you got sitting next to you hour after hour. Look who you been offering half of your spam sandwich.   (216)

This momentary aside, which reveals what Lila could but does not say to the stranger sitting next to her, exposes the extent to which Lila's guarded presence shapes not just the events of the novel's plot but the construction of its narrative. Lila's lack of formal education and frustrated self-expression extend from the storyworld into the narrative discourse; as the third-person narrative voice captures the rhythms of Lila's anxious consciousness and inhabits the limits of her vocabulary, its representations falter, sliding up against the repetitive forms of her thinking and the roadblocks of her reticence.

Simultaneously succinct and sensational, the shocking narrative of events that Lila thrusts aside in this scene highlights the extent to which the novel's representation of Lila's life story defuses the dramatic potential of its plot to constitute itself, instead, as what one critic terms "the quietest novel I have ever read" (Windsor). If the reading of plot, in Peter Brooks's terms, functions as "a form of desire that carries us forward, onward, through the text" (*Reading* 37), the repetitive, circuitous language and structure of *Lila* continually disrupt that motion. The novel not only impedes the dramatic motion of plot but disrupts assumptions of depth and denies immersion in the revelatory richness of representational particulars. Instead of animating details of romance or tracing the traumatic origins of her anxiety, then, *Lila* answers the reader's desire for disclosure with structural and stylistic deflection. Both the passion of romance and the pain of trauma are manifested in a process of narrative shut-down; the spiraling motions of consciousness disrupt the forward movement of plot and flatten the novel's prose, resulting in a kind of narrative foreclosure that renders the anxiety of Lila's existence in its very resistance to revelation.

At first glance, the novel's tendency to resist the fast pace of dramatic storytelling in order to dwell in the quiet rhythms of the everyday appears familiar to readers of Robinson's other fiction. Describing the books in the Gilead trilogy as "quiet novels," Rachel Sykes argues that these works all shift focus away from the motion of plot to the construction of character (109). "By focusing on the interior lives of quiet characters who live in a quiet location," she posits, "Robinson's fiction is untethered from the representation of noise and exceptional or noteworthy events that typically constitute a novel's plot" (115). Instead, she argues, all three Gilead novels prioritize a framework of quiet interiority that makes room to explore the complexities of subjective experience.

Critical framing of Robinson's fiction within the context of the illuminated everyday provides another potential explanation of the aesthetic compensation Robinson's fiction offers as it turns away from the dynamic trajectory of plot. Drawing upon the context of religious phenomenology, for example, Ray Horton argues that the fictional worlds of Robinson's first three novels establish "the conditions for an experience of wonder in the everyday" (132).[1] His argument picks up on a critical tradition that highlights the transfiguration of the ordinary in Robinson's fiction; within such a framework, the narrative's stalled progress opens up a space to dwell, substantively and stylistically, on the quotidian, the heightened perception of which lends texture and depth to the fictional worlds Robinson creates.

Whereas both these frameworks highlight what is given in exchange for what is taken away, I am most interested in the complex ways that *Lila* withdraws the aesthetic compensations that critics have come to associate

---

[1] If Horton's inclusion of *Home* in his discussion complicates his argument, the incorporation of *Lila* (a novel that he does not address) might challenge its conclusions in interesting ways.

with Robinson's fiction and its "quiet" focus on the everyday. Although it defuses the dramatic potential of its plot, *Lila* simultaneously refuses to lend the reader the intimate access to character that Sykes highlights or the heightened perception that Horton sees as characteristic of Robinson's phenomenology of the everyday. Instead, the structure of the novel replicates Lila's unease; the space the narrative might clear to inhabit the ordinary incites the painful habits of an anxious mind that expands to fill its emptiness with the repetitive jolts of fretful rumination:

> Even now, thinking of the man who called himself her husband, what if he turned away from her? It would be nothing. What if the child was no child? There would be an evening and a morning. The quiet of the world was terrible to her, like mockery. She had hoped to put an end to these thoughts, but they returned to her, and she returned to them. (112)

The juxtaposition of catastrophizing questions with the cycles of daily existence highlights Lila's expulsion from the familiar rhythms of ordinary life; the "quiet of the world," which Sykes associates with depth and meaning in Robinson's fiction (114), emerges here as "terrible, like mockery." The hush of *Lila* is full of what one critic describes as "anxious turnings" (Sacks) that disrupt the layering of complexity typically associated with the representation of subjectivity; they constitute a kind of narrative static that disrupts the novel's implicit promise of access to Lila's character. Even as it adopts the rhythms of Lila's thought, then, the narrative blocks ingress to interiority, situating the reader at the *periphery* of a consciousness that continually defends and deflects.

The novel's representation of the everyday offers a similar pattern of structural foreclosure. Whereas Robinson's early fiction illuminates a universe of textured particulars, transforming the quotidian through lyrical forms of representation that locate the divine in the ordinary, *Lila* stalls the reader in an everyday world that the reader, along with its protagonist, inhabits uncomfortably. The protagonists of *Housekeeping* and *Gilead* engage the everyday self-consciously, transforming the ordinary into a form of numinous presence. Lila's self-conscious relationship to the everyday represents an opposite kind of heightening: rather than transcending the parameters of the self through an act of perception that apprehends a world infused with divine presence or imagistic beauty, Lila's perception of the world continually returns her to an embodied presence that she experiences as awkward and amplified. The traumatic past that she carries with her—a personal history marked by abandonment, homelessness, poverty, and sexual violence—manifests in feelings of anxiety and shame that disturb the taken-for-granted experience of the everyday.[2] In his exploration of the way that repeated childhood trauma creates an ongoing experience of anxiety, Robert Stolorow invokes Freud and Heidegger:

> Like Freud (1926), Heidegger made a sharp distinction between fear and anxiety. Whereas, according to Heidegger (1927), that in the face of which one fears is a definite "entity within-the-world" (p. 231), that in the face of which one is anxious is "completely indefinite" (p. 231) and turns out to be "Being-in-the-world as such" (p. 230). The indefiniteness of anxiety "tells us that entities within-the-world are not 'relevant' at all...[The world] collapses into itself..." (p. 231). Heidegger made clear that it is the significance of the average everyday world...whose collapse is disclosed in anxiety.   ("Phenomenological-Contextual" 130)

The "collapse" of the everyday world in *Lila* reflects an anxiety that resists specific empirical location or referential origin; instead, it manifests in structures of thought and novelistic representation that refuse to settle into clarity or assume the alluring shape of coherent form. *Lila* traces the trauma of its protagonist through what it does not render; it is a character study that blocks access to interiority, a love story that refuses intimacy, a trauma narrative that withholds the specifics of trauma.

The language of reviewers uneasily blends their response to Robinson's character with the third-person narrative that represents her. "Lila's story," Cathleen Schine observes in the *New York Review of Books*, "is lovely and ugly and rough" (3). Highlighting the contrast between the lyrical beauty of the earlier novels and what one critic describes as the "angular prose" (Kakutani, "Woman" C1) of *Lila*, critics struggle to adapt to the loss of the characteristic grace associated with Robinson's writing. Although some reviewers justify the flatness of the narrative—located by

---

[2] Although I focus primarily on Lila's anxiety, the dynamic of shame is clearly related; also a consequence of complex trauma, shame carries similarly disruptive consequences for the experience of the everyday. Shame, Myra Mendible argues, "spectacles privilege and makes visible certain events and people, displacing everyday experiences with the singular, the exceptional, and the sensational" (4). Highlighting the self-consciousness associated with shame, Damian Vallelonga observes, "One becomes preoccupied with and fixated on the...deficiency in one's personality and is thereby distracted from one's current activities...If one manages to continue with one's already initiated task-projects, one typically can do so only in a distracted or preoccupied manner" (144).

various reviewers in its repetitive phrasing, "refractory" structure, and slow narrative development—as a direct reflection of Lila's limited vocabulary and frame of reference,[3] others compare it to Robinson's earlier novels to critique its aesthetic limitations. Kevin Power, for example, asserts:

> Her subject is the way in which the divine manifests itself in the habitual, the banal. In the earlier novels…there are moments when Robinson's prose reveals these manifestations with such beauty and force that they can be felt even by the secular reader…That is wonderful writing. Regrettably, Lila is starved of comparable ascensions. Robinson's prose, here, has a fatal sameness throughout. There are too many middle-length sentences full of short, similar words—there is nothing for the eye to snag on.   (2)

Power's critique slips from content—the divine everyday as the subject of Robinson's fiction—into form; although he connects the narrative's lyrical renderings of the ordinary with the transcendent religious vision of the early novels, praising the way that Robinson's words and images make even the secular reader "feel," his critique of style in *Lila* ignores the substance of the terse, repetitive prose he dismisses as inferior writing. If we read *Lila* as a novel concerned with "the habitual" and "the banal," we can see its third-person narrative voice as a reflection not only of Lila's limited verbal repertoire but of her estrangement from a typical everyday. "If something difficult happens repeatedly," Gretchen Schmelzer argues in her discussion of complex trauma, "you protect yourself from it. You build defenses, protections, and those protections become a part of who you are; they become your habits and how you see and understand the world" (165). The novel enacts Lila's everyday experience of the world—"I got shame like a habit," Robinson's protagonist proclaims (86)—with a tremendous force that the reader cannot help but feel. As it strips away the energy of imaginative transcendence and the compensation of aesthetic pleasure that define the experience of reading Robinson's earlier works, *Lila*'s slow narrative development and refractory structure (Power 1) pin the reader uneasily to a storyworld constructed through the lens of trauma and its aftermath.

Frustrating the reader's desire to experience not only the dynamism of plot but the depth of representation and the interiority of character, then, the novel adopts structural and representational strategies that register uneasily in critical assessments of the text. Describing what she terms "the

---

[3] See, for example, Williams and Sacks.

author's curious decision to tell the story in the third person," Michiko Kakutani in the *New York Times* describes the novel as "robb[ed] of the emotional immediacy of *Gilead*" ("Woman" C1, C4). Indeed, the issue of feeling—both as it applies to Lila and to the reader of the novel—emerges as central to any understanding of the work. Lila's relationship to the everyday serves as a useful critical lens through which to explore both the content of the novel—how its central character experiences daily living as a constant attempt to flee from the burden of unwelcome feeling—and what a number of critics have viewed as a disappointing form that disrupts the aesthetic pleasures of reading. Ultimately, it seems to me, the novel's third-person narrative voice conveys, with great force, Lila's feelings. Insofar as those feelings are rooted in trauma and defined by anxiety, ambivalence, and shame, however, the novel captures its protagonist's emotion at the expense of the aesthetic pleasure and representational depth we tend to associate with Robinson's fiction.

*   *   *

In *Modernism and the Ordinary*, Liesl Olson highlights the way in which the habitual rhythms of the everyday often function as a "mode of protection; habits become Woolf's 'cotton wool of daily life,' a domestic shield against surrounding trauma" (113). In *Lila*, however, trauma leaches into the world of the everyday, manifesting itself not just in momentary flashbacks or isolated panic attacks but in the persistent, habitual structures of anxiety that coopt Lila's consciousness and overwhelm even her most mundane interactions. If, as one reviewer argues, Robinson's "portrayal of the legacy of shame and distrust that abuse, neglect, and other kinds of trauma can leave is unparalleled" (Nelson 54), Lila carries the trauma of her past in a form of anxious hyper-consciousness that emerges in her relationship to the everyday world, continually forcing her out of a comfortable location in the present. Alan Stewart and Robert Neimeyer tie a history of unelaborated traumatic experiences to long-term experiences of dissociation and anxiety, tracing the way that unprocessed trauma compromises an individual's "core identity structures" (12) and "disrupt[s] the consolidation of the sensory and autobiographical processes that comprise narratives" (15). Although I don't want to argue for reading *Lila* exclusively as a narrative of trauma or disability, framing the novel in those terms highlights the way in which it refuses to compensate aesthetically for habits of mind rooted in trauma and resulting in long-term, disabling mental health effects.

Like *Beloved*'s Paul D., who locks the traumatic past in a figurative tin can and lets it escape just a little bit at a time, Lila is continually returned to a childhood in which it is too painful to settle. The novel begins with a scene in which a four- or five-year-old girl is dragged out from under a table, screaming, and locked outside in the cold all night long: "The child was just there on the stoop in the dark, hugging herself against the cold, all cried out and nearly sleeping. She couldn't holler anymore and they didn't hear her anyway, or they might and that would make things worse" (3). When, on the second page of the novel, Lila is revealed to be that child, the victim of abuse and neglect, her connection to the experience is acknowledged only to the reader: "Lila would never tell anyone about that time. She knew it would sound very sad, and it wasn't, really" (4). Lila's reluctance to locate herself in this scene of trauma sets in motion a pattern of dissociation and deflection that permeates the rendering of her life story throughout the text. Even after Lila is rescued from that angry, abusive household by Doll, she spends most of her young life homeless, hungry, and impoverished; she is a witness to violence and, after Doll's death, her desperate circumstances force her into sex work and virtual imprisonment. In cutting back and forth between the present and the past, refusing to settle in either temporal range, the structural shifts of the novel emphasize the way in which Lila's past continually intrudes on her present.

Because of her experience of specific traumatic events and long-term structural traumas including poverty, homelessness, abuse, and neglect, the concept of "complex trauma" provides a useful frame for understanding not only the events of Lila's life but her ability to revisit and represent them. Recently, child psychologists have adopted the term to highlight the effects of sustained or recurring traumatic experiences in childhood. As Heather Dye documents, these events include "physical, emotional and educational neglect and child maltreatment beginning in early childhood" (382). The events underlying complex trauma, Kliethermes et al. observe,

> tend to be chronic and undermine a child's personality development and fundamental trust in relationships ... a complex traumatic event has been further defined as a traumatic event that is repetitive and occurs over an extended period of time, undermines primary caregiving relationships, and occurs at sensitive times with regard to brain development. (340)

Relevant though it may be, I am less interested in applying a specific diagnosis to Robinson's protagonist than in considering the subtle ways in which the novel captures Lila's phenomenological relationship to the everyday world, a relationship shaped by a history of complex trauma.

The strategies of avoidance and denial that Lila develops to survive adversity in her childhood carry over into adulthood as a form of emotional shut-down. Her refusal to tell anyone her history because "She knew it would sound very sad, and it wasn't, really" demonstrates her forced acclimation to a landscape of neglect that she comes to take for granted and the repression of feeling—what Milot et al. describe as "psychic numbing" (93)—that she develops as a response. As she oscillates between what Van der Kolk describes as the "under or over-reactivity" (224) that is the legacy of complex trauma, Lila continually resists locating herself in an affective realm that she is unable to regulate or represent: "I got feelings I don't know the names for. There probly ain't any names. Probly nobody else ever had 'em. I tell you what, I wouldn't wish 'em on a snake" (184). The worlds of traumatized persons, Stolorow argues, "are fundamentally incommensurate with those of others," defined as they are by "an anguished sense of estrangement and solitude" ("Phenomenology of Trauma" 467). The isolation that Lila experiences from inhabiting such a world manifests in feelings that she renders as unintelligible to herself and unrecognizable to others. Her unwillingness or inability to share her story with others reflects not just her affective dysregulation but her psychic sequestration. The act of pulling her experience into language presupposes location in a shared referential reality that Lila cannot assume; first denying ownership of the feeling that her "sad" narrative implies to others, she then posits a feeling so singular and overwhelming that it can't be named. Tied to a third-person narrative that would speak for her, Lila continually asserts her estrangement from any language that would pull her private suffering into a shared space. After identifying the distorted thoughts and inability to process emotion that often result from complex trauma, Milot et al. address the way that such dynamics are exaggerated by a corresponding failure of self-expression:

Many neglected children have difficulty using words to describe their internal world and their subjective experience (Beeghly and Cicchetti, 1996), and they also lack the ability to relate their feelings with external or internal stimuli (i.e. to understand the reasons [causes] underlying their feelings). Traumatised children may also fail to differentiate between positive and negative feelings, which leaves them with no clear comprehension of what they are experiencing. (96–7)

Lila's traumatic history emerges not only through what the novel represents but through the way in which it disrupts the process of representation. Her inability to name her emotions reflects and exaggerates her sense that she inhabits an everyday world incommensurate with that of others.

Lila's inability to inhabit her feelings comfortably manifests in an ungrounded narrative that continually touches upon experiences too painful to linger over: "You always seem to need to touch the place it might hurt to touch. And not just once, either" (233). When she does return to the past, she often dwells not on single acts of violence or dispossession but on a taken-for-granted assumption that nothing can be taken for granted. The cumulative effects of poverty and abandonment, constitute an ordinary in which deprivation is routine. Lila's chronic experience of hunger, toil, and homelessness is marked by a matter of factness evident, for example, in the narrative's description of her work as a child laborer, traveling from farm to farm: "They would be up in the tops of trees all day long, and they would never spill a basket or break a branch. It was work children did best" (44). Moving quickly past the grueling temporal and material conditions of child labor to emphasize the consistency and efficiency of their performance, the passage ends with an aphoristic echo that naturalizes these dehumanizing and exploitative dynamics: "It was work children did best." The narrative renders Lila's childhood perspective on her repeated experience of displacement in similar terms as it pushes quickly past the unsanitary conditions of the various labor camps she inhabits to render even an improvised everyday welcome:

> When they were children they used to be glad when they stayed in a workers' camp, shabby as they all were, little rows of cabins with battered tables and chairs and moldy cots inside, and maybe some dishes and spoons. They were dank and they smelled of mice, and Marcelle made everybody sleep outside except when it rained, but they always had a cabin, and they kept everything they carried in it during the daytime.   (44)

Like many of Lila's recollections of her youth, this one emphasizes her matter-of-fact acceptance of an impoverished, abusive, and itinerant existence marked by her exclusion from norms of home, family, and security.[4] In the midst of that uncomfortable ordinary, Lila and the other children find ways to make themselves at home:

---

[4] Lila imaginatively converts this bare facsimile of a house, more storage unit than domestic space, from a dank, moldy structure to a home that she pretends is hers: "And Lila and Mellie and the boys, when they weren't working, played that [the cabin] was their house" (44).

They were given crates of fruit that was too ripe or bruised, and the children ate it till they were sick of it and sick of the souring smell of it and the shiny little black bugs that began to cover it, and then they would start throwing it at each other and get themselves covered with rotten pear and apricot. Flies everywhere. They'd be in trouble for getting their clothes dirtier than they were before. Doane hated those camps. He'd say, "Folks sposed to live like that?" But the children thought they were fine.   (44–5)

The abject imagery of this passage envelops the children in a cloud of rot and sour smells and bugs and dirt, challenging the boundaries of the properly human that define "ordinary" life. Rather than serving as a source of pride, Lila's accommodation to difficult circumstances—her ability not only to survive by eating what others would discard but to playfully coat herself in that detritus—emerges retrospectively as a mark of degradation. Lila recalls Doane's dismissal of what the children accept as ordinary living ("Folks sposed to live like that?") and, in the sentences that follow, anticipates an even more exaggerated reaction from others. Ashamed not only of this past but of the extent to which it seems natural to her, Lila struggles to edit her history in such a way that she can carry it into her relationship with Ames; policing even her imagined disclosure of the past, Lila "pretended he knew some of her thoughts, only some of them, the ones she would like to show him" (45). Not even in imagination can she envision sharing the contents of her history or consciousness without first editing and sanitizing them. In doing so, she must filter out both the traumas that threatened to overwhelm her and the shame that results from her ability to survive them; not only did she "live like that," but she made herself at home there.[5]

It is thus not surprising that textured recollections of Lila's childhood often emerge when she feels temporarily at ease, a feeling that she experiences, ironically, in material circumstances that others would find overwhelming. Sneaking off alone to the basement of the brothel on a dark, frigid morning to stoke the fire, for example, Lila lapses into a rare reverie about her childhood:

---

[5] This transition from an initial sensory experience, to Doane's interpretation of it as disgusting, to her expectation of Ames's interpretation, charts the process of Lila growing into her sense of shame. The novel sets this vivid description immediately before a brief, almost tossed-off, acknowledgment of how and why she hides things from Ames; although Lila as a child manages to cobble together an improvised everyday in the midst of difficult material circumstances, she gradually absorbs cultural assumptions that deauthorize even that experience.

Just standing there in the dark felt so good to her. She'd get all black and filthy with the coal dust, and when she came upstairs who knew what they would say... She was standing there, leaning against the warmth with her eyes closed, and she began to have bright dreams about waking up before dawn with Doll's arm for a pillow and the sound of a fire and Doane talking with whoever else was awake first. It was always Doane who got the fire going, and then Arthur would start the coffee when they had it. And Doll coaxed her awake. They would fry whatever there was, the light coming up and the birds singing. Dew on everything, beaded on cobwebs so it fell like a little rain when you broke one.   (196)

Standing in the dark, Lila relaxes her mode of constant vigilance; she immerses herself in a dank and dirty space she welcomes as familiar. "All black and filthy with coal dust," Lila leans into a warmth that takes her back to the home of Doll's body, the one constant in her itinerant upbringing, and to mundane routines—however tentative and contingent—that constituted some version of the everyday. The facts of privation—the lack of a pillow, the uncertainty of food and drink, the need to wake up before dawn to labor—are absorbed into the assurance of rhythm and the lyrical depiction of nature. The passage begins and ends with the acknowledgment of Lila's position in a dank, inhospitable basement—"standing in a coal hole"—(196) that serves as an objective correlative for a discomfort that Lila settles into with equanimity; if, as Van der Kolk argues, victims of complex trauma experience "trauma-related hyperarousal and numbing on a deeply somatic level" (237), the temporary thawing of Lila's "frozen" reaction may speak to the embodied experience of relaxing into a warmth that emerges only in contrast to this familiar landscape of darkness and cold.

*   *   *

As *Lila* continually pivots between the present and the past, introducing bits and pieces of Lila's history, the effects of trauma seep into the form as well as the content of the narrative. The novel links the recurring themes of isolation and alienation not only to the material conditions of Lila's past but to the psychic disruptions that take the present hostage. Images of poverty, disconnection, contamination, and coarseness continue to surface in the stream of consciousness reflections that regularly interrupt the forward motion of the plot with a series of asides that come to constitute a familiar narrative refrain. Although the love story between Lila and Ames constitutes a major part of the novel, that narrative is continually interrupted by Lila's nervous revisitings of the past and anxious ruminations about the future; the everyday of the novel's present is thus subsumed within the trauma that underlies both.

Lila's unwillingness to let herself be known slows the development of intimacy between the novel's main characters and interrupts the developing narrative of their relationship. The mere prospect of inviting Ames into her intimate space—sharing her thoughts as well as the cabin that she temporarily inhabits as a squatter—causes Lila to shut the door to further contact:

> If they could be there the way they were in her mind . . . then he could know them. She would want him to know them. No. Why did she let herself think that way? If he saw this place he would be embarrassed at how poor she was, how rough she lived. He wouldn't quite look at her, he'd try not to look at anything else, and he wouldn't say much at all.   (45)

Here, as elsewhere, Lila's expectation of humiliation surges into the narrative discourse, temporarily foreclosing narrative possibility; her anticipation of what Ames will not do and will not say crowds out representation of the developing romance. In her work on trauma and dissociation, Carola Kaplan builds on the theories of two psychoanalytic scholars, Stolorow and Philip Bromberg, to highlight the way that cumulative childhood trauma impacts the everyday:

> According to Stolorow, the most unfortunate result of emotional trauma is the narrowing of life possibilities. As Stolorow (2007) points out, developmental trauma may constrict emotional life "so as to exclude whatever feels unacceptable, intolerable, or too dangerous in particular intersubjective contexts" (p. 4). In this way, childhood trauma has long term incapacitating effects . . . the child fears that affects "herald traumatic states" (Stolorow, 1987, p. 72) and so, affects are "disavowed, dissociated, repressed, or encapsulated through concrete behavioral enactments, self-protective efforts that literally cut off whole sectors of the child's affective life" (p. 72).   (468)

For Lila, the structures of repression and anxiety disable the scaffolding of the everyday in the present as forcefully as the structures of poverty, neglect, and abuse unraveled any hope for an ordinary childhood in the past. "When trauma is repeated," Gretchen Schmelzer argues,

> we don't wait to get caught off-guard. Instead, we unconsciously . . . build a system of defenses against being overwhelmed and getting caught off guard

again . . . Instead of getting flooded with emotion—with terror, fear, and all
the responses to it—we build walls, moats, and methods of escape. We go
numb, we feel nothing, and we do whatever we have to in order to maintain
our distance from ourselves and others.   (13)

If trauma continually destabilizes the supports on which the lived world of
the present is built, victims of repeated trauma anticipate a future already
foreclosed by the past: "Any thoughts of the future are imagined to be as
dangerous as the trauma that was experienced, so any planning for the
future is to protect yourself from what already happened" (Schmelzer 38).
In *Lila*, the legacy of trauma forecloses the possibility of a future, interrupt-
ing the narrative trajectory of romance along with Lila's ability to move
closer to Ames. The novel's anxious structure interrupts, deflects, repeats,
and resists, continually unmaking the ground on which a fictional world
would be built.[6]

Insofar as anxiety governs Lila's existence, her romance with Ames
emerges primarily as a narrative of evasion. On the rare occasions when
she expresses her thoughts to him, and the reader, her nervous backtracking
overwhelms the story. Having made the mistake of speaking to him as if she
knew him,

> She turned and walked away, instantly embarrassed to realize how strange
> she must look, hurrying off for no real reason into the dark of the evening.
> The lonely dark, where she could only expect to go crazier, in that shack
> where she still lived because it was hard for her to be with people. It would
> be truer to say hid than lived.   (36)

Expelled from the ease of the everyday into the rhythms of a "crazy" mind
that refuses to settle, Lila remains homeless even after she comes to live with
Ames: "She knew he was thinking and praying about how to make her feel at
home. She had never been at home in all the years of her life. She wouldn't
know how to begin" (107). Typically, as Olson describes, the habits of
ordinary life function as a mode of protection, "a domestic shield against
surrounding trauma" (113). Whereas others rely upon familiar routines and
surroundings to facilitate the ease of daily life, Lila returns again and again

---

[6] As Schmelzer concludes, "with repeated trauma, there are always the three different forms
of trauma: the trauma that did happen, what you did to survive and the protections you used,
and what didn't happen because of the trauma" (194).

to an anxiety that she figures as her only home. Like everyday life, Rita Felski argues, "home constitutes a base, a taken-for-granted grounding" ("Invention" 22). Try as Lila might to banish her painful self-consciousness, the motion of swirling thought emerges as the only thing she can take for granted in her dislocated existence: "These thoughts were waiting and familiar, like a house where you once belonged though you just hated to go there" (231). Adverse childhood experiences, as Brett Zyromski et al. document, continue to reverberate in lived experience years after the fact; the overwhelming effects of complex trauma, including anxiety, continually pull the past into the present: "From an existential position, all of the most serious sources of anxiety would be present in those who have lived with ACEs" (159). Painfully familiar patterns of rumination continually overwhelm the specifics of plot events in the novel; even as Lila enters the narrative of pregnancy, its much-anticipated climax in the birth of a baby is subsumed within the insistent and persistent cycles of worry: "She just wished it was over and she had a child or no child and she could stop thinking" (231).

As Lila's anxiety overwhelms her consciousness and denaturalizes her relationship to the backdrop of the everyday, it consumes the narrative discourse as well. The constant restatement of the same theme and language mirrors the structure of Lila's anxiety, rendering the rhythm of her existence not in a series of habitual acts and textured descriptions but in the cyclical return of shameful feelings and catastrophic thoughts. Worry disrupts the novel's motion toward plot development, as Lila's repetitive ruminations on her own humiliation—felt and imagined, present and future—interrupt the flow of events to return the narrative again and again to the same concerns. Multiple times, Lila repeats the fear that her body reveals her shameful past, that she is unable to trust others, that her efforts to seek calm, safety, and comfort are doomed to failure. In *Ugly Feelings*, Sianne Ngai explores the literary representation of noncathartic emotions, arguing that feelings associated with obstructed agency challenge models of emotion that culminate in purifying release. Indeed, she argues, such feelings are associated with "a noncathartic aesthetic: art that produces and foregrounds a failure of emotional release" (9) in texts that seem "oddly impassive" (10). If saying the same things over and over emerges as a marker of anxiety, the repetition of key words and phrases focused on shame, trust, safety, and comfort returns the reader of *Lila* again and again to feelings that cannot be assuaged, released, developed, or transformed.

Critics' uneasiness with the novel may be traced, in part, to its refusal to compensate aesthetically for Lila's inability to locate herself solidly in the space of the novel and its constructed worlds. "In order to dissociate one's disability from stigmatizing associations," David Mitchell and Sharon Snyder argue, "disabled people are encouraged to 'pass' by disguising their disabilities. Prosthetic devices, mainstreaming, and over compensation techniques, all provide means for people with disabilities to 'fit in' or to 'de-emphasize' their differences" (3). In *Lila*, Lila's inability to "pass" manifests itself not only in the burning flush of shame continually written on her body but in a narrative that is itself markedly disabled. The legacy of trauma seeps from the storyworld of the novel, where it manifests itself in the crippling self-consciousness of shame[7] and the repetitive negative thinking of anxiety,[8] into the narrative discourse. Such a dynamic not only disrupts the forward motion of plot in *Lila* but renders the kind of textured description that characterizes *Housekeeping* and *Gilead* much more difficult to sustain. Defining texture as "the experiential quality of textuality," Peter Stockwell argues, "intensity and depth of reading produce a sense of richness around a particular reading experience. Since richness is a product of readerly disposition and the investment of emotional resources . . . the feeling of a richly textured literary work can be correlated very directly with a sense of readerly involvement" (14, 62–3). Stripped of the literary forms of compensation that Robinson develops in her early fiction, *Lila* refuses a prosthetic aesthetic that would obscure the dynamics of its protagonist's paralyzing anxiety. The structure of the novel reflects Lila's anxious everyday experience by constantly revisiting her detachment from the lived world of the novel. Rather than fostering the illusion of access, *Lila* adopts a more radical stance, replacing the narrative construction of her interiority with the disrupted rhythm of an everyday world that remains flat and inaccessible. Anxiety interrupts not only Lila's thoughts and actions but the novel's ability to conform to the conventions of genre; it disrupts the love story, defuses the drama of suspense, denies access to the interiority of character study, and interrupts the flow of literary style. Panic-driven cycles of rumination continually usurp the progression of plot and what Stockwell describes as the "richness" of description; as pre-programmed scenarios of anxiety and shame assume control of Lila's thoughts, the third-person narrative disrupts the depth associated with character and the process of pattern formation associated with story.

---

[7] See Myra Mendible and Damian Vallelonga for explorations of the relationship between shame and self-consciousness.

[8] Cf. McEvoy.

Describing the "anxious turnings" of a novel that "brims with moody, crooked metaphors" (Sacks) and "goes nowhere" (Power 1), critics of *Lila* implicitly reinforce the connection between Lila's anxiety and the novel's noncathartic aesthetic. In "Avoidance Theory of Worry and Generalized Anxiety Disorder," Thomas Borkovec et al. explore the connection between worry and what they term "semantic satiation": "Interviews of clients with GAD and introspective observations both suggest that worrying about a concern tends to be repetitive (i.e., mentally saying the same things basically over and over). Empirically, content analysis of stream of consciousness reports has shown that worry is characterized by significant decreases in topical shifts" (86). In content terms, anxiety hijacks consciousness as worry crowds out both the dynamic subtleties of individualized reflection and the relaxed assurance of taken-for-granted experience. As Lila seeks feeling that she can live comfortably with, shame stifles the narrative, undermining our illusion of access to character by subsuming Lila within the repetitive motions of her own anxiety.

Insofar as it is focalized through Lila's perspective, the repetitive structure of her anxiety belies the narrative freedom of a broader third-person point of view. The narrative voice is locked into the rhythms of Lila's anxiety and the possibilities of representation foreclosed by her speech. The development of theme is replaced by its narrative reiteration. Whether framed through third-person narrative—"she still didn't trust him" (95)—or first-person dialogue—"I just can't trust you at all" (58)—the lack of linguistic or stylistic variation renders repetition painful:

"Can't trust nobody." (69)

"Can't trust nobody." (78)

"Nobody to trust." (82)

"I don't trust nobody." (89)

"I can't trust you." (89)

Rather than serving as a key that unlocks access to the depth and specificity of Lila's consciousness, this rote revisiting of the same words echoes the structure of anxiety at the expense of defusing meaning. Lila's anxiety emerges in patterns of word choice and narrative form associated with the linguistic expression and psychological function of worry:

The cognitive psychology literature has demonstrated that the repetition of a word leads to the temporary weakening of the links to the rest of its associative network of meaning. By implication, if worrying contains the repetition of crucial, worry-related words, this repetition will result in lowered access to other elements of meaning (especially the affective and other response elements) contained within their network.

(Borkovec et al. 86–7)

Lila's tendency to repeat the same phrases and revisit the same painful images reflects a desire to inoculate herself against hurt: "She had thought a thousand times about the ferociousness of things so that it might not surprise her entirely when it showed itself again" (230).

This link between the structure of anxiety and the repetitive forms of verbalization implicit in that structure carries implications for both the characterization of Lila and for the experience of reading the novel. If the return to the refrains of her worry seeks to dull the affective experience anxiety generates for Lila, textual repetition implicates the reader, as well, in that process of shuttering feeling. The reader's apprehension of this repeated cycle of disavowing feeling is reinforced by a kind of stylistic numbness that permeates the stripped-down, repetitive narrative. Repetition of concept and even language creates the effect of flattening the narrative, foreclosing meaning and depth. Exploring what he terms "the constructive, semiotic role of repetition," Peter Brooks argues that repetition in fiction can serve to "bind" and "shape" textual energies set in motion by the plot, facilitating "the construction of thematic wholes and narrative orders" (*Reading* 124). In *Lila*, however, the return to familiar signs and structures of anxiety serves to shut down the gathering energies of the text.

That anxiety emerges as a form of heightened presence that opposes the transcendence of Robinson's early fiction. Whereas the early novels move into everyday experience, transfiguring the ordinary in the act of inhabiting it, Lila's phenomenology of anxiety operates through a cycle of repeated detachment and expulsion. Although momentary glimpses of the lyrical language and imagistic beauty of Robinson's early fiction emerge in *Lila*, the narrative refuses the reader the luxury of lingering there. Unable to dwell in the ordinary, Lila is always in motion away: "I don't trust nobody. I can't stay nowhere. I can't get a minute of rest" (89). The novel, like its protagonist, refuses to sit still. Realistic fiction often operates by developing a backdrop of the everyday that grounds characters in a storyworld; Robinson's narrative registers its protagonist's unease in its tentative creation and undoing of a textual landscape that must be continually, exhaustively remade. The structure of the novel replicates the process of negotiating a world in which nothing or no one can be taken for granted, as Lila's dialogue with Ames highlights:

> "I don't trust nobody."
>
> He said, "No wonder you're tired."
>
> She thought, That's a fact. (58)

The skittish narrative flits from worry to worry, reiterating Lila's over-whelming self-consciousness even as it labors hard not to rest on the anxious ruminations of her mind.

The breakdown of style and the structure of unembellished repetition in the novel provide a rendering of Lila's consciousness that captures the workings of her mind through form and content, even as it challenges traditional models of depth and interiority. "Stylistic foregrounding in descriptions of characters," Ralf Schneider suggests, "adds to the complexity of the mental model of character" ("Cognitive Theory" 616). As *Lila* reveals, however, mental models of character that understand complexity only in terms of depth and correlate extravagant description with rhetorical power bypass equally complex forms of consciousness that manifest in a subtractive phenomenology. Childhood trauma, as Stolorow explores, often results in "a severe constriction and narrowing of the horizons of emotional experiencing…so as to exclude whatever feels unacceptable, intolerable, or too dangerous in particular intersubjective contexts" ("Phenomenological-Contextual" 126). In such a case, the need to disavow feeling, which constitutes a threat, not only disrupts but actively undermines the healthy development of relationships: "Repression was grasped here as a kind of negative organizing principle, always embedded in ongoing intersubjective contexts, determining which configurations of affective experience are *not* to be allowed to come into full being" ("Phenomenological-Contextual" 126, emphasis mine). In Robinson's representation of Lila's affective experience, repression shapes the structure of the novel, as well as the contents of its protagonist's consciousness. The narrative voice not only reports but enacts, again and again, Lila's effort to deny the disturbing complexities of feeling or, failing that, to reduce them to the physical dynamics of bodily sensation: "She had told herself more than once not to call it loneliness, since it wasn't any different from one year to the next, it was just how her body felt, like hungry or tired, except it was always there, always the same" (34). Always there, always the same, the repetitive narrative exhaustively circles the periphery of Lila's consciousness, frustrating expectations of depth and blocking access to interiority. The novel thus adopts the structural dynamics of traumatic anxiety that Stolorow describes, invoking repression "as a kind of negative organizing principle" ("Phenomenological-Contextual" 126). Lila's strategy of mental shut-down holds important implications for a stream of consciousness narrative fueled by the need—in arresting the very motion of the thoughts it would represent—to undo itself: "And she'd take some sort of hard work that would wear her out, and then she'd sleep. No dreams and no thinking. No Gilead" (48). Mediated through the feverish forms of Lila's anxiety, the reader's access to her character occurs at the expense of repeatedly enacting Lila's effort to empty the contents of her consciousness; this Gilead novel tests the representational supports of a fictional world that leans perilously toward its own erasure, figured here simply as "No Gilead."

Lila thus inverts the project of representation that Ames self-consciously adopts in *Gilead*. Although the first-person narrative of *Gilead* doesn't focus in depth on the relationship between Ames and Lila, its richly textured representations situate Lila's muted presence in the glow of her husband's perception. Reflecting on the way his wife talks, for example, Ames observes,

> She always has to be coaxed to stay in company even a little while, and then it's all I can do to get a word from her. I believe she worries about the way she talks. I love the way she talks, or the way she talked when I first knew her. "It don't matter," she would say, in that low, soft voice of hers. That was what she said when she meant she forgave someone, but it had a sound of deeper, sadder resignation, as if she were forgiving the whole of the created order, forgiving the Lord himself. It grieves me that I may never hear just those words spoken by her again . . . It was as if she were renouncing the world itself just in order to make nothing of some offense to her. Such a prodigal renunciation, that empty-handed prodigality I remember from the old days. I have nothing to give you, take and eat. Ashy biscuit, summer rain, her hair falling wet around her face.   (148–9)

Ames's narrative recasts Lila's understated voice and simple, ungrammatical speech, coaxing meaning from her statement by situating her words in the subtle timbre and tone of her delivery. Lending dimension through context, Ames's narration envelops Lila's straightforward comment in texture and emotion, shaping the reader's response to her reticence by wrapping her words in layers of sensory prose that culminate in the lyrical beauty of these final images.[9]

In contrast, *Lila*, rather than adding layers of complexity to its protagonist's thoughts, acts, and words, provides a bare bones account of even her most emotional interactions. As Joan Acocella points out in her review in *The New Yorker*, the scene in which Lila proposes to Ames emerges very differently in *Gilead* and *Lila*; in the former, Lila proposes after Ames sees her in the garden, among "the wonderful roses" she has planted, while in her version, "she is not in a nice, symbolic garden. She is walking down a dusty road, with Ames beside her." In addition to the variance in plot details and the tension between a lushly beautiful setting and its gritty counterpart, *Lila*'s version is notable for what it does not say. The starkly unembellished dialogue of the scene in which Lila asks Ames to marry her leaves the reader struggling to contextualize the events that unfold:

> She said, "I got to get some things at the store." So they turned and walked back into Gilead.
>
> He said, "I suppose you still don't trust me at all."
>
> "I just don't go around trusting people. Don't see the need." They walked on a while.
>
> "The roses are beautiful. On the grave. It's very kind of you to do that."
>
> She shrugged. "I like roses."
>
> "Yes, but I wish there was some way I could repay you."
>
> She heard herself say, "You ought to marry me." He stopped still, and she hurried away, to the other side of the road, the flush of shame and anger so hot in her that this time surely she could not go on living. (80)

If Ames's lyrical framing of the impact of Lila's voice renders it "deeper and sadder," the third-person narrative of *Lila* backs away from texture and detail, distancing itself from dialogue by eliminating the adverbs that would place the reader in the scene and rendering even Lila detached from

---

[9] Ames's representation of this scene gives it a theological valence connected to his sacramental moment with his father. The collapse of images associated with Lila and with Ames's own experience (the ashy biscuit, for example) raises the question of how accurate Ames's reading of Lila's tone and words might be.

words that "she heard herself say."[10] As Marco Caracciolo explores in *The Experientiality of Narrative*, the reader's imagination of a fictional character's experiences involves a process of "consciousness-enactment" the intensity of which is often linked to the level of detail provided by textual cues: "The fine grained quality or texture of . . . description adds perceptual depth to the reader's imaginings . . . a stylistically marked passage can facilitate consciousness-enactment by sharpening readers' sense that they are sharing the idiosyncratic experience of a fictional being" (125). In contrast to the detail-oriented narrative strategies that Caracciolo explores, "strategies through which stories can create a precise experiential 'feel,' compensating for the representational abstractness of language" (125), this pivotal passage in *Lila* strips away and empties out textured description.

Although the narrative faithfully transcribes the exchange of language between Ames and Lila, it is not until she experiences the familiar flush of shame that accompanies the anticipation of her rejection that her emotion carries her back into the textured dimensions of the scene; the reader, along with Lila, thus experiences the *feeling* of this key plot moment only through the lens of retrospective regret:

> He just stood there. She could feel him watching her. Of all the crazy things she had ever done. It was that feeling that she had had walking along beside him that put that notion in her mind. It comes from being alone too much. Things matter that wouldn't if you had a regular life. Just walking along beside that old man, past the edge of town, not even talking most of the time, with the cottonwoods shining and rustling and shading the road. She never really looked at him, but he was beautiful, gentle and solid, his voice so mild when he spoke, his hair so silvery white.   (81)

This retrospective framing of the scene situates Lila's impulsive proposal in the context of her expulsion from the ordinary. The sudden eruption of lush descriptive language harkens back to the fullness of an everyday moment that the narrative articulates solely in the anticipation of its inevitable loss. The sensory details that only now appear—things "that wouldn't [matter] if you had a regular life"—testify to Lila's estrangement from the ordinary. The sudden burst of lyrical language as the narrative describes "the cottonwoods

---

[10] In *Gilead*, Ames describes Lila as delivering these words with "a twinkle in her eye."

shining and rustling and shading the road" emerges in the tentative security of an everyday moment that Lila experiences as anything but routine. Her spontaneous proposal is precipitated not by a moment of passion but by its opposite. "Just walking along beside that old man . . . not even talking," Lila apprehends Ames's presence without looking at him; when she describes him as "beautiful," then, it is not his physical desirability but his mildness, his gentleness, his solidity, that she identifies as moving her. The unfamiliar comfort Lila derives from Ames's presence as she finds herself tentatively relaxing into the everyday frees her to perceive and to feel; having denied the reader the experience of that feeling in its initial representation of the proposal scene, however, the narrative introduces Lila's moment of heightened perception only as it is subsumed by the return of her anxiety; for the reader, then, it is a moment experienced solely in the context of its inevitable undoing.

The narrative only briefly returns to shade in the outlines of the key proposal scene, sketching out the context of Lila's proposal and the fact of Ames's acceptance, before it turns away from that exchange to the predictably recurring dynamic of Lila's shame. The anxiety that robs her of the ability to settle into the ordinary moment manifests itself in a painfully lengthy paragraph that, instead of satisfying the reader's desire for intimate knowledge, teeters on the edge of its own dissolution.

> What was she thinking about? It was never going to happen. She might be crazy, but he wasn't. She tried to remember that he said those words— You're right. I will—in a way that really meant, That's the strangest thing anybody ever said to me in my whole life. It wasn't hard to hear them that way, except from him. He always seemed to say what he meant. Near enough. But she could see how it might've been different this time. She lifted the loose plank and took out the jar where she kept her money . . . So all together it came to about forty-five dollars. If she hadn't been buying things, cigarettes, margarine, there'd have been more. Still, forty-five dollars would take her a long way on a bus . . . She knew he wouldn't come to her place, and she couldn't go to his. He might be looking for her, since it was tomorrow, or he might not be looking for her. She would go in to town in the next few days to get her ticket, so if he happened to see her he wouldn't make much of it. She might never know—maybe he meant what he said, but if he didn't, and she saw him again, she wouldn't be able to stand the shame. Or she would, and that would be another, harder shame. (81–2)

Although her consciousness focalizes the third-person narrative, Lila exists in the present that the novel reports—her return to the shack where she lives to count up her minimal funds—only as a suspended presence. The anxious circlings of Lila's mind write and rewrite the past, anticipate and catastrophize the future, until the strains of the narrative, like wringing hands that refuse to settle into a lap, twist themselves into undoing. Her mind's frenetic motions take us away from the emotional drama of the proposal scene and the narrative momentum of the plot to suspend us in Lila's anxiety, an anxiety deflected onto the enumeration of details like the counting of her cash and the lists of items purchased—cigarettes, margarine, tins of deviled ham—that deplete that sum. This material and financial accounting temporarily suspends not only Lila's confrontation of her feeling about the proposal but the reader's access to it. As Lila parses Ames's response to her proposal over and over again in her mind, the desire that motivated her to suggest marriage is subsumed within the desire to escape her own anxiety over anticipated rejection. As she plots her escape from intolerable feeling—the shameful memory of the recent past and the anticipation of a humiliating future—her inability to dwell in the moment manifests itself not only in the plans she makes for literal flight but in the disrupted temporal dynamics of a narrative fracture that occludes the flow of the present: "He might be looking for her, since it was tomorrow." Even as the frantic pace of her thinking escalates, creating a tenuous proliferation of disassociated sentences, the force of Lila's anxiety shuts down the flow of narrative, as if to disembody the present moment—"it was tomorrow"—by collapsing it beneath the pressure of past and future. Time, as Gretchen Schmeltzer observes, "is one of the greatest casualties of trauma...[Our] stories and our sense of our selves depend on time because time is what gives us the experience of continuity—of having a past, present, and future...People who experience trauma stop believing in a future...Any thoughts of the future are imagined to be as dangerous as the trauma that was experienced, so any planning for the future is to protect yourself from what already happened" (37–8).

As the lyrical and luminous everyday gives way to spare prose that calls attention to Lila's awkward positioning in even the novel's most straightforward scenes, her physical discomfort extends into a form of emotional austerity that Lila embraces as the only alternative to overwhelming feelings. In the constancy of her anxiety, feeling, for Lila, is always a crisis; her experiences of abandonment and trauma reinforce a phenomenology of alienation that penetrates into both physical and emotional realms. Arguing that "whatever you loved had a claim on you and you couldn't help feeling it no matter what" (242), Lila seeks agency in the only way she knows how, by choosing to disavow emotional connection: "Stepping back into the loneliness, a dreadful thing, like walking into cold water, waiting for the numbness to set in that was the body taking the care it could, so that what you knew you didn't have to feel" (256). Consciousness in *Lila* is manageable only in pieces; the numbness Lila cultivates emerges as a small price to pay for temporary relief from uncomfortable feeling.

Having internalized the labels of orphan, itinerant, and outcast, Lila lacks not only the practiced experience of social conventions or the practical knowledge of how things work in Gilead, but the ease that Bourdieu, in his concept of the habitus, associates with the internalization of structures of perception, conception, and action (*Logic* 60). Even after her marriage to Ames, her constant self-consciousness and fear of the gaze renders her every motion stiff and her performance of even the most familiar domestic tasks subject to an imagined scrutiny. Sudden reference to silverware—"Damn knives and forks" (92)—interrupts the narrative description of Lila's general sense of anxiety and unease around Ames's friends, as well as the description of her wedding day:

> They went to the old man's house after the wedding and the dinner Boughton's daughters had made for them. Lila had never understood the whole business of knives and forks, that there was a way you were supposed to use them. But he sat beside her, close to her, her husband, all their kind feelings toward him now owed to her, too.   (93)

Lila's history of hard work lends her pragmatic skills that render her competent at tasks; the conventions of middle-class life and discourse, however, elude her, overwhelming her ability to feel at home even in her own kitchen: "It was strange, but if Lila pretended she was just there to do the cleaning it made things easier. She knew how to do it, and she could stop thinking about what else might be expected of her" (123). After sneaking off to "sweat and get her hands dirty. So she could sleep at night," Lila acknowledges the necessity of washing up and making herself presentable before she returns to her new home: "She learned about propriety without anybody ever telling her there was a word for it" (90–1). "Everyday life," Felski observes,

> comprises not just an array of behaviors and activities but also distinctive attitudes or forms of consciousness. It is often equated with a habitual,

distracted, mode of perception ... We act without being fully cognizant of what we are doing, moving through the world with the uncanny assurance of sleep-walkers or automatons. Everyday life thus epitomizes the quint-essential quality of taken-for-grantedness.   ("Introduction" 607–8)

Even after she marries Ames and moves into a home that becomes her own, Lila cannot shed the excruciating self-consciousness that heightens her awareness of every move, no matter how minor, performed in the real or imagined presence of others. Although she trades places and positions, the "uncanny assurance" Felski associates with being at home in the ordinary world continues to elude her.

Lila's history of abandonment, neglect, poverty, and abuse not only denies her the supporting structures that facilitate the rhythms of daily life—familiar spaces, casual interactions, habitual motions—but renders her very presence oddly tentative. Lila turns to popular culture representations of lived experience, not for their heightened drama or visual spectacle, but for the vicarious opportunity they offer to inhabit what she describes elsewhere as "a normal life" (226): "She went to the movies just to see people living, because she was curious. She'd more or less decided that she had missed out on it herself, so this was the best she could do" (210). Lacking the grounding of referential language, relationship, or property, Lila experiences herself as depthless and dislocated. Whereas she goes to the movies "to see people living," she locates her own existence in the shadowy realm of representation:

> Her name had the likeness of a name. She had the likeness of a woman ...
> She had the likeness of a life, because she was all alone in it. She lived in the
> likeness of a house, with walls and a roof and a door that kept nothing in
> and nothing out.   (68)

The slippage from images of vacant interiority to permeable materiality emphasizes the absence of an everyday that would cushion Lila's location in the lived world.

As a victim of repeated trauma, Lila, in Stolorow's terms, "quite literally lives in another kind of reality, an experiential world felt to be incommensur-able with those of others. This felt incommensurability, in turn, contributes to the sense of alienation and estrangement from other human beings that typically haunts the traumatized person" ("Phenomenological-Contextual" 133). The taken-for-granted world of others, rather than lending Lila support, only highlights her own insubstantiality, as her reaction to entering Ames's office illustrates:

> The room just felt like he should be in it. The whole church felt that way. People who live in rooms and houses don't know about that. It seems natural to them ... But a whole roomful of somebody's days and thoughts and breath, things that are faded and they don't see it, ugly and they don't care, things worn by their habits, it seems strange to walk in on that when you're almost nothing more than a cold wind.   (158–9)

Lila's reflections on what feels "natural" to others mark her exclusion from the taken-for-granted dynamics of daily living; spatialized and materialized images of the everyday—"a whole roomful of somebody's days and thoughts and breath"—bracket the products of consciousness with a cushion of everyday acts and autonomic bodily processes that support thought. The ability *not to experience* the world in its full intensity—*not to perceive* what is there—emerges here as the ultimate sign of security. As Rita Felski argues, "Faced with an agonizing multiplicity of choices and decisions, buffeted by an endless array of stimuli and sensations, we could not function in the world without the protective cushion of habit" ("Introduction" 617). Locked out of both the routines of ordinary domestic life and the emotional stability that accompanies those routines, Lila finds herself governed by the repetitive patterns of an anxiety that crowds out other feeling and disrupts the text's narrative of her emotional connection with Ames. "I got shame like a habit," Lila observes, "the only thing I feel except when I'm alone" (86).

*   *   *

From the beginning of the novel, it is clear that Lila's location in the present is defined by the traumas of her past. If, as Peter Brooks argues more generally, we seek "through the narrative text as it unfurls before us a precipitation of shape and meaning" (*Reading* 35), for the reader of the Gilead trilogy, the "movement toward totalization" that Brooks describes (91) is propelled by the desire to locate the source of Lila's reticence and render her elusive character intelligible. Even the heightened experience of trauma, however, registers with surprising understatement in the novel. When continued allusions to Lila's desperate foray into sex work finally take the shape of specific recollection late in the text, the narrative's detailed recounting of this dramatic interlude excludes any representation of her vulnerable body or her forced sexual encounters with strangers. Although reiterated allusions to Lila's checkered past create an appetite for the revelation of particulars, the reader's access to the brothel, when it finally occurs, is limited to the communal spaces of the parlor, the kitchen, and the two rooms where the girls sleep, dorm style, on simple cots. The drama that the narrative seems geared toward unveiling—the climactic revisiting of Lila's shocking past rendered through the lens of heightened representation—dissolves in the face of particulars that deflect and redirect.

It is the everyday that absorbs the brunt of the trauma in this scene; the novel renders the enormity of Lila's feeling in the realm of forced domestic unease that is palpable from the opening of her recollection of the brothel:

> It came over her, before he had even closed the door behind him, the thought of that house in St. Louis. Misery must have been what she was looking for, because she felt it the minute she walked in that door. The twilight of the parlor made her feel as if she had stepped into deep water with her eyes open. Breathing came hard and sound reached her a heartbeat after she should have heard it. She could hardly speak. Nothing was the way it was in daylight.   (188)

Representationally, the trauma of forced prostitution registers on Lila's body only as an involuntary shift out of the "protective cushion" that envelops the embodied subject in its everyday interactions; entrance into this space disrupts the very autonomic systems that underlie daily existence, rendering breathing "hard" and calling attention to naturalized sensory processes now mediated and delayed. The after effects of trauma are rendered proleptically and registered in the disruption of Lila's very ability *to be*; as it simultaneously defuses and internalizes the dynamics of sexual violence and abuse, this representation renders Lila's violation in surprisingly intimate yet frustratingly distanced terms.

The idea of the home as a "safe" space that facilitates the ease of daily life by blocking out the world is inverted here as the "whorehouse" becomes a sensory deprivation chamber that locks the girls in and the world out. Lila's recollection of her time as a sex worker reflects what Carola Kaplan describes as the experience of "traumatic spatiality," a feeling of radical displacement that often accompanies traumatic dissociation (470). The narrative lingers not on the violation of forced sex acts but on the empty facade of domesticity against which those acts are staged. When the brothel closes down because one of the girls is sick, the few possessions that the girls own are locked away in a credenza "that was the shape of a coffin" (190). The ensuing spatial vacuum merely renders visible an already existing phenomenology of disorientation and dislocation:

> When a house is shut up like that in the middle of a summer day the light that comes in through any crack is as sharp as a blade. And there would be a pot of potato soup simmering from morning to night, and the steam from it would bring out the tobacco smells and the sour old liquor smells in the rugs and the couches and the drapes. And she'd put the poker deck and the checkerboard in that damned credenza, and anything else that could help the time pass. Not that they could have seen the spots on the cards, dark as it was. In a day or two they'd start saying they were better, and they could open a window a crack. Just the darkness made some of them cry.   (190)

Domestic imagery is invoked only to be turned upside down as the image of simmering soup elicits but immediately disrupts a promise of sensory comfort. The association of that soup with warmth and solace quickly dissolves into the acrid odors of tobacco and sour liquor that its steam leaches from furnishings—rugs and couches and drapes—that function as mere props in a house where living rooms are not for living and bedrooms are not for sleeping; all the girls crowd into two rooms to sleep on cots "so that the other rooms stayed nice for entertaining" (189). Similarly, the comfort of the cyclical rhythms of the everyday collapses into the burden of undifferentiated time that will not pass. When not working, the girls are forced out of being; the sensory deprivation their Madam enforces to discourage reports of sickness parallels a broader dynamic in which their performance of commonplace acts is enlisted to bolster the illusion of an otherwise elusive everyday. The delayed representation of this unspeakable period in Lila's life promises climax or revelation; trauma in this scene, however, registers not in sex or violence but in the obstruction of the ordinary.

This scene also highlights what happens at the level of narrative discourse and representational strategy; it not only flaunts its refusal to reveal the source of Lila's trauma but thematizes the process of putting away any claim to sensationalism. Midway through the scene, Lila voluntarily hands over the knife that Doll used to kill the man Lila thought to be her father; with the removal of the prop that would function as a mechanism for violent confrontation or escape, the narrative also puts away the promise of catharsis. If the presence of that weapon offers Lila the possibility of a way out, its absence assures that the reader, too, is "shut up" in a landscape emptied of dramatic force; as the sun emerges through the cracks of curtains "as sharp as a blade," the threat of injury is relocated into the realm of the everyday and rendered only through the mediation of analogy. In narrative terms, the stripped-down everyday that would bear the weight of Lila's trauma obscures even as it enacts the violence of her forced experience as a sex worker. Refusing to shine a light on her sexual abuse, the novel locates trauma in the closed-up spaces of the everyday that it enforces through the withdrawal of "textural richness."

On the one hand, the novel's refusal to represent Lila engaging in the forced sex work it has repeatedly alluded to represents another example of repression as "a kind of negative organizing principle" of the novel and its protagonist. At the same time, however, Lila's framing of her time in the brothel primarily as an assault on the everyday captures the way that complex trauma resists localization; chronic and diffuse, it filters into every aspect of experience and identity. In his review of *Lila*, Rowan Williams observes, "The madam's spite and petty tyranny are described with a sort of expressionless resignation that conveys the emotional abuse and outrage more completely than any overt plucking of the strings" ("Living" 70). Indeed, the scene's uninflected prose reveals the degree to which Lila has absorbed trauma into her very being; its muffled echoes in the text reflect the depth of its internalization.[11] Framing her self-imposed entrapment in the brothel in oddly monotonous terms, the narrative defines the everyday quality of Lila's experience there as a kind of living hell: "Maybe that's how she knew to come here, thinking it might be where she belonged. But it was taking so long. Worse every day, because it was the same every day. It wasn't the end of anything" (198). Lila herself articulates the reader's desire for an explosive climax that would unleash the bottled-up violence at the center of her story as she contemplates burning herself up in the fire she builds to stoke the house's boiler:

> She knew a boiler could burst if something happened, it got too hot or heated up too fast. Then the coals would fly everywhere and the whole damn house would burn down, probably. She could fill it up, leaving just enough room for her to crawl in after and close the door. Boom! She'd go

---

[11] Lila's long history of abuse is marked in the complexity of her relationship with the madam, her abuser; the effects of complex trauma are evident in the way that she dreads her every encounter with her oppressor but simultaneously covets her approval.

flying, a flaming piece of her right into that girl's face, that Peg, and another one into Rita's lap, where she was always picking at her fingernails until they were bloody, and another one into the room where they kept the dress-up clothes when the gentlemen weren't around.   (198)

As Lila contemplates this violent act of self-immolation, the narrative imagines a dramatic force that promises relief from its ongoing, repetitive rhythms, "worse every day, because it was the same every day." Immediately, however, Lila's anxious rumination tamps down the fire she has briefly conjured in its anticipation of a more destructive force. The powerful image of Lila's body bursting into flaming pieces quickly dissolves into a projected mockery that returns her to the powerless rhythms of her lived experience: "And Mack would see her, all fire like that, and he'd probably be laughing, thinking he'd done it. He'd touch her cheek and the fire would come away on his hand and he'd probably just lick it off" (198). As the explosive flames that would render Lila dangerous to others are subsumed within his offhand response, Mack's casual gesture defuses the force of Lila's fire, redirecting it inward and relegating it to the familiar mark of shame that burns on her cheeks.

Once again, the enormity of trauma refuses to register in the culminating force of plot; its absorption into the anxious rhythms of the everyday renders its presence both routine and inaccessible. Denied location or articulation, trauma cycles through the novel with an understatement that belies its impact, as the narrative highlights:

> How could it be that none of it mattered? It was most of what happened. But if it did matter, how could the world go on the way it did when there were so many people living the same and worse? Poor was nothing, tired and hungry were nothing. But people only trying to get by, and no respect for them at all, even the wind soiling them. No matter how proud and hard they were, the wind making their faces run with tears. That was existence, and why didn't it roar and wrench itself apart like the storm it must be, if so much of existence is all that bitterness and fear? . . . The quiet of the world was terrible to her, like mockery. She had hoped to put an end to these thoughts, but they returned to her, and she returned to them.   (112)

In Lila's formulation, the constant lived experience of suffering pulls trauma out of the realm of the event into the landscape of the ordinary. Its constancy—"It was most of what happened"—belies the intensity of the pain it engenders as the exceptional becomes commonplace. The novel's refusal to register traumatic events in heightened terms, to roar and wrench apart the narrative that would encompass them, parallels the structural dynamic that Lila calls attention to here. In the wake of continued trauma, the fear directed toward a specific object settles into an anxiety that, in Heidegger's terms, resists source or location to permeate the very experience of "Being-in-the-world as such." The repetitive rhythm of anxious thoughts—"they returned to her, and she returned to them"—testifies to the internalization of a "completely indefinite" threat that cannot be located or held separate from the self. Rather than offering sanctuary or solace, the quiet of the novel, like the quiet of the world, reverberates with a terror heightened by its routine ineffability.

In his groundbreaking theorization of the distinction between two forms of trauma, Dominick LaCapra emphasizes the importance of distinguishing between psychoanalytic accounts of universal, structural trauma, which he defines as absence, and historically specific, event-based experiences of victimization, defined as loss. His critique of the cultural and theoretical tendency to conflate the two categories highlights the importance of recognizing the devastating impact of historical violence and the concrete effects of individual assaults on specific subjects. Even as Robinson's novel *references* the traumatic losses that punctuate Lila's life story as events, however, its narrative *registers* those losses primarily in the kind of structural and ontological terms LaCapra associates with absence. In Lila's case, such losses register in a mode of being and a form of narrative that testify quietly but fiercely to the way in which trauma has reconstituted Lila's fundamental experience of being in the world. *Lila* takes what LaCapra defines as "the conventional beginning-middle-end plot, which seeks resonant closure or uplift and tends to conflate absence with loss" (182) and turns it inside out. Rather than assigning a single historical object or event as the (constructed) explanation for the dissolution of wholeness, *Lila* does the opposite; the novel blocks access to the specifics of the traumatic events its protagonist has experienced, choosing instead to enact her loss in structural terms. The circular, repetitive patterns of representation in the novel embody the structures of Lila's anxious thoughts even as they reverse what LaCapra identifies as a common response to the elusive object of a Freudian model of anxiety. Describing Freud's understanding of anxiety as "the elusive 'experience' or affect related to absence ... a 'fear' that has no thing (nothing) as its object," LaCapra highlights the dangers of the illusion that anxiety can be eliminated by constructing and then removing a threat, an object that functions as a scapegoat by localizing a fear that has no concrete referent (183). In contrast, Robinson's novel refuses to unlock the key to Lila's anxiety; diffused as it is throughout the narrative, Lila's disability references an object or an origin that the novel refers to but never fully materializes in representational terms. The result of such a radical embrace of indeterminacy is a destabilization of the everyday that pulls the traumatic events that the novel enumerates out of the object realm into what LaCapra describes as "life in the here and now" (183). As trauma circulates throughout the text, refusing to settle, Robinson's narrative frustrates the reader's desire to locate its origin or limit its effects.

Lila's experience also suggestively complicates the dichotomy of the universal versus the particular that underlies LaCapra's distinction between absence and loss. Even as the location of specific traumas as historical events usefully distinguishes their impact from the shared ontological trauma of the human condition, *Lila* challenges the very concept of the event by rendering its protagonist's traumatic experience in strikingly diffuse terms. Lila's chronic and disabling experiences of anxiety and shame are clearly rooted in traumas ranging from abuse and neglect to sexual violation; both the repetitive nature of those assaults and her systemic experience of their effects, however, trouble the framing of them as discrete incidents in the novel's plot. Questioning the assumptions of subjectivity and privilege underlying the kind of clinical framing that positions shame as a distinct event, Sandra Lee Bartky describes the way that systematic impoverishment and oppression yield disabling psychological effects that manifest in everyday experience; for many of the women she studies, shame "was not a discrete occurrence, but a perpetual attunement, the pervasive affective taste of a life" (96). As the anxiety and shame born of repeated trauma seep into Robinson's narrative, those "ugly feelings," to use Ngai's terminology, dissolve the border between safety and threat, resulting in a phenomenology of trauma that expels Lila from the comfort of the everyday. Exploring the material and psychological effects of conditions of oppression on poor women and people of color, Bartky concludes, "What figures in much moral psychology as a disruption in an otherwise undisturbed life is, for a whole category of persons, a pervasive affective attunement, a mode of Being-in-the-world" (97). For Lila, and for the oppressed subjects Bartky describes here, the experience of subjectivity cannot be separated out from the disabling effects of specific traumatic events. Bartky's call for a "phenomenology of the emotions" (98) acknowledges what Robinson's novel suggests: that the belatedness of trauma manifests not simply in the spontaneous and unpredictable return of traumatic events but in the lived experience of an everyday defined by diffuse experiences of anxiety and shame that penetrate into the very rhythms of being.

Perhaps for that very reason, it is the emerging threat of trauma as a "discrete occurrence" that temporarily restores Lila's estranged relationship with the everyday at the end of the novel. The building tension associated with Lila's pregnancy appears to come to a head when she finds herself, in the final weeks of her pregnancy, experiencing sharp pains as she is stranded at home with her elderly husband in a ferocious blizzard. In contrast to the spiraling rhythms of anxiety and shame that disrupt even the most mundane actions and interactions throughout the novel, Lila's response to this very real threat is markedly calm:

> He put his arm around her and brought her slowly up the stairs to his room. He took off her slippers and found a pair of his socks to put on her feet and then helped her into his bed, pulling the blankets up to her chin. His, she thought, because it reminded her of that old gray sweater, when she loved how his it was. Loneliness and mice and the wind blowing and then that wooly old thing against her cheek, smelling like him. She'd put her head on his shoulder that one time when he hardly knew her name. She laughed to remember.
> "What?"
> "Nothing. It just does feel good. Cold and all." (235–6)

In contrast to the repression and displacement of feeling that characterizes Lila's phenomenological orientation throughout the novel, her spontaneous laughter and simple rejoinder to Ames—"It just does feel good"—breaks the pattern of numbness in the narrative. The physical cold, like the very real prospect of impending loss, bears down on her with a familiarity that returns her to sensation and restores texture to the narrative:

> "We'll be fine." He nestled against her. That sound of settling into the sheets and the covers has to be one of the best things in the world... She could see the light in the room with her eyes closed, and she could smell the snow on the air drifting in. (238)

As she sees the light with her eyes closed and smells the snow in the air, Lila's heightened perceptual immersion in the scene reflects an assurance restored along with her equilibrium. The near certainty of the impending traumatic event relieves the pressure of consciousness by providing a direct object for her anxiety, crystalizing it into fear. Marveling about the fact that "Fear and comfort could be the same thing" (240), Lila finds herself liberated to settle into routine acts. Circumstances that would lead others to panic and terror reassure her by offering an objective correlative for what Bartky describes as her "mode of Being-in-the-world" (97).

The narrative, too, settles in, offering an extended ten-page interlude filled with the kind of textured representation of the ordinary seldom offered throughout the novel. In this anomalous section at the end of the novel, as Rowan Williams observes, "a strong, lyrical passion infuses [Lila's] reflections" ("Living" 70): "And here they were, the two of them, waking and sleeping through the long afternoon, in the crisp sheets that smelled like snow, the baby stirring a little sometimes, the old man young in his sleep and his comfort and she as still as could be, wanting nothing" (241). Although Lila's thoughts continue to slide toward future disaster—circling around the imminent death of her child and herself, or imagining that her child, even if he survives, will inevitably reject her—she returns to a present, imagined and actual, that her consciousness inhabits with surprising ease:

> But there would be years when the child would just want to sit on her lap. He'd favor her over anybody. He'd be crying and she'd pick him up, and . . . that would be all that was left of it, because she had her arms around him. Comfort. That's strange, too. When she used to lie there almost asleep, with her cheek on the old man's sweater, the night all around her chirping and whispering, the comfort of it was a thing she'd have promised herself the whole day long.
>
> Thinking that way made her want to turn onto her back, to feel how good it was to be lying there, her body resting at a kind of simmer, the baby nudging a little, just so she'd know it was there. She could feel her body resting, the way you can tell that a cat asleep in the sun knows it's sleeping. The pleasure of it just too good to go to waste.   (244)

The fatalistic memory and anticipation of inevitable loss—whether it be in the form of death or desertion—remains constant in this scene. In fact, it is the very assurance of catastrophe that allows Lila to relax into the everyday, whether it be the feeling of her body in the bed or the imagining of how it would feel to hold her child in the years before he would, inevitably, grow old enough to realize the need to disavow her. As the wind rattles the walls and the snow piles up, the violent force of the outside world echoes the manic motion of Lila's consciousness, creating an equilibrium that temporarily relieves the pressure of being in the world. Lila relaxes into the inevitability of trauma, only now liberated to feel a comfort cushioned by the everyday. "Her body resting at a kind of simmer" (244), Lila settles into the likelihood of loss with a relief that displaces, if only temporarily, what Catherine Schine describes as the "uneasy tremor" of daily life that runs through the novel (3).

6

Race and Imaginary Intimacy in *Jack*

I began this study by acknowledging the tensions in Robinson's discussion
of her role as a novelist pushed to represent what she describes as "the course
of ordinary life" ("When I Was a Child" 21). Dismissing as mundane
the process of building the scaffolding of the everyday in her novelistic
worlds, she laments,

> As a fiction writer I do have to deal with the nuts and bolts of temporal
> reality—from time to time a character has to walk through a door and close
> it behind him, the creatures of imagination have to eat and sleep, as all
> other creatures do. I would have been a poet if I could, to have avoided this
> obligation to simulate the hourliness and dailiness of human life. (20)

In *Jack*, her newest novel, she reveals that the black sheep character of the
Boughton family, whose troubled past includes theft, imprisonment, alcoholism, and the abandonment of his infant child, is both an avid reader of
poetry and a poet. Estranged not only from his family but from "the course
of ordinary life," Jack lives largely in his imagination; instead of liberating
him from the "nuts and bolts" of quotidian existence, however, his consciousness coopts the rhythms of everyday life in a form of immaterial
constraint. In many ways, Jack's story emerges as the story of his inability
to settle into "the hourliness and dailiness of human life."

In the essay above, Robinson also positions herself as turning away from
her quotidian surroundings to engage in relationship with the inhabitants of
imagined worlds: "I have spent years of my life lovingly absorbed in the
thoughts and perceptions of—who knows it better than I?—people who do
not exist...Sometimes, when I have spent days in my study dreaming a
world while the world itself shines outside my windows, forgetting to call my
mother because one of my nonbeings has come up with a thought that
interests me, I think, this is a very odd way to spend a life. (25) Robinson's
acknowledgment of the way her immersion in a dream world disrupts
routine, unintentionally slighting the ordinary world and its occupants,

The Elusive Everyday in the Fiction of Marilynne Robinson. Laura E. Tanner, Oxford University Press (2021).
© Laura E. Tanner. DOI: 10.1093/oso/9780192896360.003.0006

sets the stage for considering how her newest novel negotiates the relationship between imagination and the everyday. Returning again and again to Jack's perception of his essential marginalization, the novel repeatedly highlights the "fraudulence in his attempts to seem like a fairly ordinary man" (246). Whereas *Gilead* traces its protagonist's use of writing to sustain his presence in the lived world after death, Jack's retreat into imaginative space reflects and reinforces his alienation from everyday life.

Through its focus on an interracial relationship in St. Louis after the Second World War, *Jack* interrogates the imaginative privilege of such self-imposed marginalization by increasingly highlighting its lived consequences for the black woman Jack romances. The aesthetic sensibility that supports Ames's effort to honor and immortalize the ordinary isolates Jack in imaginative space; his desire to have Della accompany him there implicates him in the destruction of her everyday world. By setting their romance in a time and space where quotidian divisions of geography and law exaggerate the policing of the black body that Franz Fanon marks as central to the phenomenology of African-American life, the novel raises the stakes of turning away from "the world itself" in favor of imaginative immersion. Even as their unsanctioned marriage objectifies and exacerbates Jack's existential challenge, it not only renders their combined existence illegal but threatens Della's home, her safety, and her livelihood. By inviting the reader to pursue Jack's imaginative "interests," the novel constructs an uncomfortable romance troubled by the encroachments of the wider world it would exclude.

* * *

As the most recent of the Gilead novels,[1] *Jack* follows up on the portrayal of a character who describes his existence as a "lifelong exile from the ordinary world" (*Home* 20). The plot events that constitute his life story emerge gradually over the course of three novels. A petty thief, liar, and mischief maker, Jack leaves Gilead after he discovers that the young girl he slept with is pregnant, only to learn a few years later of his daughter's death from an untreated infection. An alcoholic who spends many hours in bars and two years in jail, he fails to return home for his mother's funeral. When he does come back, he reveals that he has left a wife and a son behind. The gaps in Jack's life emerge as proof of an inaccessibility that defends against intimacy.

---

[1] Because this book is going to press before the official publication of *Jack*, reviews of Robinson's most recent novel have not yet emerged.

In *Home*, Jack is repeatedly figured as "distant" and "remote," evasive and estranged.[2] *Jack* fills in many of the missing details of Jack's life, dwelling on the early days of his relationship with Della, a young African-American schoolteacher he meets accidentally on the streets of St. Louis. Rather than closing the distance associated with Jack's remoteness in the earlier novels, however, the novel dwells in and on it. Throughout *Jack*, Jack's failed attempts to locate himself in the ordinary world are equaled only by his frustrated desire to unrealize his uncomfortable being. His apprehension of himself as "a stranger in the ordinary world" manifests in a constant sense of uneasiness, an exclusion from the "rituals of productive life," a feeling that he is a "conspicuous and awkward" figure (196, 80, 269). The novel contains scene after scene of Jack "paralyzed with unease" (247), struggling to embody the relaxed posture of those around him: "It made no sense to be sitting there, trying to seem relaxed and casual, legs crossed, arms crossed, twiddling a foot, nowhere to look" (164). As Glory reflects of Jack in *Home*, "it seemed he was attentive to strategies of evasion and places of concealment, never to the skills of the ordinary" (61).

Such strategies of evasion and concealment extend into the narrative of *Jack*, which circulates around the dispersed consciousness of a protagonist whose identity emerges primarily in negative terms. If the everyday implies "a mundane, material embeddedness in the world" (Felski, "Invention" 16), *Jack* highlights the consistently forced nature of an everyday presence that lacks material or psychic grounding: "His name was a lie... Also his manners and the words he used and the immutable habits of his mind. Sweet Jesus, there was no bottom to it, nothing he could say about himself finally" (118). *Gilead* and *Home* establish Jack's exclusion from the routines of family, religion, and community; as Jack peels away layers from the outside in, he extends the awkward tentativeness of his physical presence from his clothes to his words to his very consciousness. The "immutable habits of his mind" continuously unsettle his relationship to the everyday; the reader's access to Jack's consciousness, then, only reinforces the apparent tenuousness of his lived existence.[3] He locates his alienation from the ordinary world

---

[2] See *Home* 31, 62, 170, 71, 42, 85, 230.

[3] Throughout the novel, he attempts to manage his uncomfortable encounters in the lived world "by toying with words, a sort of fidgeting of the brain" (34). Rather than lending him control, however, this retreat into consciousness only extends his discomfort from the realm of action to speech to thought. Intimidated by the "modest good order and general teacherliness" of Della's apartment, for example, "he kept searching his memory for a word that rhymed with 'scruple.' Quadruple. He was calming himself, which meant he was nervous. Jesus was there

at a cellular level: "It is some spontaneous, chemical thing that happens. Contact between Jack Boughton and—air...A rosy heat of embarrassment around any ordinary thing. No way to hide it" (7). Continually asserting the certitude of his dislocation, Jack images his identity not as a stable core but as a cloud of chaos; linking the instability of his presence to "the wind he brought in with him when the house was warm and asleep" (140), Jack ponders the disruption he carries into the routines of his family's domestic life:

> It was like a black cloak that swept around him, setting off disturbances among the crystals on the lampshades, leafing books left open, losing places in them. Scattering letters, half-written or half-read...If they asked him why he had done [these things], he could not say, "I am at the center of a certain turbulence." That would sound flippant at best, a little deranged if they took him seriously.   (140)

Jack registers the disturbance of his presence in the once secure everyday objects that, in his wake, lose their place. The turbulent energy Jack brings with him is a force of "displacement" that encompasses a physical and psychic agitation over which he cedes control (140). Unable to settle into the quotidian world, Jack struggles "to understand the transparent barrier between himself and ordinary life" (135). His vexed relationship to the everyday echoes the self-consciousness that Ames and Lila express in *Gilead* and *Lila*. Whereas the "transparent barrier" between those characters and ordinary life may be explained by the pressure of terminal illness or the trauma of extreme poverty, however, the lack of an external source for Jack's experience of liminality leads him to render his dislocation in literary and ontological terms.

Jack's literary imagination governs his presence in the storyworld as well as the narrative discourse of *Jack*. A poet and scholar who constantly invokes verse lines and literary allusions as referents for his quotidian experience, Jack experiences a textual relationship to the everyday world. The focalization of the third-person narrative through his perspective collaborates with that self-conscious phenomenology by blurring the distinction between concrete experience and its symbolic construction. Throughout the novel, Jack situates plot events in relation to literary landmarks, delicately stepping

---

among the pictures on the upright piano, the only one in color. 'Quintuple' doesn't rhyme. How can that be? Sweet Jesus, don't let me say anything strange" (112–13).

outside the lived world even as he participates in it: "Chicago seemed more and more like an episode in *Pilgrim's Progress*, an enchanting byway where the hero's soul is imperiled by excesses of sound sleep and personal hygiene" (297). The tension between inhabiting the everyday and authoring a narrative—what Robinson refers to as "dreaming a world"—that emerges here in the meeting of the quotidian and the allegorical also surfaces in the clash between realistic and melodramatic representation. In both his constant references to literary works (much of his early dialogue with Della revolves around discussions of Shakespeare, Milton, and the Bible) and his descriptions of himself, Jack consistently translates the quotidian into the heightened realm of the tragic. In the absence of external circumstances that would explain his alienation from domestic spaces and conventional moral codes, Jack attempts to ground his behavior in the certitude of his essential immorality. In opposition to a Protestant tradition of doing good works to persuade the self of its assured salvation, Jack seeks an explanation for his injurious acts in his predestination for perdition, a frame of reference that structures even as it damns. Professing his atheism, he adapts the religious doctrines embraced by his father in personalized terms that demonstrate what Peter Brooks describes as "the melodramatic imagination" (*Melodramatic* 10):

> Melodrama represents both the urge toward resacralization and the impossibility of conceiving sacralization other than in personal terms. Melodramatic good and evil are highly personalized: they are assigned to, they inhabit persons who indeed have no psychological complexity but who are strongly characterized. Most notably, evil is villainy; it is a swarthy, cape-enveloped man with a deep voice.   (16–17)

Constructing himself as the literary or biblical anti-hero, Jack turns himself into the villain of his own tale; no less than seven times in the novel, Jack figures himself as "The Prince of Darkness" destined to leave a path of destruction in his wake (48). Throughout the novel, Jack continually rewrites quotidian experience to privilege "the cosmic moral sense of everyday gestures" (Brooks, *Melodramatic* 10). Within a melodramatic epistomology, Brooks argues, "Everything appears to bear the stamp of meaning, which can be expressed, pressed out, from it" (10). In "pressing out" the heightened meaning of his everyday gestures, Jack crafts a narrative that highlights his tragic flaws even as it distances him from the real-world repercussions of his actions.

From its inception, the relationship between Jack and Della invokes familiar literary tropes and romantic conventions. A chivalrous gentleman responding to a lady in distress, he rescues her in a rainstorm. When Jack describes his unexpected, fairytale-like introduction to Della to Hutchins, the minister responds, "That's a nice story" (189). Indeed, Jack finds himself drawn to the story of their relationship, lamenting that he may never know "the end of this strange tale" (59). In *Home*, Glory makes the literary quality of their romance explicit when she observes, "Jack had courted her as if she were the virtuous lady in an old book. Poetry. Flowers, no doubt" (229). Accustomed to moving through the streets of the city while crafting lines of poetry in his head, Jack also frames his relationship with Della as a kind of fiction: "He thought, I have been outside time and St. Louis, I have been in a dream, a Russian novel" (134–5).

Even as Jack's self-conscious relationship to the ordinary propels him out of the everyday and into a literary/symbolic landscape, he is unable to settle comfortably there; his sense of constant unease manifests in intermittent disruptions of his own imaginative constructions. Although the romance between Jack and Della plays out in the exchange of texts and the recitation of poems, *Jack* calls attention to its protagonist's forced translation of lived experience into literary terms. After imaging himself repeatedly as the "Prince of Darkness,"[4] Jack intermittently steps back from that melodramatic representation, observing, for example, "I'm an unsavory character. No, that makes me sound interesting" (108). Like Robinson, who reports "forgetting to call my mother because one of my nonbeings has come up with a thought that interests me," Jack positions himself in an imaginative world that threatens to overshadow the everyday. The "interesting" character or story, as Jack goes on to explore, holds a seductive power that the ordinary does not. When Della shares the neighborhood gossip that Jack is worshipping in a black church, a phenomenon "that makes you a little interesting" (205), he explains his avoidance of the simple truth using the same term:

> He didn't say, They gave me lunch. That would not be interesting. A white stranger with a clerical manner is experiencing a religious stirring, the Spirit acting on his frozen soul here, now, among us. He could see the

---

[4] See 40, 48, 62, 66, 237, 251.

poetry in their misconception, could see why he might seem interesting to them. To Della.   (206)

The critical distance that allows Jack to analyze the false assumptions and hyperbolic imagery underlying the construction of this "interesting" narrative does not forestall his own tendency to exercise poetic license. Although he sometimes dismisses his own poems as "ridiculous" (63), Jack remains absorbed in the metaphorical at the expense of the mundane: "Despite certain attempts at reform, as far as he was concerned, truth versus poetry was really no contest" (206).

Simultaneously indulging in and critiquing the textualization of his own lived experience, Jack inhabits a largely theoretical world. He admits to his "fascination with damage and its consequences," regardless of who bears them (44). Even as he falls into despondency, he reports finding "each phase in his descent rewarding in its own way" (147). His eagerness to let literary texts speak for him extends to a kind of detached fascination with his own difficult emotions; referencing his favorite Frost poem, he reflects: "He was acquainted with despair. The thought made him laugh. He had to admit that he found it interesting, which was a mercy, and which made it something less than despair, bad as it was" (118). Attentive to the seductive appeal of literary tropes and archetypal characters, Jack turns to poetry both to express the truth about himself and to hide it. Nervous about meeting Della's sister for the first time, he tucks a book of poetry into his pocket to create a good impression; quoting the opening lines from a poem that he often cites, he observes: "An honest account of himself, yet somehow romantic. Poetry does that, another perjured witness. Maybe he liked poetry because it also could not help lying" (235). Shifting realms from the imaginative to the everyday transforms beauty into lies, renders a book of poems both a gateway to deeper truth and a spurious accessory.

*   *   *

The sense of separation that renders Jack's relationship with the world aloof and uncertain surfaces in a passionate relationship he describes as "intimacy at a distance" (253). Given the racially segregated world he and Della inhabit, their romance necessarily exists outside the boundaries of the everyday: "Their lives were parallel lines that would not meet" (84). Even as Jack articulates the difficulty and the danger of an interracial relationship, its terms collaborate with his fundamental sense of estrangement from the ordinary world: He would "love her, anyway, at the same sanctified distance they had agreed to…Solitude could be the proof and seal of marriage"

(219). "Sanctif[ying]" Jack's tendency to escape from "the intimacy of the ordinary" (*Home* 209), the marriage they enact outside the bounds of law reinforces the primacy of a purely imaginative everyday. Jack's days are punctuated by participation in shared routines that unfold solely in his imagination. From his room in a different city, Jack "imagined her sitting in that overstuffed chair in the evening lamplight, reading while he read, listening while he told her how long the days would be if he did not almost believe she was with him there. 'This is our marriage,' she would say. 'This is what we promised each other'" (289). As he writes Della into the scene he creates, Jack piles up words in a way that acknowledges even as it obscures the distinction between experiential and narrative presence; "listening while he told her how long the days would be if he did not almost believe she was with him there," he renders Della simultaneously inside and outside the narrative, a participant in the story he imagines her listening to him deconstruct. In the relationship that Jack terms "a marriage of true minds" (263), the firmament of consciousness displaces the intimacy of the ordinary.

Insofar as their courtship, relegated of necessity to brief interludes in marginal spaces, precludes the everyday, it collaborates in Jack's abstracted relationship to the ordinary world, "making an imaginary something out of literally nothing" (84). The connection between the two lovers in the graveyard scene, the most extended scene in the novel, occurs not despite difficult circumstances but because of them; in the dark of night, after a year of holding Della in his imagination, Jack meets her unexpectedly in a white cemetery. In this liminal space, having violated the boundaries of spatial segregation and social decorum, the two trespassers step out of the conventions of ordinary life[5] in a self-conscious fashion that Della highlights: "And we are not in the land of the living. We're ghosts among the ghosts" (42). In this space where imagination supersedes perception—"Maybe I'm remembering you now, since I can't really see you" (48)—Jack dissolves into a character or a chimera: "he had let himself feel concealed by the darkness, as if only a rough sketch of him, so to speak, the general outline of a presentable man, would be walking along beside her" (41). If, as he observes earlier, "strangers in the abstract always turn out to be fairly drearily particular on acquaintance" (34), Jack takes comfort in the way the dark hollows out the particulars of his embodied presence, reducing him to the "rough sketch" or abstract form of a man. Offering Della his arm, he observes,

---

[5] Jack describes this as shedding the "outward man," the individual whose everyday needs, like getting a haircut, can be addressed concretely (42).

"You need not think of it as the arm of any particular gentleman. Kindly intent, disembodied. Civility in the abstract" (24). Jack and Della connect outside the bounds of ordinary life, two minds that, aside from the occasional disruption of wet grass or damp air, exist in dialogue with Shakespeare, Milton, and the Bible. At a narrative level, this seventy-page scene is so littered with literary quotations and biblical references that these textual signposts, rather than the frames of time and space that often ground the lived interactions of realistic fiction, function as the backdrop for interaction in the storyworld.

From the beginning of the novel, Jack's self-conscious relationship to the ordinary world blurs the boundary between plot events and imaginative or discursive constructions. His self-reflexive meditations often highlight his tendency to inhabit an everyday that unfolds in the space of his imagination. At one point, he questions whether it is Della's voice he hears or the echoes of his own consciousness:

> She said, "Maybe everything else is strange."
> Well, this happened to be a thing his soul had said to him any number of times, wordlessly, it was true, but with a similar inflection, like an echo, like the shadow of a sound. She, the actual Della, might not have spoken at all, since the thought was so familiar to him.   (33)

Second-guessing his tendency to inhabit the space of his own consciousness, Jack interrogates whether the words he hears emerge from the lips of "the actual Della" or originate in his own being. Even as Jack's disclaimers highlight Della's status as "the woman he had recruited into his daydreams to make up for a paucity of meaning and event he sometimes found oppressive" (63), however, his position as focalizer of the narrative lends him the power to author her story. The passage above continues:

> So he did look at her, her head lowered pensively, and he asked her what she had said. "Your voice is very soft."
> "Oh, nothing."
> That meant she chose not to say it again, whatever it was. "Nothing" was a finger to the lips, a confidence she had thought better of. A confidence. Then she realized she should not be so much at ease with him. She decided to be reticent about the kinds of thoughts she didn't usually allow herself, after almost speaking them. If she had said those words, it meant she liked the night well enough, and he felt a tentative kind of pride in the thought.

The night and the place were his own, more or less, and she was his guest in them, now that she had begun to seem a little more at ease.   (33)

As the paragraph takes shape, the narrative Jack constructs generates its own force. Making something out of nothing, he not only expounds on Della's actual words—"Oh, nothing"—but transforms her simple response into a temporal narrative ("Then she realized...") founded on Jack's supposed knowledge of her motivations, both conscious and unconscious: "She decided to be reticent about the kind of thoughts she didn't usually allow herself." Although Jack begins by questioning the relationship between the empirical and the imagined, Della's noncommittal response inspires a translation of her words that reads increasingly like pure projection. Della remains the "guest" in Jack's story, the visitor in the imaginative space he creates.

At times, his imaginative status as host so overwhelms the story that Jack's voice appropriates the role of omniscient narrator in the novel:

So Della went back to Memphis, to the embrace of her family, to dinners made sentimental by favorite dishes and old stories and smiles of abiding love. She will be an impostor of sorts, to all appearances herself and inwardly a stranger to them all, patient with their insistent kindness, waiting to be gone... The world around her falling away, she will still be gracious, her voice still soft.   (271)

This passage, which begins a new section of the novel, flows seamlessly from the past tense simple reportage of Della's move to a definitive statement of her future thoughts and actions. The narrative obscures Jack's focalization through an assertion of omniscience that extends across time and space, breaking down the boundaries between external and internal to reveal not only what will happen to Della but how she will feel. It is only at the end of the paragraph that these insights are revealed as Jack's speculations, emerging not out of knowledge of the plot or the character but out of the routine constructions of his imagination: "It was almost a habit with him to imagine her loveliness, the same through every change, rarefied, not vanishing, the very idea of loveliness" (271). As the specifics of Della's life fade into her abstraction into "the very idea of loveliness," Jack's idealizing impulses destabilize the boundaries of narrative voice as well as the conventions of the everyday.

*   *   *

The romance that is at the center of the novel can be read as one of several attempts on Jack's part to find an objective correlative for his experience of alienation from the ordinary. His guilt at the harm he creates in Gilead leads him not only to flee but to embrace the appearance of social liminality that objectifies his sense of himself as predestined for perdition. "Disguised as a social reject" (238), he dwells in marginal spaces, purposefully trading in the respectable suit he purchases with his family's money for something stained and appropriately "raffish" (117). Although the disconnect between his upbringing and his self-presentation surfaces in the articulate formality that encourages those who mock him to call him "Professor,"[6] he continually seeks to solidify his liminal status, rendering himself as visibly derelict as he feels. Uncomfortable in his own skin, Jack reiterates the fact that "he felt conspicuous and awkward" over and over in the novel (260);[7] his experience of marginalization extends from his (dis)location in his family's home to the disreputable boarding house where he lives, the street corners that he frequents while drunk, and the very body that he inhabits. Merleau-Ponty's idea of the lived body explores the phenomenological orientation of the subject by highlighting the way that we interact with the world around us, pulling it into the space of our lived experience: "Besides the physical and geometrical distance which stands between myself and all things, a 'lived' distance binds me to things which count and exist for me, and links them to each other. This distance measures the 'scope' of my life at every moment" (286). Lamenting, "Why were there an infinite number of ways to feel awkward?" (300), Jack fails to bind himself to any of his surroundings; his sense of unease reflects an existential homelessness marked in his fidgeting body and his anxious habits of mind.

Viewed within this context, Jack's relationship with Della relocates the uncomfortable ordinary that he experiences, lending its ontological status social, juridical, and quotidian visibility. On the one hand, the novel appropriates the conventions of romance to offer a love story in which two people fight against great odds to be together. Della, the heroine of the narrative, remains largely an idealized figure whose consciousness is inaccessible to the reader. Describing her as "the creature of his imagination" (253), Jack sweeps Della off her feet and courts her in a romantic way that promises to transcend the quotidian. At the same time, I will argue, Jack is drawn to Della for exactly the opposite reason. With her at his side, his uncomfortable

---

[6] See 71, 128, 196.   [7] See also 141, 158, 240, 300.

relationship with the ordinary finds grounding. Given the legal and cultural strictures against interracial relationships in Missouri at the time, the most commonplace acts—eating dinner at a restaurant, walking down the street together, living in the same home—threaten responses ranging from disapproval to racist violence and job loss to imprisonment. In Della's company, Jack's very existence becomes unlawful. Her presence provides a clear referent for Jack's experience of estrangement from the ordinary world, lending form to an otherwise inaccessible and inexplicable dynamic of alienation. The hypervigilance and self-consciousness that disrupt Jack's most mundane activities now make sense; the always fraught activity of moving through the everyday world becomes suddenly intelligible: "Well of course he was vigilant. Della was on his arm" (268). Given their racial identities, Jack and Della find it "impossible to walk naturally" together (268). Jack's psychic experience of displacement attaches itself to empirical cause in the context of race. Midway through the novel, the narrative observes, "Say there were two cities, one black, one white... he, as a white man in the black city, felt conspicuous... Out of place, in other words" (158). Clinging to racial and geographic boundaries to explain his displacement through much of the novel, Jack eventually breaks down the dichotomy that underlies his own model: "When he walked through black St. Louis, he felt conspicuous and awkward. He felt no less conspicuous and awkward when he walked through white St. Louis" (269). Despite Jack's attempt to locate his experience of dislocation in Della's racially marked presence, the novel unveils the forced process by which Jack externalizes his own discomfort.

Even as Jack appropriates Della's skin color to ground his sense of estrangement, he ignores its relevance to the language he uses to express that discomfort. When Jack employs a figure of speech to claim that Della is more "at ease in [her] skin" than he is, she calls him out by pointing to the literal signification of his metaphor:

He said, "You're very sure of yourself. At ease in your skin. While I..."
She stopped. "You actually said that."
"What? Well, yes, I suppose I did... It's a thing people say, isn't it?... I'm terribly sorry. It's true, though, isn't it?"
"No. Much of the time it isn't true. When I find myself trapped in a white cemetery, it definitely isn't true." (49)

Jack draws attention to his own habitual unease by juxtaposing his awkward demeanor with Della's poise; exposing the gap between Jack's metaphorical statement and its literal implications for a person with black skin, Della references what Franz Fanon terms "a racial epidermal schema." In *Black Skin, White Masks*, Fanon uses the notion of "bodily schema," a concept similar to Merleau-Ponty's understanding of the lived body, to explore the way that cultural constructions of race complicate and disrupt the dynamics of embodied subjectivity for the black subject (110). The general concept of the bodily schema, Fanon articulates, describes "A slow composition of my *self* as a body in the middle of a spatial and temporal world ... It does not impose itself on me; it is, rather, a definitive restructuring of the self and of the world—definitive because it creates a real dialectic between my body and the world" (110–11). In a white world, Fanon emphasizes, the person of color experiences that dialectic only with great difficulty; by rendering the subject in/as the black skin that culture overdetermines with a set of constructed meanings, a racial epidermal schema disrupts any attempt to anchor the self in the everyday world. In *Between the World and Me*, Ta-Nehisi Coates describes this lived experience of blackness as "the breach between the world and me" (115). In contrast to the taken-for-granted quality of a comfortable everyday, Coates highlights "feeling ill at ease" during even the most routine activities (24); addressing his son, he remarks, "when I was about your age, each day, fully one-third of my brain was concerned with who I was walking to school with, our precise number, the manner of our walk, the number of times I smiled, who or what I smiled at" (24). In *Black Is the Body*, Emily Bernard echoes Coates's description of an everyday defined by the "need to be always on guard" (90) when she observes, "My earliest experiences of blackness were defined by an unpleasant and uncomfortable hypervigilance. Being black meant that you had to be constantly aware, that you could never really be at ease" (85). In the white world, Fanon summarizes, "the man of color encounters difficulties in the development of his bodily schema. Consciousness of the body is solely a negating activity. The body is surrounded by an atmosphere of certain uncertainty" (110). Although the space of the white cemetery heightens Della's sense of unease, that dynamic is not limited to certain external spaces, but manifests in a self-consciousness that, she asserts, exists "much of the time."[8]

---

[8] Although Della calls attention to the problematic metaphor Jack employs, the narrative initially conspires to endorse his assessment of Della's equanimity. She is most often situated in the comfortable space of her own home, where she appears very much at ease and seemingly unconcerned about the real-world implications of their romance.

What Fanon describes as "an atmosphere of certain uncertainty" surrounding the person of color uncannily echoes Jack's image of his own unanchored presence in the everyday. Describing how his contact with the world destabilizes the very atmosphere, Jack observes: "It is some spontaneous, chemical thing that happens. Contact between Jack Boughton and—air...A rosy heat of embarrassment around any ordinary thing" (7). If entropy, as Jack suggests, "should have a nimbus" (7), the novel's repeated metaphors of atmospheric destabilization—"I am at the center of a certain turbulence" (140); "It was that turbulence he carried with him, that black wind" (215)—position Jack in a realm of self-conscious negation that locates him primarily in the experience of dislocation. By positioning Jack's rhetorical constructions of his ontological unease against Della's necessary negotiation of a racist world, the novel temporarily exposes the gap between the two. Jack's experience of an uncomfortable ordinary invokes what Robinson describes in an interview as an "ontological discomfort" that she links to her own imaginative creativity, observing, "There's a certain kind of ontological discomfort that seasons thought...it was that discomfort that made me feel like writing, the feeling of difference" (Mason). By setting Jack's "feeling of difference" against Della's, the novel extends the notion of an uncomfortable everyday into the realm of consciousness even as it gestures toward the social and corporeal pressures that hover at the margins of the text.

In Jack's case, the discomfort that may contribute to his status as thinker and writer implicates him in imaginative destruction as much as artistic creation. His heightened consciousness manifests in what he renders as his "fascination with damage and its consequences" (44): "I am aware instantly and almost obsessively of anything fragile, with the thought that I must and will break it" (228). Lacking what Felski describes as the "mundane, material embeddedness in the world" that is the mark of the everyday ("Invention" 16), Jack acknowledges his obsession with shattering surfaces to coerce an interface with the world he cannot take for granted. Victor Shklovsky's famous claim that art "exists that one may recover the sensation of life; it exists to make one feel things, to make the stone stony" (4), is predicated on the idea that in everyday existence "perception becomes habitual, it becomes automatic" (3). In such a context, art defamiliarizes to bypass the taken-for-granted quality of the everyday. In Jack's case, his detachment from the ordinary renders imagination a means of forcing an encounter rather than recovering sensation. Jack's abstracted relationship with the ordinary coopts the embodied apprehension of the quotidian world Shklovsky assumes; in the light of the poetry he reads, Jack observes at one point, "everything seems like a metaphor" (115). His desire to draw closer to the quotidian, to immerse himself haptically as well as imaginatively in the world, continually threatens to break it open: "That's how the world is, touch anything, change everything. Caution is needed... What would be left if the fragile were tested, pushed nearer the edge of the shelf, if that tension were sprung and the fragile thing, the essence of it, lost" (61). Jack's abstract and often poetic renderings emerge from a "feeling of difference" that the novel both confirms and interrogates in its representation of the relationship between Jack and Della, who comes to embody "the fragile thing" to which Jack is drawn.

Most of the novel hovers in the space of romance, evoking the everyday not as the taken-for-granted foundation of events but as the hazy and ungraspable backdrop of an "ordinary world" (196) against which Jack defines himself. *Jack* breaks down the boundary between the image and its referential counterpart, situating the narrative in the border between plot events and the imaginings that precipitate, reflect on, or recast them. By locating Jack's story primarily in the space of his consciousness, the narrative dwells in the "habits of mind" (118) that come to constitute the primary vehicles of his everyday. In *Critique of Everyday Life*, Henri Lefebvre reflects on an established dichotomy between two spheres of life; whereas the lower sphere assumes the "direct, immediate character of the 'lived,' a sort of irrefutable concreteness," in the upper sphere "people move and act amid formal and conventional abstractions, or more precisely, amid signs and signals" (53). Despite the significance of these critical distinctions, Lefebvre argues, for the individual, "external or internal constraints are all mixed up together" (61). In *Jack*, what Lefebvre terms "speculative thought" (47) displaces the "immediate character of the 'lived'" to form the essential building blocks of the narrative.

The novel frames its most sustained representation of an encounter between Jack and Della, for example, as a disruption of his imaginative construction of her. In the extended scene at the beginning of the novel, Jack and Della meet as darkness falls in a white cemetery where they both hide out until morning:

> Here, in a cemetery, in the middle of the night, he was caught off guard by an actual turn of events, something that mattered, a meeting that would empty his best thoughts of their pleasure. Those dreams of his had been... privileged because they were... certainly never to be exposed to the chill air of consequence. (15)

Fascinated by his own imaginings of damage, destruction, and despair, Jack ceaselessly patrols an imagination that threatens to spill over dangerously upon contact with the lived world. If, as Jack observes, "all his conniving was mainly just an exercise of imagination" (249), the novel supports Jack's imaginings by setting "actual turn[s] of events" in liminal spaces like the dark and deserted cemetery and registering their real-world consequences primarily in abstract reflections or mediated forms. In the world Jack inhabits, thoughts and images assume an immediacy that reverses the dynamics of representation, rendering imagination primary and reality a faint copy: "There were times when his imaginations of destruction were so powerful that the deed itself seemed as bad as done. So he did it. It was as if the force of the idea were strong enough that his collaboration in it was trivial" (236).

As Jack's interactions with Della vacillate between what Lefebvre terms the "irrefutable concreteness" (54) of an everyday anchored in time and space and the "abstractions" (53) of consciousness, the narrative blurs the distinction between figure and ground to unsettle both. The cemetery offers Jack and Della temporary escape from what Jack terms "the land of the living" (42); leaving the ordinary world and its conventions behind, they establish a connection grounded, despite occasional sensory detailing of the wet grass or Della's scratchy hat, primarily in language, imagination, poetry, and philosophy. As they spend their time together imagining another world, Jack invokes Milton: "Before their eyes in sudden view appear/The secrets of the hoary deep; a dark/Illimitable ocean, without bound,/Without dimension, where length, breadth, and height/And time, and place, are lost" (58). While demonstrating Jack's erudition and access to a classical education, the passage from Book II of *Paradise Lost* portrays Satan's traveling through the gulf of Chaos to undertake his corruption of humanity. Jack's citation of Milton implicates the liminal space of their nighttime encounter—a place where the conventions of everyday life, including time, place, and dimension, are suspended—in a trajectory of devastation. The novel introduces Jack and Della's romance as the meeting of two consciousnesses, set in a graveyard where they become "ghosts among the ghosts" (42); given their unequal access to a position of transcendence within racialized systemic structures, however, Jack's symbolic eclipse of the material world threatens to rebound most dangerously within the parameters of *Della*'s everyday life. Citing the historical and theoretical connection between whiteness and the power of representation, philosopher George Yancy emphasizes the way that the black body bears the consequences of a white imaginary, which include

African-American unemployment, inferior health care, and police brutality. "For black people," Yancy argues, "such conditions constitute a space of existential being-in the world," a space of "being and suffering" that is not solely discursive ("Fragments" 16). Even as Jack acknowledges the threat he poses to Della, his metaphors conspire in abstracting the concrete harm he represents to the realm of the invisible and the imaginary: "'I'm at my best unseen,' he tells her. 'The Prince of Darkness. The Prince of Absence, for that matter'" (48).

Jack's tendency to imaginatively step back from his embodied interaction with Della also manifests in the way the narrative, distracted by the metaphorical shaping of his literary sensibility, intermittently loosens its grip on referentiality. Filtered through the lens of Jack's focalization, the text slips away from its anchoring in the ordinary world and back again:

> Her sleeve stirred against him. The plum-colored cloth of her coat. He had once asked himself which colors yield to darkness first, and which of them float in it for a while. Twilight has nothing black about it, so black would be absorbed much more gradually than plum. She was clothed in twilight. That is the kind of thought I'll have when this is over and she is gone. Those ridiculous poems I never write down. In fact, she will be a respectable woman with a job and a street address, reading her newspaper over breakfast in the morning light. I'll walk by, and she won't see me.   (63)

Jack's tentative immersion in lived experience, grounded in the perception of color and touch, follows the habits of his mind to spiral into a form of imaginative transcendence that abstracts Della's form so completely—"She was clothed in twilight"—that it pushes the immediacy of her concrete presence into an anticipated absence recoverable only in memory or in the realm of "ridiculous" poetry. Jack responds to what Robinson terms a feeling of "ontological discomfort" by turning away from the woman next to him to a series of imaginings that distance him from her. Writing himself out of their lived interaction into the solitude of retrospective regret, he reestablishes "the transparent barrier between himself and ordinary life" (135). Jack secures Della in an imagined everyday of home, job, and daily routine that marginalizes his own presence: "she will be a respectable woman with a job and a street address, reading her newspaper over breakfast in the morning light. I'll walk by, and she won't see me" (63). Even as she leans against him, Jack locates Della in the close proximity of an inaccessible space constructed by his imagination. Whether "clothed in twilight" or reading the newspaper,

Della's presence testifies primarily to *Jack*'s "being and suffering" (Yancy, "Fragments" 16).

Despite its framing as a love story, *Jack* never depicts the years when he and Della find a way, however tentative, to live together (in *Gilead*, for example, Jack describes buying a home in St. Louis where he lives with his wife and son until they are forced to move). Instead, their relationship highlights the way that Jack experiences life at a remove. Detached from the ordinary world and the people in it, Jack remains oddly unaffected by even intimate encounters.[9] Not surprisingly, then, the novel locates Jack's relationship with Della primarily in the space of his haunted and isolated consciousness. Despite brief encounters in a series of liminal spaces (beginning with the cemetery in which they find themselves together at night), their romance finds no hold on the everyday. In fact, it might appear, the near impossibility of being with Della fuels the intensity of Jack's connection to her. What Jack describes as Della's "unmarriage to her unhusband" (271) assumes the form of "intimacy at a distance" (253). As "the creature of his imagination" (253), Della's presence in the storyworld is often subsumed within the rhythms of Jack's consciousness rather than what Robinson describes as the "nuts and bolts" realities of eating, sleeping, and working. The "sanctified distance" (219) that they maintain between them becomes the mark of their connection. Insofar as "strangers in the abstract always turn out to be drearily particular on acquaintance" (34), Jack sustains Della's presence in his mind as an abstraction spared the test of lived experience. If, as I have argued throughout this study, Robinson's fiction expands the experience of the everyday to include the habits of consciousness as well as body, *Jack* tests the limits of the imaginative everyday by rendering Jack's relationship with Della largely in terms of absence presence: "Their lives were parallel lines that would not meet . . . making an imaginary something out of literally nothing" (84).

* * *

As it explores the tension between ordinary and imaginative worlds, *Jack* raises the question of how we read Della's presence in the novel. The Gilead novels are remarkable for highlighting the significance of perspective; introducing a series of minor characters that the reader first accesses through the subjective lens of others, the novel series then takes up the mantle of those

---

[9] Even after his physical connection with the girl that was the mother of his child, Jack "would not know her if he saw her . . . He believed that he had gone through certain things with her, but at such a remove they could hardly have changed him" (213).

formerly inaccessible characters to lend insight into their consciousness. Jack's interracial relationship with Della, however, raises the stakes of her inaccessibility in the novel. The abstracted representation of their love story calls to mind Toni Morrison's famous remarks in "Unspeakable Things Unspoken" about how the literary form of romance negotiates the shadow of black presence in American fiction:

> In 1850 at the height of slavery and burgeoning abolitionism, American writers chose romance. Where, I wonder, in these romances is the shadow of the presence from which the text has fled? Where does it heighten, where does it dislocate, where does it necessitate novelistic invention; what does it release; what does it hobble? The device (or arsenal) that serves the purpose of flight can be Romanticism versus verisimilitude.   (378)

If Jack's imaginative sensibility and poetic creations render him a figure of the artist, the novel's focus on his interracial relationship with Della troubles Jack's romanticism in its flight from verisimilitude. Romance, Richard Moreland argues, "offers its readers [assurance] that 'plans' (and fictional plots) translate intention and principles directly into events, unimpaired by historical contingencies" (512). The literary form of *Jack* pulls away from the "drearily particular" (*Jack* 34) both in its characterization of Della and in the conventions that establish its storyworld. The narrative's tight focalization through Jack's perspective reinforces the primacy of his imaginings of Della, while his writerly sensibility shapes the representation of their relationship into a romance. Even as Della's blackness offers an objective correlative for Jack's feelings of difference, Jack's romanticized and often melodramatic telling appropriates her presence within a narrative of his own making.

By focusing on an interracial romance in a segregated city in the mid-twentieth century, *Jack* invokes the influence of historical contingencies even as it obscures them. Although Robinson's other Gilead novels situate her characters in historical time and space, *Jack* pointedly obscures those reference points. As Jodi Rios observes in *Black Lives and Spatial Matters*, St. Louis, the setting Robinson chooses for *Jack*, is a city marked spatially and historically as a site of racial conflict and turmoil:

> Located at the geographical and cultural intersections between North/ South and East/West, St. Louis walked the line on the issue of slavery for over a century, navigating between the self-interest of local slaveholding

residents and an abolitionist rhetoric aimed at…maintaining business opportunities with entities in the North and the East Coast.

The location of St. Louis at the intersection of conflicting American geographical and cultural positions is amplified by the history of a decades-long struggle over shifting spatial boundaries *within* the city. As Jeannette Cooperman documents, the local history of St. Louis assumes significance on the national stage of legal battles over racial segregation:

> In 1916, St. Louisans voted on a "reform" ordinance that would prevent anyone from buying a home in a neighborhood more than 75 percent occupied by another race. Civic leaders opposed the initiative, but it… became the first referendum in the nation to impose racial segregation on housing. After a U.S. Supreme Court decision, Buchanan v. Warley, made the ordinance illegal the following year, some St. Louisans reverted to racial covenants, asking every family on a block or in a subdivision to sign a legal document promising to never sell to an African-American. Not until 1948 were such covenants made illegal, after the U.S. Supreme Court ruled on Shelley v. Kraemer, a case originating in St. Louis.

Although historical events in the larger world, including the Birmingham race riots and the murder of Emmett Till, intrude even upon the insular setting of *Home*, which takes place within a single home in small-town Gilead, Robinson works hard in *Jack* to erase not just race relations landmarks but historical referents that would situate the novel chronologically. The April 2020 letter from Jonathan Galassi, the president of Farrar Straus Giroux, that accompanies review copies of the novel asserts that the book's "interracial romance resonates with the paradoxes of American life, then and now." The publisher's framing of its social relevance, however, sits a bit oddly against the letter's broadly sketched placement of the novel in St. Louis, "sometime after World War II."

In addition to the marked absence of dates or historical references in the novel, the landscape of the city remains blurred. The language the narrative employs, like the "sort of map" Jack drafts for Della (123), is broadly sketched and less than referential. The generic phrase, "the place," is introduced repeatedly in the novel to refer to anything from the cemetery to Jack's workplace to a restaurant to Della's apartment to the different rooming houses Jack lives in ("the place" and "the old place") to the city of St. Louis. When Della invites him to her "place" for Thanksgiving, Jack wrongly assumes she is talking about her family home in a different city (62). Although the cemetery where Jack and Della meet and the church where he finds himself are assigned proper names, the urban landscape consists mostly of generic landmarks like "the river"; even the boundaries of the racially segregated city blur as Jack moves between broadly termed "white St. Louis" and "black St. Louis" (269). Robinson's choice to focus on an interracial romance and to set the novel in a city with a history of racial turmoil only to strip away temporal and geographical landmarks leaves the reader situated hazily in referential space. In the battle between the concrete and the abstract, the mundane and the imaginary, Jack continually gravitates toward the latter. The tour of St. Louis he proposes to Della deliberately obscures the quotidian specifics of urban space:

> "Well, I could wander by your house one night and find you there and squire you through the city." He said, "'Nocturnal.' I like that word. It sounds like the change there is when the streets are empty and the houses are dark, which is a much deeper thing than just, you know, the absence of light. I could show you." (27)

In Jack's phenomenology, the sound of words exists on the same plane as the sensory data of the everyday world. If anything, he sidelines the layout of urban streets and houses to pursue "a much deeper thing"; his tour of the city, like the novel itself, disrupts the immediacy of external perception to return to the immaterial space of Jack's consciousness.

By repeatedly expressing his concern that Della will bear the brunt of the inevitable consequences of their relationship, Jack gestures toward the distinction that Yancy highlights when he argues that it is black people who must "live the reality" of racialized dynamics that whites can afford to acknowledge largely in theoretical terms ("Fragments" 16). As Andrew Smith explores in *Racism and Everyday Life*, the everyday is not merely the backdrop against which acts of racism are performed; following a lineage of race theorists who argue for the significance of the lived experiences of racism, Smith argues for attending to the significance of an everyday dynamic that necessitates the process of continually navigating a racist ordinary. Collapsing the distinction between traumatic events and the ongoing routines and mundane environments they appear to disrupt, Rhaisa Williams highlights the way that, for many black Americans, "trauma marks the ongoing" ("Choreographies" 765). Jack's language signals his awareness of structural power dynamics that render Della especially vulnerable to the lived consequences of their unsanctioned union; the narrative, however, conspires to render the real-world impacts of their relationship only at a remove. Aside from the cemetery scene, which takes place under the cover of night, the novel situates the romance between Jack and Della primarily in the safety and warmth of her home; in that circumscribed realm, Della's graceful equanimity and relaxed manner situate her comfortably in the rhythms of the everyday. Her poise extends from her "solicitude" (93) toward Jack's comfort to her grace under pressure as they discuss their relationship—"She looked at him calmly, candidly" (94)—to her practiced assurance in performing routine domestic tasks:

> Then they sat there eating together, sharing the syrup, stirring their coffee. He...realized there would be less chance of a spill if he had filled them at the table, but he was very careful. How had he found the nerve? She smiled at him and said thank you, as if it were just a pleasant, ordinary thing. She opened a little porcelain box with sugar cubes in it and dropped two in his cup and two in hers.   (97)

In contrast to Jack's exhaustively detailed self-consciousness as he enters the unfamiliar realm of domesticity (90–1), Della appears fully at home, sustaining Jack's image of a "soft" and "gracious" presence that transcends the forces of change (271). Setting the development of their romance—and Della's character—against the backdrop of a seemingly safe space, the novel's representations subtly undermine Della's assertion about the difficulty of feeling at ease in her own skin.

Notably, *Jack* denies the reader full access to any of the scenes in the novel in which Della is confronted by white authority figures; the text obscures the very moments that would fulfill the promise of dramatic climax by revealing the explosive repercussions of their romance. At the end of the long nighttime scene in the cemetery, Della puts away her notebook and heads off alone to face the white guard: "She...tottered down on the grassy slope in her high-heeled shoes, and took her place on the path of feckless humankind. When she was at a good distance, he followed along behind her" (77). At the level of both story and narrative discourse, Della's violation of racial segregation situates her "at a good distance" from Jack, whose strategic decision not to accompany her to the exit is paralleled by his focalizing presence in a narrative that reduces her interaction with the guard to a series of gestures and acts perceived from afar: "She held her head to the side, looking at the ground, waiting for the guard to stop talking to her, nodding now and then" (77). Watching the guard touch Della's arm, Jack imagines what it is that the guard wants her to say. The reader, however, only receives a clear report of the guard's words when Jack comes close enough to distract him, allowing Della to slip away. In the volley of abuse the guard directs at Jack, Della's blackness emerges as yet another signifier of *Jack*'s marginalization:

> "You! I am sick of the sight of you, buster! I should have called the cops on you a hundred times before now! This time I'm going to do it! Don't think I don't know what's been going on here. Sleeping off a drunk is one thing, but bringing along a colored gal—we've got dead people in here!" He fixed Jack with a stare, decency much offended.   (78)

As the extended depiction of Jack's interaction displaces Della's experience of this climactic scene, she exits from the narrative as well as the cemetery. Even as the story forces Della out of the fantastical interlude in the cemetery and back into the world, the narrative shifts away from the physical or psychic consequences of her disempowerment to support, instead, the abstracted rendering of Della "tak[ing] her place on the path of feckless humankind." Distancing the reader from the dramatic confrontation with white authority it seems to promise, the scene situates Della as a broadly sketched figure receding into the distance of metaphorical space and theoretical humanity. Even as Jack attempts to insert his body protectively into the space between Della and the white attendant, his presence overwhelms hers in the narrative; in the context of the racial dynamics the novel foregrounds, the limited focalization of the text assumes heightened significance. George Yancy argues for the importance of recognizing what he describes as the "social ontology of whiteness" ("Fragments" 8), the unmarked, pervasive, and systemic nature of a racialized structure that frames the lived experience of both blacks and whites:

> To be black, to fall prey to whiteness's (anti-black) epistemological and ontological modes of structuration, is to be devoid of ontological depth... Whiteness is true transcendence, an ecstatic mode of being; blackness, however, [is] locked into an ontological realm where things exist... waiting to be ordered by some external, subjugating, purposive (white) consciousness. ("Fragments" 12)

Jack's identification as a writer calls attention to his less visible role as focalizer of the narrative and participant in the white imaginary, raising the question of Della's function in a narrative that probes the ontological depths of Jack's consciousness at the expense of representing the complexity of Della's lived experience.

Although it often dwells on Jack's discomfort, then, the novel conspicuously avoids depicting the concrete impacts of his actions on Della. *Jack* opens right after the abrupt disruption of the couple's first date, revealing that Jack had abandoned Della mid-meal in a restaurant, sneaking out the back door without paying. When the narrative returns to fill in the details of that restaurant scene 100 pages later, it follows Jack through the kitchen and out the door; Della is left behind not only in the restaurant but in the narrative, which follows the shifting rhythms of Jack's consciousness at length even as it relegates Della's experience to the margins of the text. Although Jack repeatedly voices his concern about the fact that, as a single black woman in a segregated city, Della stands to lose more than her reputation—"What anyone at all might say or think would hover around them, a very real threat. To her" (243)—the narrative downplays the immediacy of that "very real threat." When Della's principal comes to her home to confront her about circulating rumors that she is violating anti-miscegenation laws, Jack fails to witness that dramatic encounter; instead, it is curtly summarized for Jack and the reader: "The sister said, to Jack, 'The principal of her school came here, right to her house, to tell her that there was talk, that there was some question about whether she was setting a good moral example. He just left an hour ago. You could have come while he was still here!'" (241–2). Although Julia highlights the urgent threat marked by the principal's sudden intrusion into the safety of Della's domestic space—"The principal of her school came here, right to her house"—the reader, along with Jack, is spared the immediacy of that interaction. Instead of probing the emotional impact or material consequences of the painful exchange he just missed, Jack responds by ruminating. He begins by repeating the fact that "every risk he took was a threat to her" (242). His consciousness, however, leads him quickly past the concrete threats posed to Della by even their most routine acts—walking down the street together, the possibility of the boarding house desk clerk calling the police—to pause in an imagining of the two of them together in his room: "He thought of the two of them whispering under the covers on that narrow bed, laughing as quietly as they could, talking about Wyoming and the end of the world, he with his arms around her dear body" (243). When, in a separate incident, Della *does* finally end up in Jack's room, she materializes there suddenly and almost magically; Jack returns from a walk when the desk clerk informs him that "a colored girl" is waiting for him upstairs (198). Although the desk clerk references the possibility of calling the police after the fact—"Don't worry, I probably won't call the cops" (198)—the narrative omits any representation of Della's encounter with that insolent, racist white character. By the time Jack (and the narrative) catch up with Della, she is sleeping peacefully in his room: "He went up to his room, and there she was, asleep on his bed, in her coat and her shoes, her handbag and hat beside her, her lovely head on his pillow" (198).

At the end of *Jack*, however, the novel introduces concrete and historically specific references to the effects of eminent domain in St. Louis that begin to press against Jack's abstracted narrative. Up to this point in the novel, Della's alignment with the safety of her domestic space has supported Jack's idealization of her unperturbable presence. As he learns that the walls of her home will soon come crashing down, however, Jack is forced to acknowledge the limits of his imaginative maintenance. Whereas earlier Jack carries a newspaper solely as a sign of his legitimacy or a prop referencing his respectability—"He would carry a folded newspaper to suggest he was a man with interests, with a foot in the larger world" (104)—toward the end of the novel, Jack reads a newspaper that penetrates the imaginary bubble he has created for himself and Della:

> She would be walking toward her side of town as quickly as she could, to escape the threat of insult or harm, to find safety, the blessed comfort of familiarity. He had not brought up with her an article he had seen in the newspaper announcing that the city had decided to demolish her side of town, churches and all, to replace it with something or other at some point in time, these decisions pending. She would know, no doubt, that she was hurrying toward a doomed refuge. (211)

The reference to a single newspaper article highlights the "historical contingencies" that Jack's imaginings have worked hard to keep at bay (Moreland 512). Although urban renewal, the federal government's mid-twentieth-century "slum" clearance program, resulted in the destruction and displacement of many black and poor communities in cities across the United States, St. Louis's urban renewal history is particularly fraught, as Margaret Garb documents in "No Place Like Home: St. Louis' Eminent Domain History." On August 7, 1954, St. Louis Mayor Raymond Tucker announced one of the country's largest urban renewal projects, which eventually resulted in the obliteration of the Mill Creek Valley neighborhood and the displacement of 20,000 families. Garb reports,

> The neighborhood, one of the few open to African Americans under the city's segregation codes...was home to black teachers, janitors, cooks, laundresses, railroad porters and musicians...Eminent domain, a seemingly obscure legal tool, has pushed whole communities out of our collective memory...we rarely recognize the urban neighborhoods that were forged under the weight of segregation, molded into vibrant working-class communities and then demolished.

Although the novel begins in the cemetery in the dark of night where Della reassures Jack, "We're not in the land of the living," frequent references in the last section of the novel to the impending demolition of her St. Louis home locate her in historical time and "recognize" in concrete terms the fact that Della is directly in harm's way.

As the news encroaches upon the narrative, the nocturnal tour of St. Louis that Jack once touted as "a much deeper thing" emerges as an illusion barely disguising the effects of racist capitalist policy on "the bad side of town" (112):

> At night the streets looked calm, solid, darkness hiding the decrepitude brought on by Eminent Domain, the giant that would fell forty churches. "Condemned" is the word they used... And all that life was condemned for the ground under it. He sat down on a stoop. Della's church would be gone, and the house she lived in gone, too, condemnation certain. (261)

If the novel has eschewed spatial and geographical orientation in favor of Jack's roughly sketched "sort of map" (123), Jack's imagination now becomes the force that locates and concretizes the future impacts of urban renewal policies, causes and effects that range from decrepitude to destruction, benign neglect to eminent domain. Describing race as "a virtually unspeakable thing" in the canonical literary history of the United States, Toni Morrison points to the subtle ways in which black presence "has shaped the choices, the language, the structure—the meaning of so much American literature" ("Unspeakable" 370, 377). What Morrison terms "the ghost in the machine" of the American novel emerges in *Jack* through the protagonist's belated recognition of damage that will no longer be obscured

("Unspeakable" 377). In "The Story of Segregation in St. Louis," Cooperman calls attention to the need to recognize "the ghost neighborhoods" that hover beneath empirical registers of the city's landscape: "What those [current St. Louis] maps don't show are the ghost neighborhoods, once-black communities ripped out of both city and county." Termed "slums" and demolished in the name of progress, those neighborhoods—and the people in them—simply disappeared:

> "We removed so-called slum neighborhoods," says Michael Allen, director of the Preservation Research Office. "Mill Creek Valley, Chestnut Valley, Carr Square, we clear-cut. Then we demolished vacant housing in The Ville," the neighborhood where Chuck Berry, Tina Turner, and Grace Bumbry grew up.
>
> Sometimes, the policy was benign neglect until it was time to condemn. Sometimes, it was eminent domain. "We have spent enormous sums of public money to spatially reinforce human segregation patterns," says Allen. "We have harnessed architecture as a barrier. And it's been very frightening to see the result." (Cooperman)

The spatial barrier Allen documents concretizes white identity at the expense of black lives; ghostly presence marks not transcendence of the everyday world but erasure within it. Black bodies, Ta-Nehisi Coates argues, "illuminate the border, illuminate what we ostensibly are not, illuminate the Dream of being white, of being a Man" (60). The seeming autonomy of white imagination, as Coates explores, depends on the literal—as well as the symbolic—manipulation of black bodies. Without your body to stand on, he tells his son, whites would "tumble out of the Dream. And then they would have to determine how to build their suburbs on something other than human bones" (105). As Coates reveals in graphic terms the cost of supporting the symbolic boundaries the white imaginary erects to enforce stable identity, he exposes not only the everyday impacts of structural racism but the illusion of transcendence that obscures the mechanisms of white world-building.

In the last seventy-five pages of the novel, Jack obsessively references the plans circulating in St. Louis to condemn homes in Della's neighborhood and seize those remaining through eminent domain. The metaphorical turbulence he associates with his presence takes hold of this historical phenomenon of material devastation, references to which interrupt the imaginative framing of Jack's focalizing consciousness in the narrative with uncharacteristic specificity. Recognizing that "an ordinary man would not dread this great, blind impulse of destruction prophesied at officious length in any newspaper" (238–9), Jack seizes on the announcement of the impending widespread demolition exactly because it literalizes the metaphors of devastation he has employed continually throughout the narrative. Indeed, one of Jack's first responses to this news is to appropriate it for "rhetorical use" (233); he seizes on the image of the wrecking ball as a weapon he deploys against Reverend Hutchins in a letter he drafts in his head: "I have read about eminent domain, a yet higher authority. A wrecking ball will break in on your parish, Reverend Sir, and the sheep will be scattered!" (232–3). Although Jack has proclaimed the inevitability of his doing harm in the past, the immediacy of the image he adopts for "rhetorical use" here breaks through its melodramatic and metaphorical framing. In response, he must "lay the flat of his hand against a shingled wall of the [church] to feel its solidity" (236). Even after reassuring himself that his imaginings have had no quotidian impact, Jack is shaken by the dissolution of the border between the real and the imaginary: "the realization startled him when he recognized the fantasy he had allowed himself was actually identical with the desolation intended for this swath of city" (236).

The pressing reality of imminent destruction calls out the self-imposed alienation that would confirm Jack's marginalization even as it would exempt him from the responsibility of social power:

> He had made an outcast of himself, yet he now knew he was not only a part of society, he was its essence, its epitome. What a lovely home you have, Miss Miles! Jesus is looking especially well this evening. Then, crash! Your gentle self in jail, all love anyone ever felt for you an agony, all hope ever placed in you dissipated like smoke. I am the Prince of Darkness. I believe I may have mentioned that. (236–7)

Though still couched in hyperbolic terms, Jack briefly acknowledges his participation in the systemic structures of white domination; spurred by the uncomfortable alignment of his fantasies with the devastatingly concrete effects of racist policies, he recasts his intimacy with Della as a cover for deception. Figuring his discursive gentlemanly presence as a violent force that, on contact, lands Della's "gentle self" in jail, Jack then retreats from his own admission of complicity to crouch within the outline of the melodramatic figure he conjures.

In the pages that follow, the looming presence of the wrecking ball directed at Della's home and neighborhood translates the abstract threat that Jack has always associated with his presence into increasingly immediate terms. Although he continues to think of himself as "the Prince of Darkness," references to eminent domain concretize the everyday impact of his largely theoretical relationship with Della: "She will come back to her unmarriage to her unhusband and live as she can, her vocation lost to what they will call turpitude. Eminent Domain will make rubble of the house she lives in, rubble of her church" (271). In this imaginative rendering of Jack's, Della struggles to "live as she can" stripped of the everyday supports of job, church, and home; her "unmarriage to her unhusband" condemns her to a negative space maintained in Jack's consciousness at the expense of her location in the grounding of the ordinary world. The impending damage of eminent domain pushes Jack's imaginings closer to consequence. As the subsequent lines of this passage highlight, Jack maintains his exteriorized and idealized vision of Della only by surrendering her dynamic presence in the lived world: "The world around her falling away, she will still be gracious, her voice still soft. It was almost a habit with him to imagine her loveliness, the same through every change, rarefied, not vanishing, the very idea of loveliness" (271). His imaginative habits once again encourage Jack to turn away from the ordinary world to his idealization of Della; the everyday costs of their romance, like the wrecking ball that hovers over her home, however, threaten the static construction of Jack's imagination with change that cannot be fully absorbed in abstraction.

On the one hand, then, *Jack* can be read within a lineage of American literary history that, in Toni Morrison's framing, appropriates black presence as a signifier of white desire: "As a writer reading, I came to realize the obvious: the subject of the dream is the dreamer. The fabrication of an Africanist persona is reflexive; an extraordinary meditation on the self; a powerful exploration of the fears and desires that reside in the writerly conscious" (*Playing* 17). As Della's presence in the novel both objectifies and idealizes Jack's fears and desires, her voice remains "still soft" and her character, "the same through every change," static and idealized (271). At the same time, the novel holds up its protagonist's writerly consciousness to view, pushing back against Della's assigned place of subordination in Jack's story. In the last section of the novel, images of Della's imprisonment and injury begin to hijack Jack's broad fantasies:

> Just stealing a few hours together could expose them to much more indignation than would any actual theft. There was a terrible vision that sometimes crossed his mind, of Della led away by police, not speaking, not crying, not looking back, proud as a martyr. And he, back in jail, having

no way to find out what had become of her. Dear Jesus, what was he doing? (250)

The prospect of spending time with Della in the flesh summons a disruptive "vision" that Jack cannot quite foreclose. Although he maintains her idealized presence, comparing her to a martyr who transcends the pain of her arrest, Jack's fantasy forces Della's proud and stoic image into a space inaccessible to Jack even in imaginative terms.

If, as Coates argues, "the Dream thrives on generalization" (50), increasingly specific threats hijack the narrative to challenge the rich promise of Jack's broad imaginings:

> He imagined himself with Della on his arm, showing her the city by night, when they [the debt collectors] appear, suddenly, anywhere, and he turns out his mended pockets and they punch him, anyway, for laughs, and what about Della? A miserable thought, bright as a dream. He might have a knife in his pocket, a switchblade, and then: Surprise! You didn't expect that, did you? There would be four of them, at most. If they got the knife away from him, who knows what might happen. They were always meaner. What about Della? She wouldn't run away. She might be all right if she were a white woman. Ah, Jesus! (258–9)

Once again, as in the "Crash!" as Della is carted off to jail in the passage above, the interjection of an exclamation—"Surprise!"—reflects the sudden intrusion of horrific particulars that disrupt Jack's romantic fantasies of his union with Della. Although Jack struggles to hold on to Della's idealized presence in the space of his dream, external threats rupture the bubble of consciousness. Americans, Morrison argues, "choose to talk about themselves through and within a sometimes allegorical, sometimes metaphorical, but always choked representation of an Africanist presence" (*Playing* 17). As the consequences of Jack's imaginings intrude violently on his allegorical constructions, his "choked representation" of Della's lived experience becomes increasingly apparent. Jack's imagination, rather than supplying the deeper meaning of a city rendered transcendent by darkness, snags on the details of an imagined harm rendered increasingly material; as the thought of a punch summons a generic knife that turns into a switchblade, the vague figures who appear out of nowhere coalesce into four men who turn against Della the very weapon Jack summons to protect her. Denied the distance of abstraction, Jack's retreat into consciousness comes to reinforce the violent encroachment of the external world rather than resist it.

Almost thirty years ago, Toni Morrison's *Playing in the Dark* highlighted the way that the racialized culture of the United States has informed the long history of literary representation; "excising the political from the life of the mind," she observes, "is a sacrifice that has proven costly" (12). In designing a character who would constitute his everyday as a life of the mind and engineering his chance encounter with a woman whose every move is circumscribed by a racial epidermal schema, Robinson's most recent novel revisits the dynamics Morrison renders visible through the lens of twenty-first-century self-consciousness. Even as the novel crafts a love story that is poignant and powerful, it disrupts the reader's immersion in the romance Jack's consciousness facilitates. Whereas Morrison tracks the complex attempts to excise racial dynamics from American literature, *Jack* both enacts and exposes what Morrison terms the phenomenon of "black surrogacy" in American literature, whereby African-American presence constitutes "an informing, stabilizing, and disturbing element" in white narratives (*Playing* 13). Jack idealizes Della from a distance even as he grasps onto her blackness as reason for and evidence of his self-imposed marginalization. In the narrative he creates, Jack is both a poet transcending quotidian concerns and a self-declared bum who chooses to trade in his respectable suit for something appropriately "cheap" and "raffish" (117); simultaneously rejecting the trappings of the everyday and appropriating them as evidence of his fundamental estrangement, Jack treats Della in the same way. "The social ontology of whiteness," as George Yancy argues, "has created and sustained a form of interpersonal distance partly informed by mythopoetic constructions about blackness" ("Fragments" 9). Both "stabilizing" and "disturbing," Della's elusive presence in the novel mirrors the interpersonal distance that renders her inaccessible to Jack in the storyworld. Whereas the white imagination that Morrison and Yancy describe covers over the markings of manipulation to create the illusion of stability, Robinson's protagonist interrupts his own narrative with a kind of self-conscious stutter that disrupts his own mythopoetic constructions. "He offered [his] name to people sometimes as if it opened to him some kind of familiarity, but he was familiar with no one, not even Della, he thought, who did not look at him though she held firmly to his hand" (244).

The conclusion of the novel moves increasingly toward unsettling the forms of romance that Jack constructs and unveiling the mantle of marginality that Jack adopts. Despite his attempt to surround himself with signifiers of marginalization and pass himself off as one of the down and out, Jack goes on to acknowledge, "He had no claim to being a veteran of these wars. No one had done him any real harm, except himself. He knew there was an old home always waiting for him" (247). Throughout most of the novel, Jack's professions of guilt emerge as melodramatic screeds that often enable and authorize his continued abdication of responsibility. Figuring himself as the Prince of Darkness, he cloaks his actions in an allegorical veil that signals his complicity even as it propels him away from real-world consequences. As the imminent destruction of Della's home penetrates Jack's consciousness, it locates his freestanding guilt and exposes the metaphoricity of his own professed dislocation: "But his side of town was under no threat. Why should he feel guilty about this? Perhaps because, an adult male from a fine family with a plausible claim to a little education, he had absolutely no influence of any kind" (262). Indeed, Jack's "influence" extends from a perceived inability to counteract racist policies to a necessary complicity in them. "To be white in America," as George Yancy argues, "is to be always already implicated in structures of power" (*Black Bodies* 226). Jack's performance of social marginality not only fails to exempt him from the racial and class privilege of his birth but collaborates in the violence of the social order. Pushed to acknowledge this power dynamic, Jack goes on to figure his relationship with Della as a form of false intimacy that allows him to violate the boundaries of her safe space: "If Della were less splendid, less burdened with others' hopes, there might be less shame in his sidling up to her, pestiferous or combustible, or something of the kind, disguised as a social reject so that he could be the perfect agent of society's malice" (238). In extending his figuration of himself from the ontological to the social ontological domain, Jack critiques the structures of imagination that would exempt him from being implicated in real-world damage.

On the one hand, the pressing realities of eminent domain lend concrete immediacy to Jack's hyperbolic claims of destructiveness, forcing him to translate his imaginings into material terms. At the same time that the specifics of mid-twentieth-century racist policies in St. Louis push him toward the concrete, however, it is Jack's symbolic imagination that allows awareness of his own complicity in the white imaginary to take hold. The very habits of mind that direct Jack away from the literal consequences of his actions locate him intimately in symbolic structures, exposing the way he is implicated in the structural dynamics of racism by virtue of his racially coded existence. Calling out his earlier assertion that Della is more at ease in her own skin than he is, Jack gestures toward the recognition of his linguistic and social power; despite his connection to Della and his identification with her marginalization, the autonomy to script and costume his own socially peripheral character emerges as an extension of the power of white world-making. As the amorphous harm he associates with his presence takes the shape of visible and material destruction, Jack is increasingly forced to place himself inside the margins of white St. Louis: "He had been a little afraid to wonder why he felt implicated in the imminent destruction, and now he knew" (273). In this context, Jack's emotional and spatial proximity to Della fails to certify his own marginality. "To encourage whites to avoid idealizations of themselves as antiracists and therefore in some sense see their subject positions as marginal in relationship to the larger structure of white power," Yancy cautions, "it is important to remind them that in racist white America there is simply no place where they can remain permanently marginal" (*Black Bodies* 225).

Stepping back to acknowledge the hegemonic force of whiteness, Jack also steps into a positionality that relocates him from the margins to the center of power: "There he was, destroying Della's world just by being who he was, where he was" (246). As the proclamation of his ontological evil broadens to encompass what Yancy terms a social ontological perspective, the symbolic terms of Jack's self-definition no longer distance him from responsibility. Having acknowledged his location in a landscape "deeply shaped by whiteness as the transcendental norm" (Yancy, *Black Bodies* 3), Jack's hypothetical existence falls out of the realm of the abstract to land forcibly in the everyday. Although whiteness, Yancy observes, must be understood "within the framework of an antiessentialist hermeneutic, it does not follow that whiteness is somehow *unreal*. Whiteness embodies a difference that indeed makes a difference on the minds and bodies of both whites and nonwhites" (*Black Bodies* 234). As what Yancy terms "a living, breathing historical construction" ("Fragments" 14), whiteness testifies to the impossibility of disentangling the everyday and the imaginary; it is sustained through habits of mind and body that would obscure the labor of performative repetition required to disguise its historically contingent formation and its urgent material, spatial, and bodily effects.

If "habits of thought," as well as routine actions, constitute the lived experience of the everyday, Jack's tendency to abstract and ontologize his own mode of being structures his experience as surely as Lila's patterns of anxious repetition structure hers. Robinson's narratives conspire with her protagonists to imagine a world framed by the shifts of consciousness that continually disrupt her characters' ability to inhabit an "ordinary" from which they feel impossibly estranged. In Jack's case, literary and symbolic mechanisms emerge not only as the tools through which he manages his anxieties but as the grounding for his performance of the everyday; scripted through the lens of a psychic experience of alienation that he struggles to concretize, his gestures, clothing, and behaviors enact the essential marginalization he feels. By the end of the novel, however, Jack's tendency to retreat to an abstract landscape where he can simultaneously acknowledge his guilt through literary or melodramatic figures and distance himself from the effects of his actions breaks down. Specific references to the historical dynamics of eminent domain in St. Louis disrupt the discursive construction of Jack's imaginative world, turning the relationship between Della's body and Jack's dream inside out. As Della's presence in the novel tests the limits and reach of Jack's imaginative everyday, the novel explores not only Jack's world but the process of world-making; in doing so, it begins to break down the boundary between the ability "to dream a world" and what Robinson describes as "the world itself" lurking just outside the writer's window.

References

Acocella, Joan. "Lonesome Road." *The New Yorker*, vol. 90, no. 30, October 6, 2014, p. 79.

Ahmed, Sara. *Queer Phenomenology: Orientations, Objects, Others*. Duke University Press, 2006.

Amery, Jean. *On Aging: Revolt and Resignation*, trans. John D. Barlow. Indiana University Press, 1994.

Atchley, Paul and Lesa Hoffman. "Aging and Visual Masking: Sensory and Attentional Factors." *Psychology and Aging*, vol. 19, no. 1, March 2004, pp. 57–67.

Atkin, Samuel and Adam Atkin. "On Being Old (A Psychiatrist's New World)" in *How Psychiatrists Look at Aging*, ed. George H. Pollock. International Universities Press, 1992, pp. 1–24.

Bachelard, Gaston. *The Poetics of Space*, trans. Maria Jolas. Beacon Press, 1994.

Baker, Simon. "Homeward Bound." *The Observer*, October 5, 2008, Books, p. 24.

Barthes, Roland. The Reality Effect" in *The Rustle of Language*. University of California Press, 1989, pp. 141–8.

Bartky, Sandra. "Shame and Gender" in *Femininity and Domesticity: Studies in the Phenomenology of Oppression*. Routledge, 1990, pp. 83–98.

Baudrillard, Jean. *Simulacra and Simulation*. University of Michigan Press, 1994.

Berg, G. and S. Gadow. "Toward More Human Meanings of Aging: Ideals and Images from Philosophy and Art" in *Aging and the Elderly: Humanistic Perspectives in Gerontology*, ed. Stuart F. Spicker, Kathleen M. Woodward, and David D. Van Tassel. Humanities Press, 1978, pp. 83–92.

Bernard, Emily. *Black Is the Body: Stories from My Grandmother's Time, My Mother's Time, and Mine*. Vintage Books, 2019.

Borkovec, Thomas D., Oscar M. Alcaine, and Evelyn Behar. "Avoidance Theory of Worry and Generalized Anxiety Disorder" in *Generalized Anxiety Disorder: Advances in Research and Practice 1st Edition*, ed. Richard G. Heimberg, Cynthia L. Turk, and Douglas S. Mennin. Guilford Press, 2004, pp. 77–108.

Bourdieu, Pierre. "On the Family as a Realized Category." *Theory, Culture and Society*, vol. 13, no. 3, 1996, pp. 19–26.

Bourdieu, Pierre. *The Logic of Practice*. Stanford University Press, 1990.

Bowlby, Rachel. "Domestication" in *Feminism Beside Itself*, ed. Diane Elam and Robyn Wiegman. Routledge, 1995, pp. 71–88.

Boym, Svetlana. "Nostalgia and Its Discontents." *Hedgehog Review*, vol. 9, no. 2, July 2007, pp. 7–18.

Brooks, Peter. "Narrative Desire" in *Narrative Dynamics*, ed. Brian Richardson. Ohio State University Press, 2002, pp. 130–7.

Brooks, Peter. *Reading for the Plot*. Harvard University Press, 1992.

Brooks, Peter. *The Melodramatic Imagination*. Yale University Press, 1976.

Caracciolo, Marco. *The Experientiality of Narrative*. De Gruyter, 2014.

Cartensen, Laura L., Derek M. Isaacowitz, and Susan T. Charles. "Taking Time Seriously: A Theory of Socioemotional Selectivity." *American Psychologist*, vol. 54, no. 3, March 1999, pp. 165–81.

Caruth, Cathy. "Introduction" in *Trauma: Explorations in Memory*, ed. Cathy Caruth. Johns Hopkins University Press, 1995, 3–12.

Casey, Edward S. *Spirit and Soul*. Spring Publishers, 1991.

Caver, Christine. "Nothing Left to Lose: *Housekeeping*'s Strange Freedoms." *American Literature*, vol. 68, no. 1, March 1996, pp. 111–37.

Chodat, Robert. "That Horeb, That Kansas: Evolution and the Modernity of Marilynne Robinson." *American Literary History*, vol. 28, no. 2, April 2016, pp. 328–61.

Clark, Clifford Edward. *The American Family Home 1800–1960*. University of North Carolina Press, 1986.

Clewell, Tammy. "Introduction: Past 'Perfect' and Present 'Tense': The Abuses and Uses of Modernist Nostalgia" in *Modernism and Nostalgia: Bodies, Locations, Aesthetics*, ed. Tammy Clewell. Palgrave Macmillan, 2013, pp. 1–22.

Coates, Ta-Nehisi. *Between the World and Me*. Spiegel and Grau, 2015.

Coles, Robert. *Old and On Their Own*. Norton, 1997.

Cooperman, Jeannette. "The Story of Segregation in St. Louis." *St. Louis Magazine*, October 17, 2014, www.stlmag.com/news/the-color-line-race-in-st.-louis/.

Cote, Rachel Verona. "The Complicated Comforts of Marilynne Robinson." *Literary Hub*, April 13, 2018.

Damasio, Antonio. *Descartes's Error: Emotion, Reason and the Human Brain*. Putnam, 1994.

Damasio, Antonio. *The Feeling of What Happens: Body and Emotion in the Making of Consciousness*. Harcourt Brace & Co., 1999.

De Certeau, Michel. *The Practice of Everyday Life*, trans. Steven F. Rendall. University of California Press, 1984.

Derrida, Jacques. "*As if* I Were Dead: An Interview with Jacques Derrida" in Ruth Robbins and Julian Wolfreys. *Applying: to Derrida*, ed. John Brannigan. St. Martin's, 1996, pp. 212–26.

Douglas, Christopher. "Christian Multiculturalism and Unlearned History in Marilynne Robinson's 'Gilead.'" *NOVEL: A Forum on Fiction*, vol. 44, no. 3, 2011, pp. 333–53.

Dye, Heather. "The Impact and Long-Term Effects of Childhood Trauma." *Journal of Human Behavior in the Social Environment*, vol. 28, no. 3, 2018, pp. 381–92.

Engebretson, Alex. *Understanding Marilynne Robinson*. University of South Carolina Press, 2017.

Epstein, Andrew. *Attention Equals Life: The Pursuit of the Everyday in Contemporary Poetry and Culture*. Oxford University Press, 2016.

Erikson, Kai. "Notes on Trauma and Community." *Trauma: Explorations in Memory*. Johns Hopkins University Press, 1995, pp. 183–99.

Esposito, Joseph L. *The Obsolete Self: Philosophical Dimensions of Aging*. University of California Press, 1987.

Esteve, Mary. "Robinson's Crusoe: *Housekeeping* and Economic Form." *Contemporary Literature*, vol. 55, no. 2, 2014, pp. 219–48.

Fanon, Frantz. *Black Skin, White Masks*. Grove Press, 1967.

Fay, Sarah. "Marilynne Robinson: The Art of Fiction." *The Paris Review*, vol. 50, issue 186, Fall 2008, p. 37.

Felski, Rita. "Introduction." *New Literary History*, vol. 33, no. 4, Autumn 2002, pp. 607–22.

Felski, Rita. "The Invention of Everyday Life." *New Formations*, vol. 39, Winter 1999, pp. 15–31.

Felski, Rita. "The Invention of Everyday Life" in *Doing Time: Feminist Theory and Postmodern Culture*. New York University Press, 2000, pp. 77–98.

Fludernik, Monika. *The Fictions of Language and the Languages of Fiction: The Linguistic Representation of Speech and Consciousness*. Routledge, 1993.

Fraiman, Susan Stanford. "Shelter Writing: Desperate Housekeeping from Crusoe to Queer Eye." *New Literary History*, vol. 37, no. 2, 2006, pp. 341–59.

Friedman, Susan Stanford. "Bodies on the Move: A Poetics of Home and Diaspora." *Tulsa Studies in Women's Literature*, vol. 23, no. 2, Fall 2004, pp. 189–212.

Garb, Margaret. "No Place Like Home: St. Louis' Eminent Domain History." *Humanities Features*, September 22, 2017, https://humanities.wustl.edu/features/Margaret-Garb-St-Louis-Eminent-Domain.

Genette, Gerard. *Narrative Discourse: An Essay in Method*. Cornell University Press, 1983.

Geyh, Paula E. "Burning down the House? Domestic Space and Feminine Subjectivity in Marilynne Robinson's *Housekeeping*." *Contemporary Literature*, vol. 34, no. 1, Spring 1993, pp. 103–22.

Gibbs, Alan. *Contemporary American Trauma Narratives*. Edinburgh University Press, 2014.

Gilbert, Sandra and Susan Gubar. *The Madwoman in the Attic: The Woman Writer and the Nineteenth-Century Literary Imagination*. Yale University Press, 1979.

Gillis, John R. *A World of their Own Making*. Harvard University Press, 1996.

Govier, Katherine. "No Place Like It, Indeed." *National Post*, November 15, 2008, Weekend, p. 19.

Grier, Katherine C. "The Decline of the Memory Palace" in *American Home Life, 1880–1930*, ed. Jessica Foy. University of Tennessee Press, 1992, pp. 49–71.

Gwinn, Mary Ann. "*Home*: Marilynne Robinson Revisits *Gilead* with Profound Results." *The Seattle Times*, September 17, 2008, Entertainment News, p. 1.

Haapala, Arto. "On the Aesthetics of the Everyday: Familiarity, Strangeness, and the Meaning of Place" in *The Aesthetics of Everyday Life*, ed. Andrew Light and Jonathan Smith. Columbia University Press, 2005, pp. 39–55.

Harries, Karsten. "Metaphor and Transcendence." *Critical Inquiry*, vol. 5, no. 1, Autumn 1978, pp. 73–90.

Hart, Jeffrey. "Now, a masterpiece—*Gilead*." *National Review*, vol. 57, no. 6, 11 April 2005, p. 46.*Gale Academic OneFile*, https://link-gale.com.proxy.bc.edu/apps/doc/A145339405/AONE?u=mlin_m_bostcoll&sid=AONE&xid=e1ed537e.

Hedrick, Tace. "'The Perimeters of Our Wandering Are Nowhere': Breaching the Domestic in Housekeeping." *Critique*, vol. 40, no. 2, Winter 1999, pp. 137–51.

Ravits, Martha. "Extending the American Range: Marilynne Robinson's Housekeeping." *American Literature*, vol. 61, no. 4, 1989, pp. 644–66.

Heller, Dana. "Housebreaking History: Feminism's Troubled Romance with the Domestic Sphere" in *Feminism Beside Itself*, ed. Diane Elam. Routledge, 1995, pp. 217–36.

Herman, David. "Narrative Ways of Worldmaking" in *Narratology in the Age of Cross Disciplinary Narrative Research*, eds. S. Heinan and R. Sommer. Walter De Gruyter, 2009, pp. 71–87.

Herman, David. *Story Logic: Problems and Possibilities of Narrative*. University of Nebraska Press, 2002.

Holberg, Jennifer L. "'The courage to see it': Toward an Understanding of Glory." *Christianity and Literature*, vol. 59, no. 2, Winter 2010, pp. 283–301.

Hollows, Joanne. "Can I Go Home Yet? Feminism, Post-Feminism, and Domesticity" in *Feminism in Popular Culture*, ed. Joanne Hollows and Rachel Mosely. Berg, 2006, pp. 97–118.

Horton, Ray. "'Rituals of the Ordinary': Marilynne Robinson's Aesthetics of Belief and Finitude." *PMLA*, vol. 132, no. 1, January 2017, pp. 119–34.

Huber, Irmtraud. *Literature after Postmodernism: Reconstructive Fantasies*. Palgrave Macmillan, 2014.

Hungerford, Amy. *Postmodern Belief: American Literature and Religion since 1960*. Princeton University Press, 2010.

Ihara, Natha. "Marilynne Robinson's *Home*." *Los Angeles Weekly*, September 25, 2008, p. 17.

Imre, Kristin. *Monotonous Feeling: The Formal Everyday in Three Modern and Contemporary Novels*. ProQuest Dissertation Publishing, 2018.

Inour, Kazuko. "'Resurrection of the Ordinary': Marilynne Robinson's Housekeeping." *Language and Culture*, vol. 16, 1989, pp. 132–49.

James, David. *Discrepant Solace: Contemporary Literature and the Work of Consolation*. Oxford University Press, 2019.

James, David. "In Defense of Lyrical Realism." *Diacritics*, vol. 45, no. 4, 2017, pp. 68–91.

Jones, Malcolm. "Wanted: More Balm in Gilead." *Newsweek*, vol. 152, no. 12, September 2008, p. 73.

Kakutani, Michiko. "Family Ties Reassembling the Shards of Its Past." *New York Times*, September 9, 2008, p. E1.

Kakutani, Michiko. "Woman Caught in the Paradox of Being Adrift and on a Journey." *New York Times*, September 29, 2014, pp. C1, C4.

Kapkin, Ihsan A. "The Aging Psychiatrist" in *How Psychiatrists Look at Aging*, ed. George H. Pollock. International Universities Press, 1992, pp. 123–40.

Kaplan, Carola. "'Sudden Holes in Space and Time': Trauma, Dissociation, and the Precariousness of Everyday Life." *Psychoanalytic Inquiry*, vol. 33, no. 5, 2013, pp. 467–78.

King, Kristin. "Resurfacings of 'the Deeps': Semiotic Balance in Marilynne Robinson's *Housekeeping*." *Studies in the Novel*, vol. 28, no. 4, Winter 1996, pp. 565–80.

Kliethermes, Matthew, Megan Schacht, and Kate Drewry. "Complex Trauma." *Child and Adolescent Psychiatric Clinics of North America*, vol. 23, no. 2, April 2014, pp. 339–61.

LaCapra, Dominick. "Reflections on Trauma, Absence, and Loss" in *Whose Freud? The Place of Psychoanalysis in Contemporary Culture*, ed. Peter Brooks and Alex Woloch. Yale University Press, 2000, pp. 178–204.

Langbauer, Laurie. *Novels of Everyday Life: The Series in English Fiction, 1850–1930*. Cornell University Press, 1999.

Lanser, Susan Sneider. *Fictions of Authority: Women Writers and Narrative Voice*. Cornell University Press, 1992.

Lefebvre, Henri. *Critique of Everyday Life*, trans. John Moore. Verso, 2002.

Lefebvre, Henri. *Everyday Life in the Modern World*. Shocken Books, 1968.

Leise, Christopher. "'That Little Incandescence': Reading the Fragmentary and John Calvin in Marilynne Robinson's *Gilead*." *Studies in the Novel*, vol. 41, no. 3, 2009, pp. 348–67.

MacDonald, Hugh. "A Dark Journey." *The Herald*, October 4, 2008, Arts, p. 13.

Madden, David J., Timothy G. Turkington, James M. Provenzale, Laura L. Denny, Linda K. Langley, Thomas C. Hawk, and R. Edward Coleman. "Aging and Attentional Guidance during Visual Search Functional Neuroanatomy by Positron Emission Tomography." *Psychology and Aging*, vol. 17, no. 1, 1999, pp. 24–43.

Mariotti, Shannon L. and Joseph H. Lane, Jr. *A Political Companion to Marilynne Robinson*. University Press of Kentucky, 2016.

Mason, Wyatt. "The Revelations of Marilynne Robinson." The New York Times Sunday Magazine, October 5, 2014, p. 24.

Mattessich, Stefan. "Drifting Decision and the Decision to Drift: The Question of Spirit in Marilynne Robinson's *Housekeeping*." *Differences* vol. 19, no. 3, 2008, pp. 59–89.

Mauro, Aaron. "Ordinary Happiness: Marilynne Robinson's Tragic Economies of Debt and Forgiveness." *Symploke*, vol. 22, 2014, pp. 149–66.

McDermott, Sinead. "Future-Perfect: Gender, Nostalgia, and the Not Yet Presented in Marilynne Robinson's Housekeeping." *Journal of Gender Studies*, vol. 13, no. 3, November 2004, pp. 259–70.

McEvoy, P.M. "Are Worry, Rumination and Post-Event Processing One and the Same?" *Journal of Anxiety Disorders*, vol. 24, 2010, pp. 509–19.

Mendible, Myra. "Introduction" in *American Shame: Stigma and the Body Politic*, ed. Myra Mendible. Indiana University Press, 2016.

Merleau-Ponty, Maurice. *Phenomenology of Perception*, trans. Colin Smith. Routledge and Kegan Paul, 1962.

Merleau-Ponty, Maurice. *The Visible and the Invisible*. Ed. Claude Lefort. Trans. Alphonso Lingis. Northwestern University Press, 1968.

Mezei, Kathy and Chiara Brigante. "Reading the House: A Literary Perspective." *Signs*, vol. 27, no. 3, 2002, pp. 837–46.

Miller, D.A. *Narrative and Its Discontents: Problems of Closure in the Traditional Novel*. Princeton University Press, 1981.

Milot, Tristan, Diane St-Laurent, and Louise S. Éthier. "Intervening with Severely and Chronically Neglected Children and Their Families: The Contribution of Trauma-Informed Approaches." *Child Abuse Review*, vol. 25, no. 2, 2 March 2015, pp. 89–101.

Mitchell, David T. and Sharon L. Snyder. *Narrative Prosthesis: Disability and the Dependencies of Discourse*. University of Michigan Press, 2001.

Montgomery-Fate, Tom. "Back at Home." *The Boston Globe*, September 7, 2008, p. K5.

Montgomery-Fate, Tom. "Seeing the Holy." *Sojourners Magazine*, vol. 35, no. 6, June 2006, pp. 38–43.

Moreland, Richard C. "'He Wants to Put His Story Next to Hers': Putting Twain's Story Next to Hers in Morrison's *Beloved*." *Modern Fiction Studies*, vol. 39, nos. 3–4, Fall/Winter 1993, pp. 501–25, https://doi.org/10.1353/mfs.0.0647.

Morrison, Toni. *Playing in the Dark: Whiteness and the Literary Imagination*. Harvard University Press, 1992.

Morrison, Toni. "Unspeakable Things Unspoken" in *Within the Circle*. Duke University Press, 1994, pp. 368–98.

Morrissy, Mary. "Return to the Margins." *The Irish Times*, October 11, 2008, Weekend, p. 13.

Munro, Alice. "What is Real?" in *The Norton Anthology of Short Fiction*, ed. R.V. Cassell and Richard Bausch. Norton, 2000, pp. 706–9.

Nacol, Emily C. "'In Those Old Days': The Old and the Aging in Marilynne Robinson's *Gilead* and *Home*." *A Political Companion to Marilynne Robinson*, edited by Shannon L. Mariotti and Joseph H. Lane. University Press of Kentucky, 2016, pp. 113–38.

Nelson, Cassandra. "Honor Thy Child." *First Things: A Monthly Journal of Religion and Public Life*, vol. 250, February 2015, p. 53.

Ngai, Sianne. *Ugly Feelings*. Harvard University Press, 2005.

O'Connell, Mark. "The First Church of Marilynne Robinson." *The New Yorker*, May 30, 2012.

Obama, Barack and Marilynne Robinson. "President Obama and Marilynne Robinson: A Conversation in Iowa." *New York Review of Books*, November 5, 2015, www.nybooks.com/articles/2015/11/05/president-obama-marilynne-robinson-conversation/

Olson, Liesl. "Everyday Life Studies: A Review." *Modernism/Modernity*, vol. 18, no. 1, 2011, pp. 175–80.

Olson, Liesl. *Modernism and the Ordinary*. New York: Oxford University Press, 2009.

Ophir, Ella. "Modernist Fiction and 'the Accumulation of Unrecorded Life.'" *Modernist Cultures*, vol. 2, no. 1, 2010, pp. 6–20.

Outka, Elizabeth. "Afterward: Nostalgia and Modernist Anxiety" in *Modernism and Nostalgia: Bodies, Locations, Aesthetics*, ed. Tammy Clewell. Palgrave Macmillan, 2013, pp. 252–61.

Phillips, Siobhan. "Merit and Mystery: Marilynne Robinson." *The Yale Review*, vol. 97, no. 2, March 2009, pp. 158–73.

Phillips, Siobhan. *The Poetics of the Everyday: Creative Repetition in Modern American Verse*. Columbia University Press, 2010.

Plant, Bob. "On Being (Not Quite) Dead with Derrida." *Philosophy and Social Criticism*, vol. 42, no. 3, 2016, pp. 320–38.

Potts, Matthew. "The world will be made whole": Love, Loss, and the Sacramental Imagination in Marilynne Robinson's *Housekeeping*." *Christianity and Literature*, vol. 66, no. 3, June 2017, pp. 482–99.

Power, Kevin. "A Spiritual Meander of a Novel That Goes Nowhere, Slowly." *Sunday Business Post*, November 2, 2014.

Rahim, Sameer. "True Religion." *The Daily Telegraph*, October 11, 2014.

Randall, Bryony. "A Day's Time: The One-Day Novel and the Temporality of the Everyday." *New Literary History*, vol. 47, no. 4, 2016.

Randall, Bryony. *Modernism, Daily Time, and Everyday Life*. Cambridge University Press, 2008.

McDermott, Sinead. "Future-Perfect: Gender, Nostalgia, and the Not Yet Presented in Marilynne Robinson's Housekeeping." *Journal of Gender Studies*, vol. 13, no. 3, November 2004, pp. 259–70.

Rios, Jodi. *Black Lives and Spatial Matters: Policing Blackness and Practicing Freedom in Suburban St. Louis*. Cornell University Press, 2020. https://cornellpress.manifoldapp.org/projects/black-lives-and-spatial-matters.

Robinson, Marilynne. *Absence of Mind*. Yale University Press, 2010.

Robinson, Marilynne. "Foreword" in *The Sound and the Fury*. Modern Library, 1992.

Robinson, Marilynne. *Gilead: A Novel*. Farrar, Straus & Giroux, 2004.

Robinson, Marilynne. *Home*. Farrar, Straus, and Giroux, 2008.

Robinson, Marilynne. *Housekeeping*. Bantam Books, 1982.

Robinson, Marilynne. "Imagination and Community." *When I Was a Child I Read Books*. Farrar, Straus and Giroux, 2013, pp. 19–34.

Robinson, Marilynne. *Jack*. Farrar, Straus and Giroux, 2020.

Robinson, Marilynne. *Lila*. Farrar, Straus and Giroux, 2014.

Robinson, Marilynne. "That Highest Candle." *Poetry Magazine*, May 23, 2007, pp. 130–9.

Robinson, Marilynne. "When I Was a Child" in *When I Was a Child I Read Books*. Virago, 2013, pp. 85–94.

Romines, Ann. *The Home Plot: Women, Writing and Domestic Ritual*. University of Massachusetts Press, 1992.

Sacks, Sam. "Book Review: *Lila* by Marilynne Robinson." *Wall Street Journal*, October 3, 2014.

Schaub, Thomas. "An Interview with Marilynne Robinson." *Contemporary Literature*, vol. 35, 1994, pp. 231–51.

Schine, Cathleen. "A Triumph of Love." *New York Review of Books*, vol. 61, no. 16, October 23, 2014.

Schmelzer, Gretchen. *Journey through Trauma*. Avery, 2018.

Schneider, Ralf. "Toward a Cognitive Theory of Literary Character: The Dynamics of Mental-Model Construction." *Style: Topics on Film and Literature*, vol. 35, no. 4, Winter 2001, pp. 607–39.

Sclater, Shelley Day. "What Is the Subject?" *Narrative Inquiry*, vol. 13, no. 2 (2003), pp. 1–14.

Seidel, Kevin. "A Secular for Literary Studies." *Christianity & Literature*, vol. 67, no. 3 (2018), pp. 472–92, doi:10.1177/0148333117736197.

Stout, Andrew C. "A Little Willingness to See": Sacramental Vision in Marilynne Robinson's Housekeeping and Gilead. *Religion and the Arts*, vol. 18 no. 4 (2014), pp. 571–90.

Sehgal, Paul. "Marilynne Robinson's Essays Reflect an Eccentric, Exasperating, Profound and Generous Mind." *New York Times*, February 20, 2018.

Sheringham, Michael. *Everyday Life: Theories and Practices from Surrealism to the Present*. Oxford University Press, 2006.

Shklovsky, Victor. "Art as Technique." *Twentieth-Century Literary Theory*, 1997, pp. 3–5, doi:10.1007/978-1-349-25934-2_1.

Smith, Andrew. *Racism and Everyday Life: Social Theory, History and Race*. Palgrave, 2015.

Smith, Zadie. "Two Directions for the Novel" in *Changing my Mind: Occasional Essays*. Penguin, 2009, pp. 71–96.

Stewart, Alan and Robert A Neimeyer. "Emplotting the Traumatic Self." *The Humanistic Psychologist*, vol. 29, nos. 1–3, Fall 2001, pp. 8–39.

Stewart, Garrett. *The Value of Style in Fiction*. Cambridge University Press, 2018.

Stewart, Susan. *On Longing: Narratives of the Miniature, the Gigantic, the Souvenir, the Collection*. Duke University Press, 1993.

Stockwell, Peter. *Texture: A Cognitive Aesthetics of Reading*. Edinburgh University Press, 2009.

Stolorow, Robert D. "A Phenomenological-Contextual, Existential, and Ethical Perspective on Emotional Trauma." *The Psychoanalytic Review*, vol. 102, no. 1, February 2015, pp. 123–38.

Stolorow, Robert D. "Existential Anxiety, Finitude, and Trauma." *World, Affectivity, Trauma: Heidegger and Post-Cartesian Psychoanalysis*. Routledge, 2011, pp. 35–52.

Stolorow, Robert D. "Identity and Resurrective Ideology in an Age of Trauma." *Psychoanalytic* Psychology, vol. 26, no. 2, April 2009, pp. 206–9.

Stolorow, Robert D. "The Phenomenology of Language and the Metaphysicalizing of the Real." *Language and Psychoanalysis*, vol. 6, no. 1, 2017, pp. 4–8.

Stolorow, Robert D. "The Phenomenology of Trauma and the Absolutisms of Everyday life: A Personal Journey." *Psychoanalytic Psychology*, vol. 16, no. 3, July–September 1999, pp. 464–8.

Sykes, Rachel. "Reading for Quiet in Marilynne Robinson's Gilead Novels." *Critique: Studies in Contemporary Fiction*, vol. 58, no. 2, 2017, pp. 108–20.

Tanner, Laura E. *Lost Bodies: Inhabiting the Borders of Life and Death*. Cornell University Press, 2006.

Tuan, Yi-Fu. *Space and Place: The Perspectives of Experience*. University of Minnesota Press, 1977.

Tyndall, Paul and Ribkoff, Fred. "Loss, Longing, and the Optative Mode in Marilynne Robinson's *Housekeeping*: On the spiritual Value of Ruth's Wandering Narrative." *Renascence: Essays on Values in Literature*, vol. 66, no. 2, Spring 2014, pp. 87–102.

Vallelonga, Damian S. "An Empirical-Phenomenological Investigation of Being-Ashamed" in *Phenomenological Inquiry in Psychology: Existential and Transpersonal Directions*, ed. Ron Valle. Springer, 1998, pp. 123–56.

Van der Kolk, Bessel. "The Developmental Impact of Childhood Trauma" in *Understanding Trauma: Integrating Biological, Clinical, and Cultural Perspectives*, ed. Laurence J. Kirmayer, Robert Lemelson, and Mark Barad. Cambridge University Press, 2007, pp. 224–41.

Vogelzang, Robin. "The Likeness of Modernism in Marilynne Robinson's Fiction." *English Studies*, vol. 99, no. 7, 16 October 2018, pp. 744–54.

Weese, Katherine. "Narration from beyond the Grave in Marilynne Robinson's *Housekeeping*." *Narrative and the Supernatural: The Function of Fantastic Devices in Seven Recent Novels.* McFarland, 2008, pp. 71–86.

Williams, Rhaisa Kameela. "Choreographies of the Ongoing: Episodes of Black Life, Events of Black Lives." *Biography*, vol. 41, no. 4, Fall 2018, pp. 760–6.

Williams, Rowan. "Living the Good Life." *New Statesman*, vol. 143, October 10–16, 2014, pp. 68–70.

Wilson, Frank. "Home, by Marilynne Robinson." *Pittsburgh Post-Gazette*, September 7, 2008.

Windsor, Gerard. "Marilynne Robinson Returns to Gilead with Lila." *Sydney Morning Herald*, October 18, 2014.

Wood, James. "Acts of Devotion: Review of *Gilead*." *New York Times*, Section 7, Column 1, Book Review Desk, November 28, 2004, 1.

Woolf, Virginia. "Phases of Fiction." *Collected Essays*, vol. 2. Harcourt, 1967, pp. 56–102.

Yancy, George. *Black Bodies, White Gazes*. Rowman and Littlefield, 2017.

Yancy, George. "Introduction: Fragments of a Social Ontology of Whiteness" in *What White Looks Like: African-American Philosophers on the Whiteness Question*. Routledge, 2004, pp. 1–24.

Zhang, Dora. "Naming the Indescribable: Woolf, Russell, James, and the Limits of Description." *New Literary History*, vol. 45, no. 1, Winter 2014, pp. 51–70.

Zyromski, Brett, Colette T. Dollarhide, Yahyahan Aras, Sarah Geiger, J.P. Oehrtman, and Halley Clarke. "Beyond Complex Trauma: An Existential View of Adverse Childhood Experiences." *Journal of Humanistic Counseling*, vol. 57, no. 3, October 2018, pp. 156–72.

Index

For the benefit of digital users, indexed terms that span two pages (e.g., 52–53) may, on occasion, appear on only one of those pages.